Selected praise for

MERCEDES LACKEY

"Lackey has created an intelligent,
self-possessed heroine."
—*Publishers Weekly* on *The Fairy Godmother*

"Wry and scintillating take on the Cinderella story…
Lackey's tale resonates with charm as magical
as the fairy-tale realm she portrays."
—*BookPage* on *The Fairy Godmother*

Selected praise for

TANITH LEE

"Lee's prose is a waking dream,
filled with tropical sensualities."
—*Booklist*

"Tanith Lee is an elegant, ironic stylist—
one of our very best authors."
—*Locus*

Selected praise for

C.E. MURPHY

"A swift pace, a good mystery, a likable protagonist,
magic, danger—*Urban Shaman* has them in spades."
—Jim Butcher, author of the bestselling series
The Dresden Files

MERCEDES LACKEY

is the author of the Heralds of Valdemar series, the Five Hundred Kingdoms series, plus several other series and stand-alone books. She has collaborated with such luminaries as Marion Zimmer Bradley, Anne McCaffrey and Andre Norton. She lives in Oklahoma with her husband, Larry Dixon, and far too many birds. Her next Five Hundred Kingdoms title, *One Good Knight,* will be available March 2006 from LUNA Books.

TANITH LEE

was born in 1947, in England. Unable to read until she was almost eight, she began to write at the age of nine. To date she has published almost seventy novels, ten short-story collections and well over two hundred short stories. Lee has also written for BBC Radio and TV. Her work has won several awards, and has been translated into more than twenty languages. She is married to the writer/artist John Kaiine. Readers can find more information about Lee at www.TanithLee.com or www.daughterofthenight.com.

C.E. MURPHY

holds an utterly impractical degree in English and history. At age six, Catie submitted several poems to an elementary school publication. The teacher producing it chose (inevitably) the one Catie thought was the worst of the three, but he also stopped her in the hall one day and said two words that made an indelible impression: "Keep writing." It was sound advice, and she's pretty much never looked back. She lives in Alaska with her husband Ted, roommate Shaun and a number of pets. More information about Catie and her writing can be found at www.cemurphy.net.

WINTER MOON

NEW YORK TIMES BESTSELLING AUTHOR
MERCEDES LACKEY

WORLD FANTASY AWARD WINNER TANITH LEE

AND C.E. MURPHY

LUNA™
www.LUNA-Books.com

LUNA™

First edition November 2005

WINTER MOON

ISBN 0-373-80239-0

The publisher acknowledges the copyright holders of the individual works as follows:

MOONTIDE
Copyright © 2005 by Mercedes Lackey

THE HEART OF THE MOON
Copyright © 2005 by Tanith Lee

BANSHEE CRIES
Copyright © 2005 by Catherine Murphy

Printed in U.S.A.

CONTENTS

MOONTIDE

Mercedes Lackey

Dedicated to my fellow "Lunatics"
at www.LUNA-Books.com,
without whom I would be a great deal less sane

Dear Reader,

The world I created for the Five Hundred Kingdoms stories is a place where fairy tales can come true—which is not always a good thing. But it is important to remember that most people living in this world go about their lives blissfully unaware of the force that I call "The Tradition" and its blind drive to send certain lives down predestined paths. As long as their lives are not touched by The Tradition, as long as they do not find themselves replicating the story of some tale, song, or myth, most people go about their business never even guessing that such a force exists.

Such are the characters in this story, "Moontide." There is no mention of The Tradition, nor of Fairy Godmothers. These folks have magic, indeed, but it is small magic for the most part. Do not underestimate the small magics, however. A great deal can be done with a very little magic at the right time and place. And even more can be done with a heart full of courage, and someone you can trust at your side.

Mercedes Lackey

Lady Reanna watched with interest as Moira na Ferson took her chain-mail shirt, pooled it like glittery liquid on the bed, and slipped it into a grey velvet bag lined with chamois. It was an exquisitely made shirt; the links were tiny, and immensely strong; Moira only wished it was as featherlight as it looked.

"Your father doesn't know what he's getting back," Reanna observed, cupping her round chin with one deceptively soft hand, and flicking aside a golden curl with the other.

"My father didn't know what he sent away," Moira countered, just as her heavy, coiled braid came loose and dropped down her back for the third time. With a sigh, she repositioned it again, picked up the silver bodkin that had dropped to the floor, and skewered it in place. "He looked at me and saw a cipher, a nonentity. He saw what I hoped he would see, because I wanted him to send me far, far away from that wretched place. Maybe I have my mother's moon-magic, maybe I'm just good at playacting. He saw a little bit of uninteresting girl-flesh, not worth keeping, and by getting rid of it he did what I wanted." Candle- and firelight glinted on the fine embroidered trim of an indigo-colored gown, and gleamed on the steel of the bodice knife she slipped into the sheath that the embroidery concealed.

"But to send you here!" Reanna shook her head. "What was he thinking?"

"Exactly nothing, I expect." Moira hid her leather gauntlets inside a linen chemise, and inserted a pair of stiletto blades inside the stays of a corset. "I'm sure he fully expected to have a half-dozen male heirs by now, and wanted only to find somewhere to be rid of me at worst, and to polish me up into a marriage token at best. He looked about for someone to foist me off on— which would have to be some relation of my mother's, since he's not on speaking terms with most of *his* House—and picked the one most likely to turn me into something he could use for an alliance. You have to admit, the Countess has a reputation for taking troublesome young hoydens and turning out lovely women." The ironic smile with which she delivered those last words was not lost on her best friend. Reanna choked, and her pink cheeks turned pinker.

"Lovely women who use bodkins to put up their hair!" she exclaimed. "Lovely women who—"

"Peace," Moira cautioned. "Perhaps the moon-magic had a hand in that, too. If it did, well, all to the good." An entire matched set of ornate silver bodkins joined the gauntlets in the pack, bundled with comb, brush, and hand mirror. "There can be only one reason why Father wants me home now. He plans to wed me to some handpicked suitor. Perhaps it's for an alliance, perhaps it's to someone he is grooming as his successor. In either case, though he knows it not, he is going to find himself thwarted. I intend to marry no one not of my own choosing."

Reanna rested her chin on her hands and looked up at Moira with deceptively limpid blue eyes. "I don't know how you'll manage that. You'll be one young woman in a keep full of your father's men."

"And the law in Highclere says that no woman can be wed against her will. Not even the heir to a sea-keep. And the keep will be mine, whether he likes it or not, for I am the only child." Moira rolled wool stockings into balls and stuffed them in odd places in the pack. She was going to miss this cozy room. The sea-keep was not noted for comfort. "I will admit, I do not know, yet, what I will do when he proposes such a match. But the Countess has not taught me in vain. I will think of something."

"And it will be something clever," Reanna murmured. "And you will make your father think it was all *his* idea."

Moira tossed her head like a restive horse. "Of course!" she replied. "Am I not one of her Grey Ladies?"

Moira's midnight-black braid came down again, and she coiled it up automatically, casting a look at herself in the mirror as she did so. As she was now—without the arts of paint and brush she had learned from Countess Vrenable—no man would look twice at her. This was a good thing, for a beauty had a hard time making herself plain and unnoticed, but one who possessed a certain cast of pale features that *might* be called "plain" had the potential to be either ignored or to make herself by art into a beauty. Strange that she and Reanna should have become such fast friends from the very moment she had entered the gates of Viridian Manor. She, so dark and pale, and Reanna, so golden and rosy—yet beneath the surface, they were very much two of a kind. Both had been sent here by parents who had no use for them; daughters who must be dowered were a liability, but girls schooled by Countess Vrenable had a certain cachet as brides, and often the King could be coaxed into providing an addition to an otherwise meager dower. Especially when the King himself was using the bride as the bond of an alliance, which had also been known to happen to girls schooled by the Countess. Both Moira and Reanna were the same age, and when it came to their interests and skills, unlikely as it might seem, they were a perfectly matched set.

And both had, two years ago, been taken into the especial schooling that made them something more than the Countess's fosterlings. Both had been invited to become Grey Ladies.

It sometimes occurred to Moira that the difference between girls fostered with Countess Vrenable and those fostered elsewhere, was that the other girls went through their lives assuming that no matter what happened, no matter what terrible thing befell them, there would be a rescue and a rescuer. The Grey Ladies knew very well that if there was a rescue to be had, they would be doing the rescuing themselves.

There was a great deal to be said for not relying on anyone but yourself.

"You're not a Grey Lady yet," Reanna reminded her, from her perch on the bolster of the bed. "That's for the Countess to decide."

A polite cough beside them made them both turn toward the door. "In fact, my dear, the Countess is about to make that decision right now."

No one took Countess Vrenable, first cousin to the King, for granted. And it was not only because of her nearness in blood to the throne. She was not tall, yet she gave the impression of being stately; she was no beauty, yet she caused the eyes of men to turn away from those who were "mere" beauties. It was said that there was no skill she had not mastered. She danced with elegance, conversed with wit, sang, played, embroidered—had all of the accomplishments any well-born woman could need. And several more, besides.

Her hair was pure white, yet her finely chiseled face was ageless. Some said her hair had been white for the past thirty years, that it had turned white the day her husband, the Count, died in her arms.

"You are a little young to be one of my Ladies, child," the Countess said, in a tone that suggested otherwise. "However, this move on your father's part holds...potential."

The older woman turned with a practiced grace that Moira envied, and began pacing back and forth in the confined space of the small room she shared with Reanna. "I should tell you a key fact, my dear. I created the Grey Ladies after my dear husband died, because it was lack of information that caused his death."

She paused in her pacing to look at both girls. Reanna blinked, looking puzzled, but too polite to say anything.

The Countess smiled. "Yes, my children, to most, he died because he threw himself between an assassin and the King. But the King and I realized even as he was dying that the moment of his death began long before the knife struck him. We know that if we had had the proper information, the assassin would never have gotten that far. Assassins, feuds, even wars—all can be averted with the right information at the right time." She passed a hand along a fold of her sable gown. "My cousin has kept peace within our borders and without because he values cunning over force. But it is a never-ending struggle, and in that struggle, information is the most powerful weapon he has."

As Reanna's mouth formed a silent O, the Countess turned to Moira. "Here is the dilemma I face. There is information that I need to know in, and about, the Sea-Keep of Highclere and its lord. But conflicting loyalties—"

Moira raised an eyebrow. "My lady, I have not seen my father for more than a handful of days in all my life. I know well that although my mother loved him, he wedded her only to have her dower, and it was her desperate attempt to give him the male heir he craved that killed her. He cast me off like an outworn glove, and now he calls me back when he at last has need of me. I have had more loving kindness from you in a single day than I have had from him in all my life. If he works against the King, it is my duty to thwart him." She met the Countess's intensely blue eyes with her own pale grey ones. "There are no conflicting loyalties, my lady. I owe my birth to him—but to you, I owe all that I am now."

What she did not, and would not say, was a memory held tight within her, of the night her mother had died, trying to give birth to the male child her father had so desperately wanted. How her mother lay dying and calling out for him, while he had eyes only for the son born dead. How he had mourned that half-formed infant the full seven days and had it buried with great ceremony, while his wife went unattended to her grave but for Moira and a single maidservant. She had never forgiven him for that, and never would.

The Countess held herself very still, and her eyes grew dark with sadness. "My dear child, I understand you. And I am sorry for it."

Reanna sighed. "Not all of us are blessed with loving parents, my lady," she said.

The Countess's lips thinned. "If you *had* loving parents, child, I would be the last person to remove you from their care," she replied briskly, and Moira suddenly understood why she felt she had joined some sort of sisterhood when she came to foster under the Countess's care. None of them had been considered anything other than burdens at worst, and tokens of negotiation at best, by their parents.

Which makes us apt to trust the first hand that offers kindness instead of a blow, she thought. Which was, of course, a thought born of the Countess's own training. The Countess taught them all to look for weaknesses *and* strengths, and to never accept anything at its face value, even the girls who were not recruited into the ranks of the Grey Ladies.

But then her mind added, *And it is a very good thing for all of us that milady is truly kind, and truly cares.* Because she had no doubt of that. The Countess cared deeply about her fosterlings, whether they were Grey Ladies or not.

But it did make her wonder what someone with less scruples could accomplish with the same material to work on.

"Would that I had a year further training of you,

Moira," the Countess said, frowning just a little. "I am loath to throw you into what may be a lion's den with less than a full quiver of arrows."

"I am thrown there anyway," Moira replied logically. "My father *will* have me home, and you cannot withhold me. I would as soon be of some use." And then something occurred to her, which made the corners of her mouth turn up. "But I shall want my reward, my lady."

"Oh, so?" The Countess did not take affront at this. One fine eyebrow rose; that was all.

"Should I find my father in treason, his estates are confiscated to the Crown, are they not?" she asked. "Well then, as we both know, your word is as good as the King's. So should information I lay be the cause of such a finding, I wish your hand and seal upon it that the Sea-Keep of Highclere, my mother's dower, remains with me."

Slowly, the Countess smiled; it was, Moira thought, a smile that some men might have killed for, because it was a smile full of warmth and approval. "I have taught you well," she said at last. "Better than I had thought. Well enough, my hand and seal on it, and if you can think thus straightly, I believe you may serve your King." And she took pen and parchment from the desk and wrote it out. "And you, Reanna—you may hold this in surety for your friend," she continued, handing the parchment to Reanna, who waved it in the air to dry. "I think it best that you, Moira, not be found with any such thing on your person."

Moira and Reanna both nodded. Moira, because she knew that no one would be able to part Reanna from the paper if Reanna didn't wish to give it up. Reanna— well, perhaps because Reanna knew that the Countess would never attempt to take it from her.

"All right, child," the Countess said then. "I am going to steal you away from your packing long enough to try and cram a year's worth of teaching into an afternoon."

In the end, the Countess took more than an afternoon, and even then, Moira felt as if her head had been packed too full for her to really think about what she had learned.

The escort that her father had sent had been forced to cool its collective heels until the Countess saw fit to deliver Moira into their hands. There was not a great deal they could do about that; the Countess Vrenable outranked the mere Lord of Highclere Sea-Keep. The Countess was not completely without a heart; she did see that they were properly fed and housed. But she wanted it made exquisitely clear that affairs would proceed at *her* pace and convenience, not those of some upstart from the costal provinces.

But there was more here than the Countess establishing her ascendancy, for the lady never did anything without having at least three reasons behind her action. The Countess was also goading Lord Ferson of Highclere Sea-Keep, seeing if he could be prodded into rash behavior. Holding on to Moira a day or two more would be a minor irritation for most fathers, especially since his men had turned up unheralded and unannounced. In fact, a reasonable man would only think that the Countess was fond of his daughter and loath to lose her. But an unreasonable man, or a man hovering on the edge of rebellion, might see this as provocation. And he might then act before he thought.

As a consequence, Moira had more than enough time to pack, and she had some additions, courtesy of the Countess, to her baggage when she was done.

In the dawn of the fourth day after her father's men arrived with their summons, she took her leave of Viridian Manor.

As the eastern sky began to lighten, she mounted a gentle mule amid her escort of guards and the maidservant they had brought with them. She took the aid offered by the chief of the guardsmen; not that she needed it, for she could have leaped astride the mule without even touching foot to stirrup had she chosen to do so—but from this moment on, she would be painting a portrait of a very different Moira from the one that the Countess had trained. This Moira was quiet, speaking only when spoken to, and in all ways acting as an ordinary well schooled maiden with no "extra" skills. The rest of her "personality" would be decided when Moira herself had more information to work with. The reason for her abrupt recall had still not been voiced aloud, so until Moira was told face-to-face why her father had summoned her, it was best to reveal as little as possible.

That said, it was as well that the maid was a stranger to her; indeed, it was as well that the entire escort was composed of strangers. The fewer who remembered her, the better.

This was hardly surprising; she had been a mere child when she left, and at that time she hadn't known more than a handful of her father's men-at-arms by sight. She had known more of the maidservants, but who knew if any of *them* were still serving? Two wives her father had wed since the death of her mother; neither had lasted more than four years before the harsh winters of Highclere claimed them, and neither had produced another heir.

Of course, father's penchant for delicate little flowers did make it difficult for them. Tiny, small-boned creatures scarcely out of girlhood were his choice companions, timid and shy, big eyed and frail as a glass bird. Moira's mother had looked like that—in fact, if she hadn't wed so young (too young, Moira now thought) she might have matured into what Moira was now— ethereal in appearance, but tough as whipcord inside.

She felt obscurely sorry for those dead wives. She hadn't been there, and she didn't know them, but she could imagine their shock and horror when confronted by the winter storms that coated the cliffs and the walls of the keep with ice a palm-length deep. She was sturdier stuff, fifteen generations born and bred on the cliffs of Highclere, like those who had come before her. Pale and slender she might be, but she was tough enough to ride the day through and dance half the night afterward. So her mother still would be, if she'd had more care for herself.

The maidservant was up on pillion behind one of the guards. There were seven of them, three to ride before, and three to ride behind, with the seventh taking the maid and Moira on her mule beside him. They seemed competent, well armed, well mounted; not friendly, but that would have been presumptuous.

She looked up at the sky above the manor walls as they loaded her baggage onto the pack mule, and sniffed the air. A few weeks ago, it had still been false summer, the last, golden breath of autumn, but now— now there was that bitter scent of dying leaves, and branches already leafless, which told her the season had turned. It would be colder in Highclere. And in another month at most, or a week or two at worst, the winter storms would begin.

It was a strange time for a wedding, if that was what she was being summoned to.

"Are you ready, my lady?" She glanced down at the guard at her stirrup, who did not wait for an answer. He swung up onto his horse and signaled to the rest of the group, and they rode out without a backward glance. Not even Moira looked back; she had said her farewells last night. If her father's men were watching, let them think she rode away from here with no regret in her heart.

They thought she rode with her eyes modestly down,

but she was watching, watching everything. It was a pity she could not simply enjoy the ride, for the weather was brisk without being harsh, and the breeze full of the pleasant scents of frost, wood smoke, and occasionally, apples being pressed for cider. The Countess's lands were well situated and protected from the worst of all weathers, and even in midwinter, travel was not unduly difficult. The mule had a comfortable gait to sit, and if only she had had good company to enjoy it all with, the trip would have been enchanting.

The guards were disciplined but not happy. They rode without banter, without conversation, all morning long. And it was not as if the weather oppressed them, because it was a glorious day with only the first hints of winter in the air. As they rode through the lands belonging to Viridian Manor, there were workers out harvesting the last of the nuts, cutting deadfall, herding sheep and cattle into their winter pastures, mostly singing as they worked. The air was cold without being frigid, the sky cloudless, the sun bright, and the leaves that littered the ground still carried their vivid colors, so that the group rode on a carpet of gold and red. There could not possibly have been a more glorious day. And yet the guards all rode as if they were traveling under leaden skies through a lifeless landscape.

They stopped at about noon, and rode on again until dark. In all that time, the guards exchanged perhaps a dozen words with her, and less than a hundred among one another. But when camp was made for the evening, the maid, at least, was a little more talkative. Lord Ferson had provided a pavilion for Moira to share with the maid; if it had been up to Moira, she would have been perfectly content to sleep under the moon and stars. She felt a pang as she stepped into the shelter of the tent, wishing she did not have to be shut away for the night.

She let the maid help her out of her overgown, and sat down on the folding stool provided for her comfort while the maid finished her ministrations. "I have not seen Highclere Sea-Keep in many years," Moira said, in a neutral tone, as the maid brought her a bowl of the same stew and hard bread the men were eating. "Have you served the lord long?"

"Eight years, milady," the maid said. She was as neutral a creature as could be imagined, with opaque brown eyes, like two water-smoothed pebbles that gave away nothing. She was, like nearly every other inhabitant of the lands in and around Highclere, very lean, very rangy, dark haired and dark eyed. The Sea-Keep had always provided its servants with clothing; hers was the usual garb of an upper maidservant in winter— dark woolen skirt, laced leather tunic, and undyed woolen chemise—and not the finer woolen overgown and bleached lamb's wool chemise that Moira recalled her mother's personal maidservant wearing. So her father had sent an upper maid, but not a truly superior handmaiden. This was not necessarily a slight; handmaidens tended to be young, were often pretty, and could be a temptation to the guards. This woman, old enough to be Moira's mother, plain and commonplace, and entirely in control of herself and her situation, was a better choice for a journey.

"Has the keep changed much in that time?" Moira asked, as she finished her meal and set the bowl aside. It was a natural question, and a neutral one.

The woman shrugged as she took Moira's braid down from its coil and began brushing it. Needless to say, the pins holding it in place were simple silver with polished heads, not bodkins. "The keep never changes," she replied. "My lady has fine hair."

"It is my one beauty," Moira replied. "And my lord my noble father is well?"

"I am told he is never ill," said the maid, concentrating on rebraiding Moira's plaits.

Moira nodded; this woman might not be a superior lady's maid, but she was not rough handed. "He is a strong man. The sea-keeps need strong hands to rule them."

Bit by bit, she drew tiny scraps of information from the maid. It wasn't a great deal, but by the time she slipped beneath the blankets of her sleeping roll, she began to have the idea that the people of Highclere Sea-Keep were not encouraged to speak much among themselves, and even less encouraged to speak to "outsiders" about what befell the keep. And that could be a sign that the lord of the sea-keep was holding a dark secret.

If so, then this was precisely what the Countess Vrenable of Viridian Manor wished to find out.

Highclere Sea-Keep was less than impressive from the road. In fact, very little of it was visible from the road.

The road led through what the local people called "forest." These were not the tall trees that surrounded Viridian Manor; the growth here was windswept, permanently bent from the prevailing wind from the sea, and stunted by the salt. The forest didn't change much, no matter what the season; it was mostly a dark, nearly black evergreen she had never seen anywhere else but on the coast. Though the trees weren't tall, this forest hid the land-wall and gatehouse of the sea-keep right up until the point where the road made an abrupt turn and dropped them all on the doorstep.

And there was a welcome waiting, which Moira, to be frank, had not expected.

She had not forgotten what her home looked like, and at least here on the cliff, it had not changed. A thick, protective granite wall with never less than four men patrolling the top ran right up to the cliff's edge, making it unlikely anyone could attack the keep from above. There was a gatehouse spanning both sides of the gate, which was provided with both a drop-down iron portcullis and a set of heavy wooden doors. Above the gate was a watch room connected with both gatehouses, which could be manned even when the worst of storms battered the cliff. Both the portcullis and the wooden doors stood open, and arranged in front of them was a guard of honor, eight men all in her father's livery of blue and silver, with the Highclere Sea-Keep device of a breaking wave on their surcoats.

Moira dismounted from her mule—but only after waiting for the leader of the honor guard to help her. He bowed after handing her down from the saddle, as the sea wind swept over all of them, making the pennants on either tower of the gatehouse snap, and blowing her heavy skirts flat against her legs.

There was ice in that wind, and the promise that winter here was coming early, a promise echoed by the fact that the trees that were not evergreens already stretched skeletal, bare limbs to the sky.

"Welcome home, Lady Moira," the leader of the guard said, bowing a second time. "The Lord Ferson awaits you in the hall below."

"Then take me to him immediately," she said, dropping her eyes and nodding her head—but not curtsying. The head of the honor guard, a knight by his white belt, was below her in status. She should be modest, but not give him deference. This was one of the many things she should have learned—and of course, had—under anyone's fosterage. She had no doubt that this knight would be reporting everything he saw to her father, later.

The knight offered her his arm, and she took it. Most ladies would need such help on the rest of the journey. She and the knight led the way through the gates, with the honor guard falling in behind; the maid and her journey escort brought up the rear.

Just inside the gates stood the stables and the Upper Guard barracks. These were the only buildings visible. Just past them was the edge of the cliff, and the sea.

She took in a deep breath of the tangy salt air; for once, there was no more than a light wind blowing. This was home. And despite everything, she felt an odd sense of contentment settle over her as the knight led her courteously toward the cliff edge, and the set of stairs, only visible when you were right atop them, that were cut into the living rock of the cliff. And only when you looked down from that vantage did you see the sea-keep itself.

It was built both on a terrace jutting out over the ocean, and into the cliff itself. The side facing the sea was six feet thick, and needed to be, for when the winter storms came those walls would shake with the force of the waves crashing against them, and only walls that thick could prevent the keep from tumbling down into the foam.

Today, with the sun shining and the wind moderate, the spray from the waves beating against the base of the cliff far below was nowhere near the lowest level of the terraces—which, in a storm, would be awash.

From the highest terrace at either side were two walkways leading along the cliff. These led in turn to the second reason for the existence of the sea-keeps—the beacons.

It was the duty of the lord of each sea-keep to man the beacons and keep them alight, from dusk to dawn, and during all times of fog and storm. They warned ships away from the rocks, and provided a guide to navigators. In return, because even the beacons could not protect every ship from grief, the lords had salvage right to anything washed ashore. It was from this salvage right that the lords obtained their wealth. Ships could and did sink even far out to sea; ambergris and sea coal came ashore, and also here at Highclere, true amber and jet. Seaweed and kelp were burned for—well, here Moira had to admit she didn't know precisely what they were burned for, but apparently the ash was quite valuable. And there were some types of kelp that were edible, by people and animals. She'd had kelp soup hundreds of times; it was one of her favorites. Other kinds made jelly superior to that made with calves' feet. When the tide went out, the scavengers came out to scour the shingle, and half of what they found was the property of the lord.

If a typical keep were to be set on its side, its entrance facing upward, that is how the sea-keeps were built. The stair led downward to the entrance, a kind of hatchway with two enormous double doors, which now were open to the sky and laid flat against the roof of the topmost tower.

With her knightly escort holding to her arm and walking on the outside of the stair, Moira descended the stair to the tower top, and then passed into the keep itself.

Inside, the stair broadened, and continued descending into the Great Hall. There was only one set of windows in the Great Hall—because the glass had to be very thick, recessed into the stone, and protected by an overhang on the sea side. That set of windows stood in back of the lord's dais, so that the lord of the sea-keep was haloed by light. *He* had a fine view of whoever entered his hall—but to those who came down that stair, or stood in the hall below, he was nothing more than a silhouette.

Moira was prepared for this, of course. She took only a glance to assure herself that her father was standing on the dais as she had anticipated, then paid careful attention to her footing.

I suppose it must be Father, anyway. I can't think who else would dare to stand there.

Every step echoed in the vast hall, and she was glad of her cloak, because it was nearly as cold here as it was on the cliff with the sea wind blowing. During a winter storm there were rooms in the keep that were nearly uninhabitable, they were so damp and cold, and even with a roaring fire in the fireplace, more heat was sucked up the chimney than went into the room.

At last, she reached the floor, and her escort immediately let go of her arm. He released her so quickly, in fact, that it was rather funny. Was he afraid her father would be offended if he held to her arm a heartbeat longer than absolutely necessary?

Moira kept her expression sober, however. Lord Ferson would not find it that amusing.

She walked with her head up and her eyes on the dais between two of the long, rough wooden tables that would hold anyone of any consequence here in the keep at meals. Well, except for the kitchen staff. But everyone else, except for the very lowest of bound serfs, ate in the Great Hall. Lord Ferson liked it that way; he wanted his people under his eye three times a day. Moira wasn't quite sure why that was; perhaps he thought it would be harder for anyone to foment rebellion undetected with the lord of the keep keeping a sharp eye out for the signs. Perhaps it was only because he enjoyed all the trappings of his position, and those trappings included having his underlings arrayed before him on a regular basis. She had been very young and entirely unschooled in reading men when she had left, and memory, as she had come to understand, was a most imprecise tool when it was untrained.

But except for those times when Lord Ferson had shared his position with a spouse, he had never in *her* memory had another person on the dais with him.

And as her eyes adjusted to the light, just before she sank into a deep curtsy, she realized with a sense of slight shock that he had someone up there with him now, standing deferentially behind him. There was something odd about the second person's silhouette, as if he was standing slightly askew.

"And what do *you* make of the wench, Kedric? She's learned some graces, at least." Her father's voice hadn't changed much, except, perhaps, to take on a touch of roughness. Probably from all the years of shouting orders over a roaring ocean. It was still deep, still resonant, and still layered with hints of impatience and contempt. Moira remained where she was, deep in her curtsy, head down.

"Comely, my lord. And graceful. Obedient and respectful." This was a new voice, presumably that of the man who sat at her father's feet. Not much higher, but smoother, and definitely softer. A much more pleasant voice to listen to.

"Graceful, that I'll grant, and it's as well, since I sent her away an awkward, half-fledged thing. Obedient and respectful, so it seems. But comely? Stand up, girl! Look at me!"

Girl? Can it be that he doesn't remember my name?

Moira raised her eyes and stood up. Lord Ferson had thickened a bit—not that he was fat, but he no longer had a discernible waistline. There was grey in his black hair and beard, and lines in his face. He peered down at her with a faint frown, hands on hips. "Comely, no. Properly groomed, neat, seemly, but pale as the belly of a dead fish. So girl, what have you to say to your father of that?"

"I am as God made me, my lord," she replied, in an utterly neutral tone of voice.

"Oh, a *properly* modest, maidenly, and pious response!" Lord Ferson barked what might have been a laugh, had it possessed any humor at all. "And I suppose you wonder why I brought you home, don't you, girl?"

"My lord will tell me when he feels it is needful for me to know," she said, dropping her eyes, as much to keep him from reading her dislike of him as to feign maiden modesty.

"Another proper answer. You've been taught well, that I'll grant." Lord Ferson snorted. "You, men—report back to your captain. Go on, Kedric, escort the lady to her chambers. You'll be joining us at dinner as is the custom, daughter."

"Yes, my lord," she replied, and dropped another curtsy—this one not nearly as deep—as the man, dressed in fool's patchwork motley (though oddly enough, it was patterned in black-and-white rather than colors) descended from the dais at her father's orders. He offered her his arm, and she took it, examining him through her eyelashes.

He was just as pale as she, though she couldn't tell what color his hair was under the fool's hood that covered his head. For a fool, he had a strange air of dignity, and of melancholy, though one didn't have to look much past the hunched shoulder to understand the reason for the latter. He also was not very tall—just about her height—and quite slender, with long, sensitive-looking hands. There did seem to be something wrong with his shoulder. He wasn't a hunchback, but it did seem to be slightly twisted upward. Perhaps an old injury—

"If you will come with me, my lady Moira," he said, with a slight tug on her hand. He truly had a very pleasant voice, low and warm.

"Certainly, though I know the way," she replied as he guided her to the door beneath the stair that led deeper into the keep.

But he shook his head. "You are not to be quartered in your old chamber, my lady," he said, directing her down another stair, this one a spiraling stone stair cut into the rock of the cliff that she knew well, lit by oil lamps fastened to the wall just above head height at intervals. "You have been given new quarters from those you remember. The old nursery chamber would not suit your new stature."

She bit off the question she was going to ask—*And what is my stature?* It was best to remember that she needed to tread as carefully here as if she was in an enemy stronghold, because, if the King and the Countess's suspicions were correct, she might be.

"What is my disposition to be, then?" she asked instead.

"You are to have the Keep Lady's suite for now," came the interesting reply. Interesting, because as long as Lord Ferson had evidenced any intention of remarrying, he had kept those rooms vacant. So if he was putting her in them now, did it mean that he was giving up the notion of taking another wife?

Or was it simply that the Keep Lady's suite was the most secure? Almost impossible for anyone to break into.

Or out of.

It had one window, which provided light to the inaptly named "solar," and that one was tucked into a curve of the keep so that all one could see from it was the cliff face and a tiny slice of ocean. From the window it was a sheer drop six stories down to jagged rocks and the water. The rest of the suite, like this stair, was carved into the rock of the cliff and never saw daylight. Moira had once overheard Ferson's second wife tell the handmaiden she had brought with her that it was like living in a cave.

At least it was not *as* drafty in a storm as some of the rest of the rooms. And the chimney always drew well, no matter what the weather.

"I regret that no handmaidens have been selected for my lady as yet," Kedric was saying, as he gestured that she should precede him through the narrow door at the bottom of the stair. "I fear my lady will be attending to the disposition of her own possessions. Lady Violetta's handmaiden departed upon Lady Violetta's death, and no suitable person has been found for my Lady Moira."

Interesting that he would know that; the comings and goings of servants were not usually part of a fool's purview.

"I hardly think I will fall into a decline because I need to unpack for myself," she said drily. "The Countess's fosterlings usually took care of each other. However, if no one objects, I would not be averse to having the woman who attended me on my journey as my servant."

"I will inform the seneschal, who will be greatly relieved, my lady," Kedric replied. "My lord is reluctant to bring in outsiders; nearly as reluctant as they are to serve here."

"Life in a sea-keep is not an easy one," she said automatically as they traversed the long corridor of hewn stone that would end in the Keep Lady's rooms. Their steps, thank heavens, did not echo here; the corridors and private rooms were carpeted with thick pads of woven sea grass, or no one would ever have gotten any sleep in this place. There was an entire room and four serf women devoted to weaving sea-grass squares and sewing them into carpets, which were replaced monthly in the areas inhabited by the lord and his immediate family and whatever guests he might have. Not that the carpets so replaced went to waste—there was a steady migration of the carpets from one area of the keep to another, until at last they ended up in the kennels and the stables as bedding for hounds and horses.

And as Kedric courteously opened the massive wooden door into the Keep Lady's quarters for her, she saw that one or another of her father's wives had made still another improvement for the sake of comfort. There were woolen carpets and fur skins atop the sea-grass carpets, and hangings on all of the stone walls.

The window—one of the few, besides the one in the Great Hall that had glass in it, a construction of panes as thick as her thumb and about the size of her hand leaded together into a frame that could be opened to let in a breeze when the weather was fair—was closed, and Moira went immediately to open it. The hinges protested, and she raised an eyebrow. Evidently Lady Violetta hadn't cared for sea air.

"I should like those oiled as soon as possible, please," she said briskly. If Kedric was—as he seemed to be—taking responsibility for her for now, then he might as well get someone in here to do that, too. "Do you know if my things have been brought down yet?"

"I presume so, my lady," Kedric replied. "If my lady will excuse me, I will see that the seneschal sends the servant you require."

Something in his tone of voice made her turn, and smile at him impulsively. "Thank you, Kedric. Yours is the first kindly face and voice I have seen or heard since I left Viridian Manor."

He blinked, as if taken entirely by surprise, and suddenly smiled back at her. "You are welcome, my lady." He hesitated a moment, then went on. "I have fond memories of Countess Vrenable. She is a gracious lady."

Interesting. "How is it that you came into my father's service?" she asked, now that there was no one to overhear. "When I knew him, he was not the sort of man to employ your sort of fool."

He raised a sardonic eyebrow at her wry twist of the lips. "And by this, you imply that I am not the usual sort of fool? You would be correct. I was in the King's service, until your father entertained him a year or so ago. Your father remarked on my...usefulness, as well as my talents. I believe he found my manner of jesting to his liking."

"And what manner of jests are those?" she asked. She knew her father. Foolery did not amuse him. The feebleminded infuriated him. But wit—at the expense of others—

"The King was wont to say that my wit was sharper than any of his knight's swords, and employed far more frequently." The corner of his mouth twitched. "Perhaps he tired of it. More likely, his knights did, and he wearied of their complaints. My Lord Ferson finds it to his liking." He shrugged. "At any rate, when he admired my talents, the King offered him my services, and he accepted. Like many another who serves, a fool cannot pick and choose his master."

Now here, Moira had to school herself carefully, for she had never, ever known the King to dispose of *anyone* in his retinue in such a cavalier fashion. So either Kedric the Fool had egregiously overstepped both the bounds of his profession *and* the King's tolerance, or—

Or the King had carefully planned all of this in order to plant the fool in her father's household.

Someone had certainly sent the information that had led to Countess Vrenable asking Moira to spy on her own father. Could that someone have been Kedric?

"When you say *talents,* I assume this means you exercise more than your wit?" she asked, carefully.

If he was, indeed, an agent of the King, he was not about to give himself away—yet. "I am a passable musician, and your father did not have a household musician. I have a wide fund of tales, and at need, I can play the scribe and secretary. And I am useful for delivering messages to his underlings, since there are no pages here, either." He shrugged. "As, you see, I am about to do for you, if my lady will excuse me?"

She tried not to allow a chill to enter her voice. After all, even if he was an agent of the King, why should he trust her? He could not yet have heard from his master that she was the Countess's eyes and ears. So far as he knew, she was no more than what she seemed to be, a girl schooled in fosterage who had no notion of what the Grey Ladies were. And if, in fact, it was difficult for him to send and receive information, he might not learn this for weeks, or even months.

Not to mention that if he was *not* the King's man— if, in fact, he *had* been dismissed from the King's service to enter Lord Ferson's—there was no reason on earth why he should have responded to that little opening with anything other than the statements he'd made. *She* needed to remember to walk cautiously....

"I do indeed excuse you, Kedric. And I thank you for your help." She smiled again, though this time it was with a touch of sadness. "I hope you will not decide to exercise your wit at my expense, though I am certain my father would enjoy the results."

He had begun to turn away, but he turned back at that, and his expression had darkened. "My lady," he said, with what she was certain was carefully controlled anger, "can be absolutely certain that I will not abuse my talent in such a way."

And then he was gone, leaving her to stand, dumbfounded, staring at the closed door.

What could have brought that particular comment on? It was very nearly an outburst.

There was only one thing she was sure of now. Lord Ferson might enjoy the wit and company of his fool, but his fool did not care in the least for Lord Ferson.

She was actually rather pleased that the maid did not turn up until after she had put her own things away. One of the Countess's lessons for all her girls, and not just would-be Grey Ladies, was in how to contrive hiding places for things one did not want found. It didn't take a great deal of work, just a very sharp and exceedingly strong knife. Most chests were never moved from where they were set; working at the bottom, one could remove one or more of the boards and create a hiding place between the bottom and the floor. The backs of wardrobes could often be removed as well, and often enough there were panels that had not been intended to conceal, but which could usually be removed and objects put behind them. By the time the maid appeared, her chain mail, sword, and knives were all carefully hidden away, as were a few things that the Countess had entrusted her with. When the woman turned up at her door, there was nothing visible that should not have been in the luggage of a well-born and proper young woman.

"My lady has been busy," the maid said, blinking a little in surprise.

"I am well used to tending to my own things," she told the woman. "I suppose it is not fitting that I should do so now that I am grown, but I saw no need to sit with folded hands and wait for someone to come to deal with my belongings."

"I *will* tend to all such matters from now on, my lady," the woman replied, though Moira thought she saw a brief glimmer of approval. "You are correct—it is not meet that you should be doing the work of a servant, now that you are a lady."

And as if to emphasize that, she proceeded to bustle about the room, checking the contents of every chest and the wooden wardrobes. This made Moira doubly glad that she had taken the precaution of stowing away anything she didn't want the woman to find.

That did not take long, and perhaps it was only that the maid wanted to be sure where Moira had put things in order to understand where they were to be kept. Soon the maid was helping her out of her traveling gown and chemise, wrapping her in a woolen robe, and tending to her hair.

"Do you know if Lady Violetta left any fine-work stores behind?" she asked, as the maid made a better job of combing out her hair than had been possible in a tent lit by a single small lantern.

"I can find out," the maid said. "Shall I bring anything of the sort here for your use?"

"Please. And you do have a name, don't you?" she added, feeling impatient, all at once, with this nonsense of treating a servant like a nonentity. That might do for her father, but it did not suit her. She had known the names of every servant she came into contact with at Viridian Manor. It was one of the little niceties that the Countess had insisted on.

"Anatha," the maid responded, sounding surprised. "Milady."

"Then, Anatha, if you would be so kind as to find whatever fancywork and supplies any and all of my father's wives might have left behind and bring them to my solar, I would be most appreciative." She turned her head slightly so as to meet the maid's eyes. "As you know, I brought nothing of the sort with me. Such finework as we did was done for the Countess and her household. I wish my lord father to be aware that I am not idle, and I am well schooled."

"Very well, my lady." Anatha nodded. "If I may suggest the blue wool for dinner, my lady."

So, she's not entirely unfamiliar with what a lady's maid is supposed to do. Good. "The blue wool it is," she replied.

Anatha was entirely at a loss when it came to selecting jewelry and accessories, however. It was Moira who selected the silver circlet for her hair, the silver-and-chalcedony torque and rings, and the silver-plaque belt. But her cosmetic box was hidden away, and she was not going to get it out. Until she knew what her father was up to, she had no intention of doing anything to enhance her looks.

The jewelry, however, she felt she needed to wear. Similar sets had come, regular as the turning of the year, every birthday and every Christmastide. Although she had seldom worn any of it at Viridian Manor, the chest that it was all contained in made for a substantial weight, for these were not insignificant pieces, and she had the feeling that her father assumed she *was* wearing it all as a kind of display and reminder of *his* wealth and importance.

The fact that it had probably all come to him as gleanings from wrecks was something she had preferred not to think too much about. Clasping the necklets, torques, and necklaces around her throat sometimes made her shiver, as at the touch of dead men's fingers there.

But Lord Ferson would expect her to wear it now, and might be considerably angered if she failed to do so. This was not the time to anger him.

Twilight was already falling and the torches and lanterns had been lit by the time she went up to the Great Hall. There was no signal to announce dinner, as there was at Viridian Manor, but she took her cue from Anatha's behavior as to when to leave. The moment the maid began to look a bit restless, and just a touch apprehensive, she had asked for a lantern to light the way—not all the halls were well lit, and even when they were, when storms blew up, torches and lamps blew out. The lamps in the sea-keeps burned a highly flammable and smokeless fish oil, from the little ones of the sort Anatha carried, to the huge beacons above the rocks. It didn't matter how the beacons smelled, but at least the lamp oil was scented with ambergris and had a pleasant perfume. Shell plates, thinner than paper and nearly as transparent as glass, sheltered the flame from drafts. Anatha followed her, holding the lantern high, and Moira's shadow stretched out in front of both of them.

Moira took a light mantle, remembering how cold some of the hallways and the hall itself got, and as she made her way upward, the now-silent maid a few paces behind, she was glad that she had. The wind had picked up, and many of the staircases, as she well recalled, acted like chimneys, with a whistling wind streaming up them.

The Great Hall was half-full; a fire roared in the fireplace, and an entire deer roasted on a spit above it. That alone told her that, however little her father seemed to regard her, this evening was significant. Meat for the entire company was a rarity; the usual fare at dinner here was shellfish chowder and fish baked in salt for the common folk. They tasted meat three or four times a year at most.

Moira was used to the order and discipline that held in the Great Hall at Highclere, and the same was true of Viridian Manor; it had come as something of a surprise to her to hear of brawling and quarreling at the lower tables of other great houses. That discipline still held; as she entered the hall, there was no great change in the sound level. The steady murmuring continued, and those who were already here kept to their seats, though most craned their necks to look at her. Those who were still on their feet bowed with respect toward her before taking their seats on the long benches. Strict precedence was kept; there were choice seats at the tables—nearest the fire, for the lowly, and nearest the High Table for those with some pretension to rank. But the one thing that struck her after her long absence was that beneath the sound of restrained voices, there was no music.

The Countess had musicians and her own fool to entertain during meals, and sometimes the services of traveling minstrels and entertainers; that had never been the case at Highclere since her father had taken over. On occasion, Lord Ferson would call for a wrestling contest or the like at the final course, or when the women retired and the men sat over wine and ale, but traveling entertainers were few, and only appeared in summer, and he had kept no entertainers of his own until now.

And it was quite clear as she approached the dais and the High Table that he had not much changed his habits. He might have a fool, but the man was not making merry for the company; nor was there precisely "entertainment" to be shared by high- and lowborn alike. Kedric was sitting on a stool on the dais to one side of the table, fingering a lute but not singing. It wouldn't be possible for anyone more than ten paces from the table to hear the soft music.

Lord Ferson was already in his seat, though nothing had been served as yet. Moira approached the table and went into a deep curtsy in front of his seat, but this time she kept her head up and her eyes on him, and rose at his gesture.

"Take the Keep Lady's seat, girl," he said. "We have guests, but they've not yet come up."

She did as she was told, moving around the side of the table that Kedric was sitting at—but before she sat down, she took the pitcher of wine from the table and poured her father's cup full. She waited until he took it with a raised brow for the courtesy, then filled her own, and sat in her chair. There were chairs at the High Table, another touch that showed the difference between the low and the high. The high need not rub elbows and jostle for room at their dinner.

Serving the Keep Lord his wine was, of course, the Keep Lady's duty, unless he had a page, which Ferson did not—and it had also been a test, she suspected, to see just how *well* schooled she was. If so, she had passed it.

"Guests, my lord?" she said in an inquiring tone. This was a surprise, and not a particularly pleasant one. On the whole she really would rather not have the duty of being a hostess thrust on her so soon. And she could not help but feel that these "guests" might well have something to do with a marriage. Probably hers.

"You'll see," he replied simply.

And a moment later, there was a bit of a stir at the door, and she did, indeed, see.

And as soon as she did, she had to fight to keep herself from stiffening up all over.

Striding into the hall as if *he* were the right and proper lord here, was a tall, lanky, saturnine man, with a neat, trimmed beard and a long face. The trouble was that even if Moira had not recognized the emblem embroidered on his oddly cut and brilliantly scarlet, quilted silk surcoat—which she did—she would have known by the styling of the garment, by the voluminous ochre silk breeches and wrapped ochre sash instead of a belt, the pointed-toed boots, and by the matching ochre scarf tied about his head, ornamented at the front with a topaz brooch that was worth, if not a king's, at least a prince's ransom, that he was from the Khaleemate of Jendara.

And by the sigh of the phoenix rising from the flames embroidered on his surcoat, he was the eldest son of the Khaleem himself.

There was just one small problem with this scenario. Not to put too fine a point on it, the Khaleem was a pirate. His ships had been preying on this kingdom's merchants and navy for the past two hundred years, at least. And the only reason that outright war had never been declared between the two countries was that the Khaleem always disavowed any knowledge of the piracy, and would, on occasion, make a show of attempting to "root out the problem." Raids would cease for a few seasons, then it was business as usual.

She had been expecting many possibilities. This was not one of them. And, as Kedric fumbled three notes of the song he was playing, the fool was just as surprised and shocked at the identity of their "guest."

Behind the Khaleem's son came three more men. All of them were as richly dressed as he, in blue, ochre, and green, but their surcoats told those who had eyes to read them that these three were Great Captains—high of rank, to be sure, but barely more than servants when compared to their leader's son.

Lord Ferson was standing. Moira remained seated, which was perfectly proper. No Jendaran would pay the least bit of attention to a mere female anyway, so it hardly mattered what she did. "Welcome to my hall and table, Massid," her father said in that booming voice, as the man stopped at virtually the same place Moira had, and made a slight bow of his head with his wrists crossed over his chest. It did not escape Moira's attention that heavy gold cuff bracelets adorned those wrists. Lord Ferson gestured to a servant, who brought a plate with half a loaf and a small bowl on it. He offered it to Massid, who tore off a small piece, dipped it in the salt, and ate it, then offered it to the other three Jendarans, who did the same.

The ceremony of bread and salt. So…suddenly my father and these people have a truce.

That truce would not bind anyone but Massid and

the three captains with him, of course, and if the Kha-leem chose to attack the sea-keep at this very moment, by his way of thinking, he would be violating no pledge. But he would be mad to try. Only a fool who wanted very much to die would attack a sea-keep with less than a hundred ships, and even then, it would take a moon, maybe two, to conquer it. Unless, of course, a storm blew up, at which point, the battle would be over and anyone not inside the walls would be dead.

Moira cast her eyes down to her empty plate, but watched all this through her lashes, so stunned for the moment that she fell back on the default expedient of appearing quiet and withdrawn. Massid of Jendara! *Here!* What could it mean?

Whatever was toward, her father was acting as if this pirate was an old and trusted ally; he gestured to the chairs on his left, the opposite side to which Moira was sitting, and the four men took their places, with Massid sitting closest to Lord Ferson.

This seemed to be the signal for service, for servants came hurrying through the doors from the kitchens laden with the serving stones.

This was an innovation Moira had never seen any-where else, nor heard of being used except in the sea-keeps. It was a long way through cold hallways from the kitchens of Highclere Sea-Keep, and a very long time ago the lords of the keep had gotten decidedly weary of eating their food stone cold. So what came through the doors first at each meal were teams of men carrying boxes full of round stones from the beaches below. Those stones had been heating in and around the ovens all day. Once the boxes were in place around the perimeter of the hall, the food came in. Baskets of bread, huge kettles of shellfish soup and stewed kelp, roasted vegetables, all the courses needed for a full formal dinner. All of these were placed on the hot stones to keep them warm throughout the meal, and only then did the actual serving begin. Anywhere else, smaller bowls and platters of food would be brought to the tables from the kitchens; here those smaller platters were served from the food left warming in the stone boxes at the sides of the Hall.

The trencher bread was served first, to act as a plate—and as part of the meal—for those who were not of the High Table. Then bowls of shellfish soup were brought to the tables—wooden bowls, for those at the low tables, silver for those at the high. Lord Ferson had never stinted the appetites of his people; until the kettles were empty, anyone could have as much of the common food as he wished, and after a long day of work in the cold, appetites were always hearty. This was one of Moira's favorite foods, but she had little taste for it tonight.

"And this is what, Lord Ferson?" asked Massid with interest, as the bowl was placed before him. Without waiting for an answer, he dipped his spoon in it and tasted it. Of course he wasn't worried about poison—he'd seen himself that everyone was served from the same common kettles.

"Interesting!" he said after the first cautious taste. "It could do with saffron, but—" he dipped for another spoonful "—quite tasty. I shall have spices sent to your kitchen, with instruction to their use, saffron among them. I believe you will find it improves an already excellent dish."

"Most gracious of you, Prince," Ferson replied, managing to sound gracious himself, given that he had no interest whatsoever in what he was given to eat so long as it wasn't raw or burned. "Instructions would be wise. I have never heard of, nor tasted, this 'saffron,' and I fear my cook would be at a loss to deal with it."

"More precious than gold, I promise you." Moira could not see Massid from where he sat, though she had the uneasy feeling that he was staring in her direction. "Though not so precious as…other things."

Without a doubt, that was intended to be a compliment directed at her, and although she wished profoundly that she could call it a clumsy one, in all truth, it was courtly and elegant. And she only wished she could appreciate it. Massid was not uncomely. He was courteous, and if only he wasn't the Prince of Jendara….

But he was. And the King could never have approved of this, or she would have been informed. So this was all happening without the King's knowledge.

Treason? Very probably. Why else keep the knowledge of this little visit—and what Moira could only assume was going to be a marriage proposal and alliance with Lord Ferson of Highclere Sea-Keep—from the King?

This was bad. This was very, very bad.

And she had absolutely no idea what to do about it.

Whatever curiosity those at the lower tables had about the visitor was completely overshadowed by the slices of venison laid on their trenchers. The High Table had a full haunch, which Ferson himself carved, but even the least and lowest got some bit of meat and the drippings that had been thriftily saved during the cooking poured over his bread. Nothing in the conversation of their superiors could possibly compete with that.

Her father and the Prince continued to make polite conversation throughout the rest of the meal, which Moira ate without tasting. It was no more than polite conversation, however, with no hints of what was being planned; there was talk of how the weather had affected shipping this past summer, and how soon the storms would start. Massid spoke largely of falconry, her father of coursing hounds against stag and boar. And if there was a code in any of that, she couldn't decipher it. By the time the sweet course came in, and the betrothal announcement she had dreaded throughout the entire meal never materialized, she felt a little of her tension ebbing. Only a little, but evidently there was going to be some negotiation going on before she was handed over.

Which was going to give her the chance to think calmly about her situation, and perhaps do something about it.

Or at least, so she hoped.

When the wine came in, after the sweet course, and all but the highest-ranked men in the keep departed for their duties or their beds, Moira rose as her father had probably expected her to do, and made the formal request to retire "with her ladies." She didn't *have* any ladies, of course, but that was the traditional phrase, and her father, deep in some conversation with Massid and his captains about horses, absently waved his permission.

She left the hall without a backward glance, although once again she felt Massid's eyes on her until the moment she left the room.

And it was all she could do not to run.

Back in her chambers, after Anatha had helped her disrobe and she had gotten into bed, she stared up at the darkness beneath the canopy of the huge bed with only the firelight, winking through the places where the bed curtains hadn't quite closed, for illumination. She needed to calm her mind, or she wouldn't be able to think.

She heard the distant sounds of walking, but nothing nearby, so at least there wasn't a guard on her door. Obviously her father didn't expect her to do anything that an ordinary lady of the sort he'd been marrying wouldn't do—such as go roaming the halls seeing what she could overhear.

Not yet. I want to save that for when I need to do it.

First, above all else, she needed to get word to the Countess—and thus, the King—of Massid's presence here.

That wouldn't be as difficult as getting *detailed* information out. She did have a way to do that immediately, though she'd hoped not to have to use it. Unfortunately, the communication would be strictly one-way; unless the Countess in her turn found a way to get a messenger to physically contact Moira, there would be no way that she could get any advice from her mentor.

She closed her eyes, and tried to reckon how likely that would be, and could only arrive at one conclusion: swine would be swooping among the gulls first. With the Prince of Jendara here, Lord Ferson would be making very sure that no one traveled into or out of his realm without his express knowledge and permission, and that would only be given to those whose loyalty he could either trust or compel. In past years, once past All Hallows' Eve—and that night had come and gone while she was en route—there had never been so much as a hint of traveling entertainers or peddlers. It wasn't just that the winter weather along the coast was harsh—which it was. Once winter truly closed in, the forest between the sea-keep and the rest of civilization became dangerous with storms and hungry wild animals. It wasn't worth the risk for an uncertain welcome at a place where, if you were truly unfortunate, you could be trapped until spring came. Any so-called minstrel or peddler who showed his face *now* would simply not be permitted past the gates at the top of the cliff, because her father would be sure he was a spy.

So she was on her own, here.

Given that, what were her possible choices?

It had been a long time since she had lived here, but some knowledge never completely faded. There was a sound in the waves below that warned that she—and the Prince—had only just arrived ahead of the bad weather. Storms far out to sea sent echoes of their anger racing ahead of them in the form of surging waves, and anyone who lived at a sea-keep learned to read those waves. So, the prince would be here till spring, whether or not he had planned to be.

The first of her options that came to mind was the most obvious. Marry the Prince. She ignored the finger of cold that traced its way down her spine at that thought, and she looked that choice squarely in the face.

She could marry the Prince, in obedience to her father. Then what?

Well, the Jendarans did not have a very good reputation when it came to treating women like anything other than property to be sequestered away from the eyes of all other men. If he regarded her in the same light as a Jendaran bride, she'd find herself confined to these rooms with a guard on the door, never seeing anyone but her maid except during Massid's...conjugal visits. Not that she was particularly afraid of *those,* but being confined to two rooms with no company but a maid would drive her mad.

Although the traditional guard is a eunuch, I don't think he brought one with him, and I don't foresee anyone of the keep men volunteering for the operation...

It would also leave Massid and her father free to do whatever it was they were planning without anyone at all able to discern what it was.

Then, when spring came and the sea calmed enough to travel on, Massid would probably send her back to Jendara, which would be even worse. She'd be a captive among his flock of wives and concubines, none of whom would speak her language, all of whom would probably be hostile. If she wasn't driven to insanity by such imprisonment, one or more of them would probably try to poison her out of jealousy if Massid showed the slightest bit of preference for her. Travelers' tales of war among the women of a Jendaran *chareen* might be partially apocryphal, but where there was smoke, there was usually flame somewhere about.

Not a good option, for herself or her King.

Next choice—try to escape.

She wouldn't get more than a single chance at that, and she would need to be very careful about the timing. *I won't get a chance at all once there's a wedding, so it will have to be before then if I try it.* That much she was sure of—or at least, she wouldn't get a chance unless something completely catastrophic happened that threw the entire keep into an uproar and removed the probable guard from her door. So any attempt would have to take place after she learned as much as she could, but before a wedding.

The autumn and winter storms were on their way, and both Ferson and Massid *must* be as aware of that as she was, so whatever her father and the Prince were planning was probably intended to take advantage of the storms. But those same storms would also make getting to and from the keep from the landward side quite difficult. Not impossible, but it took a very determined traveler to brave the wind, snow, and above all, the ice storms that pounded the coastline by winter. If she was to escape, she'd have to plan things to a nicety, and she would have to have a great deal of luck. The closest place likely to take her in was one of the two nearest sea-keeps, but there was no telling whether or not Ferson was including the Lord of Lornetel and the Lord of Mandeles in his plans. If she fled to either of them, she might find herself handed back over. So the safest direction to flee would be inland, and it would take her at least twice as long to get to another inland keep as it would to get to the nearest sea-keeps.

Escape was not a good option. It might be the only one, but it was not much better than going through with the wedding.

Whatever the King and Countess suspected, it was nothing like this, or surely they'd have given her more warnings—and more of the sort of arcane aid that resided beneath the floor of the wardrobe.

Nevertheless, there had been a lot of thought put into this plot, whatever it was.

He must have been planning this for a while—but not for too long, or he would have summoned me earlier. This scheme could not have been hatched before this time last year.

The moment she realized that, she was certain of something else.

This had not been Lord Ferson's idea. Or at least, it didn't originate with him.

It wasn't that her father wasn't intelligent, because he was. He wasn't *clever,* he wasn't good at coming up with cunning plans, but he was intelligent. He knew how to read men, to the point where some of his underlings thought he could see what was in a man's mind. He was also cautious. Living in a sea-keep tended to make you cautious; the sea was temperamental and unforgiving; slip once, and she tended to kill you for your carelessness.

He also hated risk. He always measured risk against gain. But he wasn't creative, and he never initiated anything if he could help it.

Any overtures would have to have come from the Khaleem, and the promises of reward would have had to be quite substantial before he would even have considered answering the initial contact.

Whatever Lord Ferson had been promised, it had to have been something big enough to override that intelligence and native caution. And whatever was afoot, it had to be something that Lord Ferson was quite sure of bringing to fruition without being caught.

This was probably the Khaleem's idea. He had promised her father a great deal—and might even have already paid him some of what was promised as a gesture of good faith. Until this moment, there would not have been a great deal that anyone could point to as evidence of treason. Even now—well, entertaining Massid for the winter was a dubious move, but not precisely treasonable. It could even be said, and likely Ferson would if he was caught, that he had been trying to open negotiations to end the Khaleem's piracy.

Only if he made some more overt move, such as pledging his daughter to Massid, would he enter the realm of treason, and he had timed things so word of *that* was unlikely to escape before the greater plan came to fruition.

Now, something about that tickled her mind, but she couldn't put a finger on it. Mentally, she set it aside in the back of her mind and continued pursuing her original train of thought, jumping a little as the fire popped.

Nevertheless, even with powerful incentives, and a strong likelihood of success, there was something missing from this equation. There were too many things that could go wrong, too many uncertainties. The Khaleems were not known for fidelity to their promises in the past. Lord Ferson had never been noted for being a risk taker.

Something in his life must have changed in the past

year to make him even consider such an overture, much less follow through on it.

She took in a shuddering breath. This was getting more complicated by the moment. She was going to have to watch every step she took, every word she spoke.

So far her options were marriage, and escape. Both were fraught with the potential to go wrong. There was a third option—to delay—but she didn't think that she would get very far with that—except...

Hmm.

There was a narrow path through all of this, perhaps. She had boldly told the Countess there was no way her father could force her into a marriage against her will. Legally, that is, and when she had claimed that, she had assumed any such marriage would be to a fellow countryman, who would be bound by the law and custom of the sea-keeps. But that assumed there would be someone here to oppose her father's will; she had also assumed that no actual marriage could take place before spring, and that such a wedding would involve the invitations to the other lords of the sea-keeps. At least one of *them* would have answered to an appeal from her. Especially since all of them were very jealous of their equality in power, and would resent anything that made the Lord of Highclere the most powerful of the lot.

The arrival of Massid put rest to all of those assumptions.

However....

Part of what had been tickling the back of her thoughts finally bloomed into an idea. She couldn't *depend* on the law...but she could use it.

She closed her eyes briefly and said a little prayer of thanks that she had managed to keep her father from knowing precisely what kind of person he had welcomed back into his keep. The good God must have been in the back of her mind, keeping her from betraying her intelligence this whole time, from the moment she had left Viridian Manor to this moment. Because using the law to delay was going to depend entirely on Lord Ferson's impression that she was passive, ordinary, and above all, *stupid*. Stupid enough not to realize why Massid was here, and stupid enough to believe the law would actually protect her from a marriage to anyone she didn't wish to wed. Stupid enough to blurt out her rights in public, thus reminding the rest of the freedmen of the keep that those rights existed, and make them feel unease that those ancient rights—as ancient as the ones that kept them *free* rather than serfs—were being threatened.

She was under no illusion that any of them would leap to her defense. Oh no. Those that weren't blindly loyal to Ferson—and there would be some, perhaps many—were also smart enough to know that opposing him in this could mean an unfortunate slip on an icy parapet in the middle of a storm.

However, that was not what she was aiming at. Fully half of those who served Ferson were freedmen; they were jealous of those rights that kept them free, and though they were not quick to anger, their anger burned long and sullen when it was aroused.

It would be a mistake to arouse their suspicions of the motives of their Lord at any time, but to do so when the winter storms were coming and everyone was confined here for months...that was dangerous. It had not happened in recent times, but there were tales, and plenty of them, of winters when one man ruled a sea-keep, but at the arrival of spring, another pledged fealty to the King in his place. Unfortunate slips on icy parapets in the middle of winter storms did not happen to only the lowborn.

Those who dwelled in the sea-keeps were isolated from the rest of the land at the best of times. The King was a far and distant figure; their lords and ladies stood with them through the storm as well as the zephyr. It was hard to give loyalty to one who was only a profile on a coin; easier by far to tell oneself that loyalty should go to those whom one *knew*. They might soothe their consciences by telling themselves that the King did not matter, that he cared nothing for them, so they were not obliged to care for him. But if they thought that their own lord threatened their rights—then they would begin to doubt, and every doubt served her purposes.

It was a thin plan, but at least it was a plan. First, before she did anything else, she needed to get word to the Countess of what she knew.

And she would have to be as hard to read as the stones of Highclere Sea-Keep. Her best hope of success lay with her father expecting one thing from her, and getting something quite, quite different.

Anatha woke her in the morning, the first morning in a very long time that she had not awakened by herself. Part of it was the sound of the sea beneath the walls of the keep; it had been her lullaby as a child, and the familiar sound, at once wild and rhythmic, was strangely soothing. Even the warning of storm to come in the waves below her window was not enough to keep the waves from lulling her. Part of it was the darkness of her rooms. Not even in the long nights and dull days of winter were the rooms at Viridian Manor this dark.

But the sound of footsteps in the outer room did, finally, penetrate her slumber, and the sound was unfamiliar enough to bring her to full wakefulness in the time it took to draw a breath.

Anatha did not speak, but as soon as Moira was awake, she recognized the sounds of someone tending the fire and assumed it could only be her new maid. She pulled back the bed curtains herself in time to see Anatha flinging back the shutters in the solar to let in the daylight.

"My lady!" the woman said, turning at the sound of the fabric being pulled back. "What gown do you wish?"

"The brown wool, please, Anatha," she said quietly.

"And the amber torque and carnelian bracelet." Not ostentatious, but enough ornament that her father would find nothing to fault in her appearance—and she had a use for the carnelian bracelet. "Have you found the fine-work you told me of?"

"I now know where it is stored, my lady," the maid replied, removing the gown from the wardrobe and a chemise from the chest. "I shall fetch it for you when you are dressed."

"I have been dressing myself since I was a child, Anatha," she replied. "I think I can do so now, and I should like to have the fine-work here as soon as may be. It is dull here without other ladies to speak to. I shall need something besides my duties to occupy me."

There. Let Anatha carry the tale that she was interested only in "womanly" things. And that there was some "womanly" vanity involved, probably. The gowns she had brought with her were plain and mostly unornamented; any embroidery to make herself fine she would have to do with her own two hands.

"If you will be so kind as to deal with the fine-work," Moira continued, "I shall attend to myself." She smiled at the maid's hesitation. "I doubt anyone will question your diligence so long as *I* do not."

Anatha bowed her head slightly. "Very well, my lady," she replied, as Moira pulled the chemise over her head. The door was closing behind her as Moira's head emerged from the folds of fabric.

Which was precisely what Moira had hoped for.

Quickly she removed the bottom from the wardrobe, and removed a small box. From the box she took a metal capsule fastened to a leather band, and a slip of paper as light and thin as silk. There were only a half dozen of those capsules, but she doubted very much that she would get many chances to use them all with storms coming. She took both, and the quill and ink from her desk, to the window. She needed all the light she could get to write the tiniest letters she could manage.

"Prince Massid, son of Khaleem of Jendara here," she wrote. *"Ferson's guest. Purpose unknown. Possible alliance and marriage?"*

She nibbled the end of the quill and added, *"King's fool Kedric also here."* It was all she could fit in; it would have to do.

She waved the paper until the ink was dry, then rolled it until it would fit inside the tiny capsule, and screwed the capsule up tight. She picked up her favorite bracelet, silver, with a carnelian cabochon. The metal backing the cabochon on the inside of the bracelet was hinged; the capsule fit snugly inside it with the thin leather tucked in around it.

Then she hastily pulled on the brown woolen gown, clasped the necklet around her neck, restored the wardrobe, and returned the ink and quill to their proper places.

By the time Anatha returned with two servants carrying wooden chests, she was sitting quietly on a stool, brushing out her own hair.

"I'll do that, my lady," the maid said, with faint disapproval, putting the casket she herself held down on the chest at the foot of the bed. "You two! Put those chests down next to my lady's tapestry frame in the solar and go!"

Moira surrendered the brush to Anatha, and allowed the maid to brush and braid her hair with brown silk ribbons. She sat quietly during the whole process, only allowing her fingers to rub the surface of the carnelian. Was there a faint warmth there?

Well, the first, and easiest part was done with. Now she had to find an excuse to go up to the top of the cliff this afternoon.

Prince Massid was nowhere to be seen when she went down to the hall to break her fast, but she didn't expect him to be there. Princes of Jendara did not eat with common folk, and only the evening meal was held in state at Highclere Sea-Keep. There was food set out in the morning, and again at noontide, and one was expected to help oneself. Though of course, anyone with rank to command a servant could have food brought to her room.

And I may just do that. The less Father sees of me, the better. Bread and butter, small beer, and an apple, all taken from the side tables, had served her well enough this morning; she was apparently Keep Lady now, and she should take up her duties as such.

An inspection of the kitchen and kitchen staff was definitely in order. They needed to see her; she needed to see them. In all likelihood, absolutely nothing would change, except that the order of responsibility would have been established. And this, too, was something she would have—and indeed had—learned under Countess Vrenable's tutelage.

Lord Ferson was not the sort to allow his staff to be left to their own devices even though there was no Keep Lady. He must have established strong superior servants in place when his second wife proved un-equal to the challenge of truly running the daily busi-ness of the keep. The head cook was a formidable man, muscled like a fisherman used to hauling in heavy nets, and the housekeeper his equally formidable wife whose build nearly matched his. They came after the time when Moira had been sent off to fosterage, but she found nothing to fault with either of them. She did, however, take charge of the keys to the spice cup-board and the wine cellar. Not that there probably wasn't another set, and perhaps two, but the Keep Lady was supposed to be at least nominally in charge of the spices and fine drink, and appearances had to be maintained.

She spent the rest of the morning and early afternoon inspecting the rest of the household stores with Anatha in tow, then had exactly the excuse she needed to go up to the top of the cliff when the cook came to her with the evening's menu for her approval, which included a dove pie for the High Table, and asked if she would also care to see the chicken pens and dovecote above.

"Indeed," Moira said promptly. "And I will take the opportunity to see the stables and the kennels as well. There are storms coming, and I do not think there will be another good chance soon."

"My lady has the sea sense," the cook rumbled with approval, and sent her up with two of the sturdiest kitchen maids as escort.

Fish was a staple and plentiful at the sea-keeps, but those who sat at the High Table had the benefit of a more varied diet. There would be game laid away as soon as the first storm brought real cold, but the two things that could be depended on to supply a change in menu were the chicken yard and the dovecote. Both were in the lee of the seaward wall, to keep the worst of the storms off them. There was nothing to distinguish either from every other dovecote and chicken yard she had ever seen—though both were impeccably kept—but she went through the motions of inspecting them. Then, while the maids selected doves for the pie, *she* picked a bright-eyed, strong young dove on a perch, and calmly reached toward it with the hand bearing the carnelian bracelet. The dove stared at the stone, transfixed, and she picked him up as casually as selecting an egg. The maids didn't even notice.

She took him outside, made sure that there was no one near to see what she was doing, then took off the bracelet. She had practiced this a hundred times under the Countess's sharp eye; it was a matter of moments to extract the capsule containing her message, tie it to the bird's leg securely, slip the bracelet back on, and toss the dove in the air.

The capsule, of course, had been enchanted. While it was touching her, it would freeze a bird in a kind of sleep. The moment it left her hand, it told the bird that home was not *here,* home was in the little dovecote where the Countess kept her "pets" in the solar of Viridian Manor. Pigeons were well-known for swift flight and homing ability. This one would be with the Countess by tomorrow at the latest, where, saved from becoming pie, he would live out his life as a pampered pet, and perhaps go on to sire more doves from the lines of Highclere. But the spell was strictly one way, nor would it have been wise for her to be looking for messages among her father's doves. She could never be sure when a message would arrive, and for one to fall into anyone else's hands but hers would be a disaster.

With the dove away, she turned her attention to the chicken yard, then the kennel and stables. All were immaculate, but she expected nothing less from her father. Firstly, he was a man with a powerful sense of order, and secondly, there were visitors to impress. Perhaps the Prince of Jendara was unlikely to venture up here to look at ordinary hounds and horses, but in case he did, Lord Ferson would want stables and kennels to be ready for him.

There was no mews here; the lords of the sea-keeps generally kept no birds of prey. The ducks that swam in the sea, coots and scups and the like, tasted like the

worst of fish and fowl combined. Not much in the way
of game birds populated Lord Ferson's lands, and even
if they had, they didn't vary greatly enough in taste
from dove, pigeon, and chicken for him to care to
bother. And at Highclere, no one hunted for pleasure.
This was a working, quasi-military keep; there were no
highborn fellows idling about. Hunts were purposeful,
for meat, and conducted with the intention of spending as little time on them as possible. Boar and deer
were tracked, netted, and, if deemed "fair" game,
quickly dispatched. Rabbits and hares were snared.
The gamekeepers brought the catch in to be stored,
and that was the end of it; Lord Ferson himself rarely
participated.

So the kennels here were nothing like those at Viridian Manor; there were coursing hounds, calm and purposeful, but aloof. Nor were the stables full of anything
but sturdy workhorses. Still, Moira had enough of sea-
keep blood in her that she had never really enjoyed
hunting and riding the way most of the other girls fostered with the Countess had. Riding was a way to get
from *here* to *there* quickly, and as for hunting, why
spend all day pursuing something your gamekeeper
could take down in an hour? The only thing she had really enjoyed was falconry, and then it was in watching
the swift and agile birds, riding the winds like the em-
bodiment of wind itself.

She followed the kitchen maids with their burdens
back down into the keep, noting as the door to the

upper stairs closed behind her that the sound of the waves had intensified. The storm would arrive soon, possibly around dinnertime.

She wondered how the Prince of Jendara would like it. The Khaleemate was not noted for weather.

The storm broke over the keep as she was descending into the Great Hall for dinner. She had spent the remainder of her afternoon going over the contents of the chests her maid had hunted up out of storage, and they had been surprising. Her own mother had not been noted for her needlework, preferring to cut bands of fine work from old, outworn garments and stitch them with nearly invisible stitches to new ones, rather than embroider anything of her own. Sometimes, when the sea brought salvage in the way of clothing or fabric, she would use the ornaments from those, or carefully cut long strips of brocade to hem into trim. But Lord Ferson's next wives, it appeared, had been expert needlewomen. The chests contained fine linen and silk, hemmed strips of frieze for covering with counted stitches, and skeins of fine, beautifully dyed wool for tapestry and the heavy embroidery called crewel. The smaller casket held embroidery silks and gold and silver bullion meant for a truly skilled worker with the needle—and golden needles. The latter were not for show—a needle made of gold would never snag on even the thinnest of silk, but pass through it smoothly and easily.

In this, Moira was *not* like her mother. She enjoyed needlework, and had brought her skills up to a level where even the Countess admired her work. She smiled with pleasure at the sight of such riches.

There was even a half-finished neck placket for a gown there, and she wasted no time in mounting it to the frame by the window and setting out what she would use to complete it before the sky began to darken with clouds racing before the storm. The next few days would be so dark that she would not be able to discern colors well; she would have to know what was where in her holder in order to work in the dim light.

The nearer the time came to dinner, the more her stomach knotted. Surely tonight the announcement would come—and she had no idea what to do yet.

By the time she paced into the hall, as the first bolts of lightning flashed outside the windows and the storm winds screamed at the stones, she was as taut as a harp string with tension.

But there was no one on the dais, and she took her seat with as much outward calm as she could manage. Already it was much colder in the hall than last night, and servants had set shields made of paper-thin slices of mica around any open lamp. Not that there were many of those; the one thing Highclere never ran short of was drafts, and most lamps were shielded.

The onset of the storm made no difference to the folk of the keep, except for those who would be manning the storm beacons. In this sort of weather, they would not be taking the path that clung to the cliff—that would be courting death. There were ways out to the two nearer beacons which cut through the cliff itself from the keep. The passages were narrow and claustrophobic, but better than trying to inch along the path with rain and wave striving to tear you from it. Those two near beacons marked the site of dangerous current and rocks, and were the reason the sea-keep had been built where it was. The further beacons, showing only where the coastline was, were built on the top of the cliff, much like watchtowers, and the men manning them stayed there for a week at a time.

Moira felt the stone of the keep shiver under her feet as the storm waves outside began to pound against the cliff side and the keep itself. Now the roar of the waves penetrated even the thick stone; it would be a hard night, and the storm might last two or three days altogether.

Then a bolt of lightning flashed down somewhere very nearby, for the crash of thunder that shook the entire keep came simultaneously with the flash that lit up the hall more brightly than daylight.

Moira was not ashamed that she jumped and smothered an involuntary scream. Half of the people in the hall did the same, and the other half started and clutched at something.

Her heart was pounding and one hand was at her throat as she forced calm onto herself, just as the Prince of Jendara and her father came in. She had barely gotten her heart under control. Kedric followed a few paces behind. Moira was secretly pleased that Massid was visibly shaken, wide-eyed and, she thought, a little pale under his tan.

Her father seemed to be assessing the Prince as they took their seats, and Moira thought he made up his mind about something as he gave the signal to begin the serving.

"You told me your weather was—formidable, Lord Ferson," Massid said. To his credit, his voice was steady. "I did not grasp quite what you meant. This is an order of magnitude greater than I had thought."

Moira looked down at her soup, but concentrated on every word, and especially, the nuances of expression in their voices.

"I have never known an outsider who had any grasp of what a winter storm could be like before he came to a sea-keep, Prince Massid," her father replied, and there was an interesting inflection in his voice, something Moira could not quite grasp. "Nevertheless, this is an unusually strong storm, even for this time of year. I think it is a very good thing that your ship is safe in the harbor."

The Prince of Jendara and her father exchanged a wordless glance. Moira could not see her father's expression, but Massid looked like someone who was harboring a very satisfying secret. She felt the back of her neck prickle. "As my father told you, my lord, we have never lost a ship to a storm, though our enemies have—often." He smiled then, a smile that called to mind the grin of a shark with a seal in its jaws.

"Depending on who was caught in this weather, what kind of ship and pilot they have, we may be gathering our winter harvest when the storm ends," Lord Ferson replied, and he did not trouble to hide the satisfaction in his voice.

Moira shivered. Fortunately her father's attention was on his guest, and to a man from Jendara, a woman was too unimportant to take note of. She knew very well what he meant. At a sea-keep, the "winter harvest" meant the salvage cast up on the rocks after a wreck.

"In a storm this strong," her father continued, "any ship that's been hugging the coastline had better have a sharp pilot and a good lookout to avoid the rocks, or she'll be driven straight onto them. Even with the beacons, you need luck on your side when the Winter Witch comes in, because if you don't make your turn, you're on the teeth, and there's an end to you."

He was gloating. She knew it—she knew that tone. He was gloating, and she didn't know why—

"So unfortunate." Massid shook his head, and added, silkily, "And I suppose that turning out to sea and beating away from the coast is no better?"

"You'd better be provisioned for a double fortnight. The Winter Witch can take you a long way from where you ought to be, if she catches you away from the coast. And then, of course, there's pirates." Ferson's voice took on a sly note.

Yes, and you both should know about pirates, Moira thought.

"Ah, pirates. A terrible scourge. I am told they often follow along behind one of these storms as if they knew where it was going," Massid replied—but out of the corner of her eye, Moira saw him straighten, and abruptly his tone took on a lighter cast, with no shades of meaning. "Ah, what is this?"

"Fish baked in a salt crust, my lord," replied Ferson, as if they had been discussing no more than food the moment before. "It is one of my cook's specialties. This fish, baked in this way, leaves no bones in the meat, and the herbs it is stuffed with permeate the flesh, while the flesh itself remains moist. We make a virtue of necessity, having plenty of fish and no lack of salt. The salt sticks to the skin and never touches the flesh."

"Interesting!" As the server laid a portion before the guest, he leaned over and sniffed it. "Thyme, bay, and basil, I think. How very pleasant!"

Moira knew some sort of secret dialogue had been passing between the two of them, but she simply did not have the key to understanding what was going on under the surface. It was exceedingly frustrating.

Kedric played quietly throughout the meal though his presence was not in the least soothing. At least, she didn't find it so. The time or two she took her attention off Massid and her father, she found the fool staring at *her* with a strange intensity, which was as unnerving as the unspoken conversation going on between Ferson and his guest.

Once again, the announcement she had dreaded never came, and she excused herself as soon as she could.

She didn't feel completely easy until she was in the semidarkness of the passage and out of sight of the High Table. As a child, during storms, she used to run through the passages as quickly as she could, because the lamps would snuff out seemingly by themselves. Strange currents of air would whisper or whine in corners, and all she could think about were the stories of how all those who had drowned when their ships ran up on the Teeth of Highclere followed the wind and the sea into the keep when the Winter Witch blew.

Now, as an adult, she knew that strange behavior of wind and sound was usual in a storm. No matter how well shielded the lanterns were, not all remained lit; drafts were so unpredictable that servants went through every passage at intervals, relighting the lamps that had blown out. And there was no way to keep drafts out of a place like this in storm season.

She felt sorry for anyone who had to take the passages to the beacons. There was no hope of doing anything except making your way in the darkness. No lamp flame could survive the blast that traveled along that tunnel, which was the source of the uncanny moan that signaled the beginning of a storm and didn't end until it was over.

As she neared her chambers, she paused for a moment, then, prompted by a feeling that she *ought* to, she abruptly took a different turn, going down the corridor that led to her old childhood nursery. The nursery had a window, and one of the best views in the entire keep. This wasn't an accident. The idea was that the children of a sea-keep should get used to the worst that storms could throw at the keep at an early age, and the cradle was not considered too early. Moira remembered many, many gloomy afternoons when it was too dark to have lessons or read or do needlework, lying in her bed on her stomach, peeking out through the curtains at the foot of her bed and watching rain lash the window. The curtained bed had seemed very safe when she was small, a good place to retreat to if the storm became so fierce the walls shook.

And she remembered nights, too, when lightning flashed through the cracks of the shutters while thunder vibrated the whole keep. Storms had never frightened her once she had gotten past a certain age; in fact, she'd found them exciting, exhilarating.

Though in the dark of the night, with witch fire dancing on the points of pikes, the tips of towers, and the tops of flagpoles, and the wind keening a death cry, the idea that those drowned souls might come looking for the warmth of the living could still make her skin crawl. At least they weren't looking for revenge. It was the honor and the duty of the sea-keeps to *prevent* them from coming aground....

Yes, but why was Father saying those things to the Prince of Jendara, then?

She shivered, opened the door to the nursery, and wrinkled her nose at the cold, dusty smell of the place. Clearly no one had been in here since she had left.

She felt her way along the wall, huddling into her warm shawl. The stone was like ice, the room itself as cold as a snow cave, but she wanted to see the storm over the ocean for herself. It was a sight she hadn't had since she'd left. The storms at Viridian Manor were impressive, but nothing like the Winter Witch riding the waves.

She came to the shutters and flipped the worn, wooden latch, opening them just as a bolt of lightning struck the sea outside.

In the brief flash of light, she could see that the waves were already washing over the stone terrace of the lowest level of the keep. As usual, water would be running in under the door there, and down the stairs. No matter. There was a drain for it at the foot of the stairs, and no one would go out that door until the storm was over, so it didn't matter if the stairs were slippery. She'd gone down there once or twice, daring herself to touch that foot-thick door as it trembled visibly under the full fury of the storm. All the keep children did. It was a rite of passage, to prove that you dared the witch to take you, and you were brave enough to face her down.

This was, definitely, one of the worst storms in her memory, especially for one so early.

She sat down on the chest just beneath the window, propped her elbows on the sill with her chin in both hands, and peered through the darkness, looking for the northern beacon that marked the beginning of the Teeth—and frowned.

She should see it clearly from here. No matter *how* terrible the storm, she should be seeing the beacon! Nothing could blow it out, and never, in all the history of the sea-keep, had anyone failed to light it in darkness or storm and keep it lit. This was not tiny lantern flame to be blown out—it was a great, roaring, oil-fed conflagration, shielded in a large bubble of greenish glass as thick as a thumb and surrounded by polished brass mirrors that reflected all the landward light out to sea.

Then, turning her head a little, she saw it, breathed a sigh of relief—then frowned more deeply.

It wasn't where it should be. It should be much farther away, along the cliff face. It wasn't where she remembered, and she had very vivid physical memories of planting both elbows on this windowsill, in little depressions that countless other elbows had worn into the wood, and looking straight out through the center pane to see it. Not through the pane that was left of center.

But I'm older and much taller—

No, that wasn't the problem. It couldn't be the problem. Taller would make no difference in where the beacon appeared to be from the view through this window—

But I can't be sure....

She stared at the warm, yellow light; it was, of course, much dimmer from the land side. The reflectors that sent as much light out to sea as possible saw to that. But the more she stared, and the more she positioned herself within the window frame, the more certain she was that it was not her memory that was at fault here.

But there was a way to be absolutely certain, and as she sucked on her lower lip anxiously, she decided she was going to make that test for herself. Because if something *was* wrong, she wanted to know, and she wasn't going to go to her father to try to find out. He had, after all, brought the Prince of Jendara here, and she was certain that it was without the King's knowledge or permission.

Quietly—in fact, on tiptoe, though she could not have said *why* she felt the need for stealth—she slipped back to her rooms. Anatha was not there. She was probably still enjoying her own dinner with the rest of the servants, for Moira had made it quite clear that she did *not* require her maid to dance attendance on her at every waking hour. There was no reason to leave the hall; the banks of hot stones that kept the food warm more than made up for the winds whistling in the rafters and stealing the warmth of the fires up the chimneys. And if she was in particularly good graces with the cook and the housekeeper, Anatha would be invited afterward to the warm room backing onto the baking oven, which the superior servants used as a parlor in winter.

Thank heavens. Anatha's absence made this much easier—no need to conjure up excuses for going back to the nursery.

She opened her jewelry casket underneath the lamp and found the ring she was looking for. Slipping it onto her middle finger, she stole back down the hall to the nursery, carefully closing the door behind her this time.

She positioned herself at the window with her eyes mere inches from the center pane, and making a fist, rubbed a little scratch in the glass right where the beacon shone through the storm with the diamond in the ring.

There. When the storm broke, she could come back here in daylight and see if the scratch lined up with the beacon. If it did, she had been anxious over nothing.

If it didn't—

If it didn't, there was something very, very strange going on at Highclere Sea-Keep. And she would have to find out what it was—and more important, why it was happening.

When Anatha returned to Moira's rooms, she found her mistress with her feet resting on a stone warmed on the hearth with a fur rug covering her lap, sitting beside the fire, knitting. Knitting was a very plebian pastime, and most ladies didn't even bother to learn, but Moira found it soothing. It was one of the few tasks that could be done by the uncertain light of a flickering fire and guttering lamps during a storm. And it certainly did no harm to have extra soft, lamb's-wool hose on hand in a sea-keep winter.

"A wild night, my lady," was all Anatha said. "The Winter Witch has come early."

"I thought as much—but I also wondered if my memory had been at fault," Moira replied. "Well, what are the canny old sailors saying?"

"That—that it isn't natural, my lady," Anatha replied, looking over her shoulder first, as if she expected to see someone spying on them from a corner. "The witch has never flown before all the leaves are gone, not in anyone's memory."

Once again, Moira felt an odd little sense of warning. "The leaves will certainly not outlast this storm," she replied, and yawned. "Are they saying this means a bad winter?"

Anatha looked over her shoulder, and this time, she leaned very close to Moira and whispered, "They're saying, this storm was *sent*."

Once again, that touch of warning, that sense as if a single ice-cold fingertip had been touched to the back of her neck. She thought about her father and Prince Massid exchanging cryptic comments and glances full of meaning about the winter storms.

But no one could control the weather. Even the greatest of magicians couldn't control the weather—the one who could would have a great and terrible weapon at his disposal. Such a magician wouldn't be content to serve a greater master. He himself would use that power to become a powerful ruler.

Not that Moira had any great acquaintance with magicians. They were few and far between, the genuine ones, anyway. The Countess had her wizard, Lady Amaranth, but she had never performed any magic more powerful than the spell that allowed the Grey Ladies to use pigeon-mail. And Lady Amaranth was supposed to be the most powerful wizard in the kingdom, except for those that served the King.

"How could such a storm be sent?" she replied, keeping her tone light and disbelieving. "And more to the point, why? This is a sea-keep—we are used to such storms. At most, it is an inconvenience. The men-at-arms won't be able to hunt until it's over, and we might run a bit short of fresh meat, but the High Table will not suffer. The beacons will have to be tended, and the poor fellows who have to do the tending will spend a miserable time of it. Soon or late, it doesn't matter when the Winter Witch flies, she'll have no effect on Highclere. And I hope you aren't going to tell me that God has sent the storms early for our sins! I shall be quite cross with you."

Anatha laughed at that. "No, my lady. You're right, of course. It was all just kitchen talk."

"Then I count on you to be sensible," Moira replied, with a nod. "When that sort of talk begins again, make sure you are the one who keeps her head." She yawned and set aside her work. "And I believe that I will be sensible and go to bed."

Tucked up in bed, with the curtains closed tightly all around to prevent icy drafts from waking her, Moira did not feel in the least sleepy. She turned on her side to think.

If someone was a powerful magician, and could control the weather, at least in part—he'd use that power to make himself a king. Wouldn't he?

But what if he already was a king? Or, say, a Khaleem, which was basically the same thing.

Massid had said that the Khaleemate had never lost a ship to storms. Maybe that wasn't just good luck. Maybe the Khaleems of Jendara had power over the weather.

If that was their only power, it was a cursed useful one, especially for a nation that fielded an enormous navy, and unofficially fielded a second enormous force of pirates.

But why would that be attractive to her father? It was true that bad storms could bring a few more ships to grief on the Teeth of Highclere, and that in turn would certainly increase the coffers of the Lord of Highclere Sea-Keep. But the gain would be offset by some loss; the worse the storms were, the less hunting there would be, the less fishing, and the more likely that one of those unfortunate accidents would befall whoever was supposed to be working outside. She vividly recalled a particularly wretched winter when frequent, though not violent, storms had kept everyone pent up within the walls right up until late spring. The number of fights had been appalling. Feuds had begun that were probably still being played out to this day. Ferson had lost a dozen men to accidents and to fights; it had been hard to replace them, and the keep had been shorthanded for nearly a year.

So what possible use could Ferson make of such a power that would outweigh the disadvantages?

She couldn't think of anything. So whatever had brought the Prince of Jendara here, it probably wasn't that.

She fell asleep still trying to figure out what had.

After four days of wind and storm, the morning of the fifth day broke over calm seas and a cloudless—if icy—sky.

Immediately, the scavengers went out to comb the shores for whatever the sea had cast up. Heaps of extremely useful kelp was always thrown upon the rocks, of course, but there were other things. Amber, jet, sea coal. And sometimes the sea in her fickle nature elected to toss back things that had gone to the bottom in previous wrecks. By the time Moira went down to breakfast, the keep was practically empty. Everyone who could be spared was out combing the shore, and everyone who could hunt was up in the forest doing so. The cook would make only one hot meal today, as most of his helpers would be elsewhere.

It seemed as good a time as any to send the Countess another message. But what? Moira still had no idea why Massid was here. No marriage had yet been proposed. And yet—

Frustrated, she essentially repeated her previous warning with the addition of the rumor about the storm being "sent," adding only that Massid was spending all his time in her father's company. She released the dove with a sense of futility, and carried a basket of eggs down to the cook as her excuse for being up there in the first place.

With nothing much to do, she went into the Great Hall before returning to her rooms, and stood at the window, brooding down at the ocean.

"Pining for a beloved, my lady?" Kedric's dry voice came from behind her.

"If you know anything at all about the women schooled by the Countess, you know we don't pine for anything," she replied, without turning. "And as for a beloved, you would know that we also are aware that our lives are not our own to give."

"Ah yes, you are well schooled in obedience—" The bitterness in his voice made her turn and regard him with a lifted brow.

"Perhaps, Kedric, you are insufficiently acquainted with the meaning of the phrase *noblesse oblige,*" she replied, keeping her tone cool, and just on the polite side of sarcastic. "It means that those who are born into a position of power inherit obligations and responsibilities far in excess of the benefits of privilege. It means that we are obligated to protect those who give us their loyalty and service. Sometimes that protection comes at the cost of a life. Sometimes the cost is only freedom.

But we *owe* them that. This is what *noblesse oblige* means."

She could not read Kedric's face, so she continued. "Men," she said with some bitterness of her own, "think that being willing to lay down their lives is difficult. They have no conception of what it means to be willing to lay down your life as a woman does—not for a moment of sacrifice, but for years, decades of sacrifice. To surrender it in that way so that the people you have sworn to protect *are* protected."

"And so, you lie down and let yourself—" Kedric began.

She interrupted him, a cold fury in her voice that she could not entirely repress. "Is that what you think? That this is mere, passive obedience, weak and weak willed? I thought you wiser than your motley, Kedric. It is hard, hard, to subdue the will, to force aside *I want* for *I must*. But you mistake me. Even in the most loveless and calculated of marriages, there are children to love and be loved by. I refer to the hardest sacrifice of all, for a woman to steel her will to live alone and unwedded, not because she wishes to, but because, for the sake of her people, she must—to look down the long years ahead and see nothing at the end of them but an empty bed and a lonely singleness."

He made a little strangling sound, and she sniffed, interpreting his odd expression, she thought, correctly. "What? You thought the Countess remained single because she wished to? Or because she does not care for men? Oh, she mourns the Count her husband, and she truly loved him, but she stays a single widow because it is her cousin the King's will, so that she can be the stalking horse, be dangled, like a prize at a fair, for all to see but ultimately never be won by any. And she takes no lovers, for she is the King's cousin, and like Caesar's wife, she must be above reproach. She knows that, has always known it, and she makes sure her Gr— her ladies know that there is more than one way in which the King may ask for their obedience, and what the cost may be."

"I—see," he managed. "That had not occurred to me."

"And to protect my people, if I thought it *would* protect them, yes, I would give myself over to be locked away in a seraglio in Jendara," she added, turning back to the window. "But I do not think it would protect them. I think the opposite, and I think the King would agree."

"I think he would, too, my lady." Kedric's tone was firm again.

Well, there it was. The unspoken message and alliance she had been hoping to hear. Kedric was the King's man, and he was here to be the King's eyes and ears. "The trouble is, I do not know how to prevent it," she said, sadly. "Short of throwing myself into the sea."

"You are the heir to a sea-keep, my lady, and as such you can wed any of the King's subjects you choose without his leave," Kedric said slowly, as if he was thinking aloud. "But by the law of the land and the charter by which a sea-keep is held, you *cannot* wed someone who is *not* one of his subjects without his leave."

And there it was—her escape. Or at least a way to stall for time. Her father would have to pretend that he was sending for the King's permission. Probably he would forge such a message, but *she* had been schooled by the Countess, and she had seen and learned how to recognize the King's hand and seal. She didn't think there was anyone here with sufficient talent to successfully forge a royal decree.

"That," she said aloud, "is quite true. And it is exceedingly useful to keep in mind."

"I am pleased to have given you something useful, my lady," he replied, as she turned back to look down at the ocean.

A movement along the cliff face caught her eye. It was the work crew, going out to replenish the fuel for the beacon—and that reminded her, suddenly, of the mark she had made on the window of the nursery, a mark which might give her some information, though what use she could make of it, she was not yet sure.

"You'll excuse me, I hope," she said, after a moment—but then, abruptly, added, "unless you would care to accompany me to the old nursery. I think I might have left something there that might interest you."

He looked at her askance, but nodded. "If you wish, my lady, and you think I may be of service."

She smiled without humor. "Say, rather, it might be

instructive to you to see how a sea-keep child begins its life. We are not sheltered."

"That," the minstrel said, raising his eyebrows, "I can *truly* believe."

He followed her to the nursery, and did not voice any objections to the chill, stale air as she opened the door. It was dark, as she had expected. As far as she could tell, no one had opened the shutters on the window since she herself had closed them.

She went straight to the window, and opened them—she didn't fling them open, she moved them quietly, to make as little noise as possible.

"What are you—" Kedric began. She held up a cautioning hand.

"This, you see, is the view every child of the lord of a sea-keep gets from the time it leaves the cradle," she said, as she leaned down to scrutinize the window-panes. Finally she resorted to finding the scratch she had made by touch rather than by sight. Somewhat to her surprise, it wasn't standing out the way she had thought it would. Perhaps too many fantastic tales of lovelorn maidens or tragically imprisoned heroes inscribing poems on the windows of their rooms had given her the mistaken impression that all it would take was a little rubbing with a diamond to leave a visible mark.

At length she found it, sat down on the window seat, and tried to make the mark line up with the beacon just visible from where she sat.

It did nothing of the sort. The trouble was, it didn't line up with any place that people would be able to get to. While she could certainly imagine that her father would have the cleverness to construct a false beacon, this one was apparently somewhere beyond the cliff itself, out in the water.

Which was...odd.

"It's a bit of a harrowing view for a child, I would think," Kedric said. Then he whispered, "What exactly are you doing, my lady? I hope you didn't bring me here to reminisce."

"During the storm, I made a scratch on the glass to line up with the beacon," she whispered back, "because it seemed to me that it was in the wrong place, and the only way to know for sure was to see if the mark lined up with the structure when the storm cleared.

"Here, take my seat and see for yourself," she said, louder, relinquishing her spot on the window seat. "Generations of sea-keep children grew up on this view, come storm or sunshine."

He replaced her, while she spoke in conversational tones about the beacon, the storms, and the beachcombers down on the rocks and what they might find.

He lined himself up with her mark, and peered through the window, frowning. "What keeps the beacon alight?" he asked, still frowning.

"Sea coal, but something's done to it magically," she replied. "A little of it burns with a tall, bright flame.

There are reflectors behind the flame to send as much of the light as possible out to sea. We have to get the special coal from the King and store it. He sends it to us by packhorse. It must be very hard to make, because we have to account for every bit burned, and if we use more than we've been allotted, we have to say why."

With his back to her, she could see that one of his shoulders was significantly higher than the other, and his spine was slightly twisted. It looked very painful.

Perhaps that accounted for his sourness.

"The beacon and your scratch do not match up, my lady," he said softly. "Is there any significance to the position where it does match up?"

"Of course, the beacon is meant to show sailors where the coast is, when there are storms and fog," she said aloud. "During times like those, ships hug the coastline, so they navigate by the beacons in order to avoid being lost at sea. But also a beacon has to be placed precisely, because at the spot where it has been built, there are generally shoals or rocks where ships can run aground."

He nodded. "So if, say, something were to destroy this beacon, the new one would have to be built on exactly the same spot?"

"Oh, more than that. Even if this one were destroyed, *some* sort of temporary beacon would have to be put there immediately," she replied. "It's just too vital."

She watched his lips compress and his eyes narrow, only at that moment realizing that they were a dark grey that seemed to darken even as she watched. He knew something that she didn't.

"I wish, my lady, that we could discover just *where* along your coastline this scratch does line up," he whispered.

"There is no way to tell, and I wouldn't care to go outside in a storm to try to find out," she whispered back. Then she said, in a normal tone, "If it were not for the beacons, of course, it would not be possible for trade ships to sail in the winter, nor for the coastal patrols to keep enemies from our shores. Fishermen have no need of them, of course, for when the weather is foul they wisely do not put out to sea."

"Indeed. Well, this has been very enlightening, my lady, and I thank you for your hospitality." He stood up abruptly, forcing her to step back with some haste. He sketched a bow. "There is a great deal more about this sea-keep and its daughter than meets the eye."

He held the door open for her courteously, and she stepped through. They parted at the intersection of the two corridors, and she returned to her room, feeling irritated and uneasy. *She* had shared her information with him, but he had given her nothing.

Her irritation only increased when she returned to the Great Hall, intending, if nothing else, to watch the beachcombers and her father's overseer below from the vantage point of the great window behind the High Table on the dais, thinking perhaps she might be able also to guess where the displaced beacon had been, though she could not for a moment imagine how the light had *been* displaced. As far as she could tell, though she was far from certain about this, it had been "moved" several hundred yards down the coastline and a bit farther out to sea. Which, if she was correct, would mean that any boat using it as a guide would think the promontory and rocks that the beacon stood over were there, and that once past, it would be safe to cut in closer to shore.

Which would, of course, depending on the accuracy of the beacon, put a ship directly *on* the rocks.

Was it just greed that had driven her father to storm-assisted piracy? That didn't make a great deal of sense. In summer, when storms never lasted more than a day, yes. But winter storms lasted several days, and it wouldn't do her father a great deal of good if the ship he wanted was wrecked on the first or second day of a storm. You couldn't go out on the rocks for salvage in the teeth of a winter gale, and anything washed up after a wreck would soon be taken away by the sea and tides again. If he was colluding with the Khaleem to bring in invaders—

Well, that made no sense, either. You would want the beacon where it actually *was* if you were bringing in strangers to this coast, and anyway, where would they land? The docks for the keep were small, nowhere near big enough for an invasion force. And anyway, the Khaleemate ran to pirates, not soldiers. It was one thing to turn them loose on the high seas and tax them on their booty when they returned to port. It was quite another to expect them to come in to land and act like soldiers.

So *why* shift the beacon?

And who had done it? The only thing she could think of was that it had been done by magic, and aside from Massid and Kedric, there were no obvious strangers here.

And surely Massid could not be a magician. As rare as magicians were, surely the Khaleem would not allow a son who was also a magician so far away from home.

She brooded down on the waves crashing over the rocks in torrents of white foam, and felt a chill steal over her. That left Kedric.

Kedric, who she, not that long ago, had told almost everything. So now, if he *was* her father's man, her father knew everything—from her own reluctance to be handed off in marriage to Massid, to the fact that she knew about the beacon. After all, he hadn't said he was the King's man, she had merely read it into what he *had* said.

Blessed God, I have been a fool! She stared sightlessly down into the water, feeling her heart slowly going numb, and her mind with it. She had showed him—she had told him—

What? asked an impatient and surprisingly rational voice inside her. *You told him that you would do your duty and marry Massid if you thought it would protect your people, but that you didn't think it would do any such thing. You made it clear you were unhappy about the idea, and who wouldn't be? You told him a few choice things about the Countess, but nothing that's not common knowledge, and you didn't reveal that you are a Grey Lady. You pointed out what your duty was to your people, and how much that duty could cost you. You showed him the scratch on the glass and told him why you'd made it, but so far as he knows, you have no way of telling anyone else.*

All that was true, certainly, but—

But if he's your father's man, now he has all the arguments your father needs—or so he thinks—to persuade you to marry Massid when he proposes it. There's no harm in that. He knows you are more intelligent than you appear, but there's no harm in that, either. He doesn't know about the birds, or your weapons, or any of your other skills. The only thing you showed him is that you are an intelligent young woman who suspects her father is up to no good, but who certainly can't tell anyone and can't do anything about the knowledge.

She recognized that little voice in her mind; it was the one that coolly analyzed and put fears to rest, no matter how panicked the rest of her mind was. It was seldom wrong, and that only in degree. She sometimes wondered if it was the voice of some guardian angel. Sometimes the voice sounded exactly like the Countess, though, and while she admired the Countess greatly, she would have been the first to say that the Countess Vrenable was no angel.

She unclenched her fists and closed her eyes a moment to clear her mind. If Kedric was the King's man, he had information he might be able to use. If he was her father's man, he had nothing he could use to harm her—except that he—and her father—would now know that she was intelligent enough and quick enough to suspect something was wrong.

So—not "no" harm done. Though she was not an immediate danger to any plans they had in train, she could reveal them, now or later. So she had done herself harm enough that her father might move a little faster to put her where she could do *him* no harm... which was probably with Massid.

Time to send another bird. And more than time to resume her training. When the time came, she might need every bit of strength she had.

But two weeks, and another storm, passed with nothing changing in the keep or out of it, so far as appearances went. Every day Moira tended to the affairs of the keep as the Keep Lady should. Every evening she spent dining in the Great Hall with her father and Massid. Afternoons were spent at her embroidery; she quickly finished the half-finished placket, had Anatha stitch it to one of her gowns, and started another. But there was one change that no one was aware of.

The sea-keep was carved into and out of the rock of the cliff; with that sort of construction, it was difficult to create "secret" passages and "hidden" rooms, such as Viridian Manor, with its wood-and-stone construction. It was, after all, much, much easier to build something of that sort into the walls than it was to carve it out of rock, then try to hide it.

But there was one place in Highclere Sea-Keep that almost no one ever went to this time of year.

Even a place built out of stone has need of timber. Not firewood, but properly seasoned lumber, for repairs, paneling, cabinetry, furniture, and boats.

So when a particularly fine tree was cut down—or when the lord of the sea-keep was moved to trade for one with an inland lord whose forests were not subject to near-constant wind—cut and planed planks of every possible thickness were laid down to dry and season in what was called "the timber room."

It wasn't a room at all. It was a cave, but a peculiarly dry cave, and one which allowed the planks to cure and dry naturally. The oldest bits of wood—very expensive stuff it was, of fantastical grains and coloring—were three generations old. There wasn't a great deal of that, and it was generally used for inlay work. The rest wasn't more than ten years old, twenty at most, although there were some heavy oak beams that had been seasoning since Moira's grandfather laid them down before he died.

In summer and early fall, this place was a hive of activity. In winter, though, no one bothered to look in. In itself, it was valuable, but no one was likely to steal a load of wood. Layers of planks laid down in soft sand made a floor that didn't shift much. There wasn't much light, and the noise from the ocean far below drowned out any sounds that might be made up here.

In short, it made a perfect place for Moira to practice.

There was a great advantage to being a modest maiden in winter. The loose, long-sleeved, high-necked gowns and wimples she wore allowed her to wear her fighting clothing, mail and all, and no one noticed. Heavy winter fabrics did not betray so much as a hint of chain mail. She didn't bring her sword and dagger up to the timber room, but there were plenty of pieces of wood of the right size and shape there already. So once a day—and a different time of day each time, if she could manage it—she would, over the course of an hour, first get back to her room and put on her mail and armor, then find a way to get to the timber room, where she would doff her dress and begin her stretching exercises, moving into the fighting exercises as soon as her muscles were limber. It was frustrating, not having a partner to practice with, but at least it *was* practice, and she always tried to push herself a little more each day, in speed and accuracy. When she was tired, but before she was winded, she would go back to her room, take off the armor and hide it again, and go on about her business.

It was particularly interesting to be up there during a storm. Only one lantern could be made to stay alight, and the shifting shadows made footwork and blade-work a challenge. The wind howled through here; the place was like a chimney. She was exceptionally careful about the lantern. Under these conditions, if a fire actually started up here without first being blown out, it would be uncontrollable in an instant, destroying decades' worth of valuable wood.

Though of course, with the wind howling through the place, it was unlikely that a fire *could* catch strongly enough to avoid being extinguished.

And still nothing happened. Except that Massid and her father began to play chess every night after the remains of supper were cleared away.

After the first night, she remained to watch out of curiosity. Their play reflected, she thought, their personalities. Her father played without speaking during his own turn, fiercely intent and intense, and scowling whenever he lost a piece. The Prince of Jendara was a complete contrast, outwardly relaxed, a smile on his bearded lips, apparently listening to Kedric's playing and occasionally commenting on it or the game. But as she watched him, she became aware of a predatory glitter in his eyes just before he was about to swoop down on an opposing piece, and a little smile of satisfaction when he knew he was going to win.

Or, more rarely, his smile grew icy, and his speech less easy and more punctiliously polite when he knew he was about to lose. And when that happened, there was a flash of pure rage for just the barest fraction of a moment that made her shiver.

It was particularly frightening the second night of the

second storm, when the wind and waves were crashing against the rocks below with such force that the stones of the keep groaned, and there was enough lightning they hardly needed lanterns. Chess was one game she had not mastered, so she couldn't really tell what was happening on the board, but her father was grinding his teeth in frustration, and Massid's eyes had that satisfied glitter as he toyed with his goblet. And then, all in an instant, her father's face went from angry desperation to utter triumph. He swooped down on the board and moved a piece, slamming it down in front of Massid's king. "Check and mate!" he shouted.

And for a moment, Massid's face went black with rage.

Now, that was a phrase that Moira had often heard before, but she had never actually seen it happen, and had often thought it a picturesque fabrication.

Now she knew better.

It wasn't that his face physically darkened—it was that his whole demeanor changed, and his expression for that instant was so suffused with the bitterest of hatred that it *seemed* to go black.

It only lasted a moment; it was gone so quickly that if she hadn't felt that shaken by what she had seen, she might have doubted the expression was there at all. But she *had* seen it, and it *was* there, and she knew that if, in that instant, Massid could have gotten away with it, he would have killed her father, and possibly everyone else who had witnessed his defeat.

But by the time her father looked up, Massid was

wearing an expression of rueful amusement. "I did not see that coming, my lord," he said graciously. "A most unorthodox move. I congratulate you."

Her father was not a gracious winner, but at least he didn't gloat too long. Massid's mask slipped a trifle, but he managed to maintain it long enough to excuse himself and retire for the night.

Moira went to bed feeling her insides quivering. If there was such a thing as a spirit of pure ruthlessness— too impersonal to be evil—that spirit dwelled within the Prince of Jendara.

And woe betide whoever crossed him in something he *really* wanted.

She had seen the face of the enemy. It frightened her in a way she had not expected to be frightened. It was one thing to face the possibility of having to deal with a forced marriage. It was another thing entirely to see what she had seen behind the pleasant mask.

The thought kept her in a restless half sleep that night, and she woke early to the sound that told her another storm was on the way. Her mind was preternaturally clear, and the first thing that came to her was that this storm would probably arrive on or about Midwinter Moon—the longest night of the year, and the highest tide until Midsummer Moon.

Not a good time to be having a winter storm as well. Any ships out at sea on that night would be better off well away from the coast.

In fact, if the waters surged in too high, parts of the keep would have to be temporarily abandoned. That hadn't happened in decades. Certainly not while Moira had been alive.

But the keep had probably weathered a hundred such storms, and would weather a hundred more. Whatever was in the lowest levels would be taken elsewhere; probably not much, actually, or at least, nothing much worth saving. They'd been dug as hiding places and escape routes, and there was always sea water getting in....

Well, when the storm came, they'd be flooded.

Two days, she thought, listening to the waves outside. *Three at the most.*

Part of her was still exhausted from the restless night, but the rest of her could not lie still a moment more.

She rose from her bed and dressed herself before Anatha could arrive. There was a tension in the air today, or at least, it felt that way to her.

And yet, when she ascended to the Great Hall, no one else seemed aware of it.

Everyone could read the signs of the impending storm, however, and it didn't take a sage to figure out that a storm combined with Midwinter Moon meant trouble. Small boats needed to not only be pulled into the sea caves, but winched up above the highest high-water mark. Large boats were manned with skeleton crews and sailed to the nearest safe harbor. The flotsam and jetsam that had collected since the last bad storm down in the lower keep levels was dragged out and sorted through, with anything deemed worth keeping packed properly away, and what was left over taken off to the rubbish pile for the next high tide to wash away farther down the coastline. The sea doors were checked and reinforced, supplies hauled down from storage places above, the heaviest of shutters locked in place over the most vulnerable windows.

With all this activity, Moira did not dare to slip away to the timber room to practice. With every able-bodied person scurrying on or about the keep making preparations, the cook was not bothering to lay out regular meals. Food was left in the Great Hall for people to snatch in passing.

This left her with nothing to do, staying in the Keep Lady's rooms in order to remain out of the way. Even Anatha was busy somewhere....

She tried to sit at her embroidery, and could not manage to set more than a stitch or two. At length, she rose and began pacing back and forth in front of the window. She had measured the space in steps at least twenty times, when a light tap made her jerk her head toward the door like a startled deer.

"I have been told, in no uncertain terms, that I am in the way, my lady," said Kedric, pushing the door open with one hand, the other clasping the neck of his lute.

"As am I," she admitted. "I am too much the lady to be permitted to work with my hands, and not enough of one, it seems, to be allowed to direct the work."

"Then we should obey Lord Ferson's directive and stay out from underfoot," Kedric replied lightly, and shut the door behind him.

His expression went from moderately amused to dead sober, all in an instant.

"Lady Moira, is there anyone among your father's people who is a magician or a wizard?" he asked urgently.

She started but covered it swiftly. "Why do you ask?" she replied cautiously, wondering if he had some way of detecting the spell on her bracelet and the little message capsules.

"Because I have several times been to the old nursery at night, during calm times and during storm," he replied. "And during calm nights, when someone walking guard or otherwise outside the keep might take notice, the light from the beacon is where it should be. But on nights of storm, it again comes from the wrong place. If the cause was some freakish reflection, it would not behave in such a manner, and the only way *I* know of to make such a thing happen is by—" he hesitated "—by magic."

Should she trust him? That was a good question, and she too hesitated before she answered. She still did not know who he served.

"Lady Moira," he said, as if reading her thoughts. "You must trust me. I have had word from the King and his cousin concerning *you*. The Countess Vrenable has identified you as one of her Grey Ladies. I serve the King in a similar capacity. The Countess was not aware of my presence here until after you had left Viridian Manor, or perhaps she would not have been so ready to send you here." He grimaced. "I know that you have been sending the Countess information using the doves at the top of the cliff. I also know that you have no means of getting information back in return, except by some visitor, and your father has arranged for the road to Highclere to be closed since your arrival."

She eyed him dubiously. "Then how are *you* getting word from my mistress and the King?" she demanded.

He laughed mirthlessly, and shrugged his good shoulder. "My lady, I am the king's wizard. Or one of them, anyway. I am an alchemyst. See here—" He pushed up his sleeve, and tattooed around his wrist was the image of the Serpent of Wisdom, the great snake that eats its own tail, the symbol of the alchemysts. It was the same side of his body as his hunched shoulder, and she wondered—had he always been so crippled, or had that deformity been inflicted upon him in the service of magic? "When I think it safe, I speak to my own master, who also serves the King, in the fire. But since you showed me the moving beacon, I have been extremely careful, because anyone who suspects that I am an alchemyst will know I can do this. If there is another magician about, he will have the power to duplicate what I do, and can intercept my messages in his own fire. And I ask you if there are any magicians among your father's people because the only way that *I* know of for the beacon to change its apparent position is by magic."

She shook her head, to his obvious disappointment. "Never, not since my mother died, and even she had only the touch of Moon and Sea magic she needed to be invested as Keep Lady. She was pregnant with me at that time, so both of us were bound to the service of the keep at the same time." It was her turn to laugh mirthlessly. "Trust Father to manage things so that he didn't have to bring a sage in for a second Investment Ceremony. He hates magic—"

She hesitated. Kedric crossed the room to stare into her eyes as if trying to wrest the thoughts from her head. "What?" he demanded.

"Perhaps I should have said he *hated* magic. I do not know that he still does. And perhaps the only reason he hated it once was because he could find no way to make it serve *his* demands, only those of the King and the keep."

"So if he has found a magician to answer to his will— he might have lost his distaste for the Arts Magical?" Kedric hazarded, his eyes narrowing.

"Maybe." She shook her head. "But—" she hesitated again "—all I have is speculation—"

"The speculations of a Grey Lady are as informed as many a man's certain facts," he told her. "Speak."

"I have only bits of things. Massid's presence—I *thought* it was to secure an alliance, but father hasn't even hinted at a betrothal, much less a marriage, and

Massid has made no real effort at courtship." She shook her head. "The thing is—"

"Ah," he said, holding up his finger for a moment. "Here is the other reason for my being here. Your father wishes to persuade you to an alliance with Massid, as you have assumed. I believe he intends to find a way to force you to it, and only the certainty that he cannot do so publicly has prevented him from having you bound over already. He has asked my advice on the subject. He has even toyed with allowing Massid to abduct you, by the way, and it was with great difficulty I persuaded him that this was a bad idea. I finally pointed out that the King would probably send the Corsairs in pursuit, despite the season, since you are his cousin's fosterling. I believe he wants this dealt with before the Midwinter Moon, and I believe that he intends to find a way to trick you or coerce you into agreeing within the next few days."

She turned an indignant and appalled face to him. "Surely you are in jest!"

He shook his head. "But I have a plan—"

"Well, daughter." Lord Ferson's voice was low, but strong enough to carry to the heads of the nearest tables. "I believe you may have divined my will by now, with regards to a marriage with Prince Massid."

Moira's head came up abruptly, and as she turned to face her father, she allowed her real feelings to show on her face. "Yes, I have," she said clearly, and more than loudly enough for most of the room to hear her.

It was something of a relief to be able to drop her mask at last, enough to show her anger and her resentment. "And I find it difficult to believe, my lord, that you are so willing to flout the law and the will of the King in this matter!"

If she had not been warned, she might have tried to dissemble. As it was, though her father was not aware of it, his wine had been mingled with a much more potent distilled spirit all evening, courtesy of Kedric, and she had her response ready, hoping to push him into acting without thinking.

Exactly as she had expected, her father's face darkened with the flush of anger, and the liquor seething in his veins spoke for him. "I find it difficult to believe that my own daughter, who owes me her life and her obedience, is so willing to flout *my* will!"

She stood up, and felt her hands trembling. She did not bother to try to hide her agitation; it would serve her purpose. "I am an obedient daughter, my lord, but the King's will supercedes my will and yours! Anything less is treason!"

"Nothing supercedes my will in this keep!" Ferson roared, rising to his feet, although Massid placed a restraining hand on his shoulder. "Forget that, my girl, and you will learn the truth of it to your sorrow—"

"Sorrow!" She uttered a brittle laugh. "If that is all you can threaten me with— I have rights, my lord, and not even you can take those from me, and I say I *will* not agree to this treasonous marriage!"

By now every eye was on the dais. There would be no keeping this secret from even the lowest scullery boy, and by the looks on the nearest faces, Ferson's words were not going down well. One did not threaten the Keep Lady; she embodied the Luck of the Keep. When she was contented, the storms were few, and the storm harvest rich. Moira could tell that people were beginning to think about the too-early and too-frequent storms of this winter.

They were also thinking that Ferson was talking about marrying the Luck of the Keep to an enemy, and that when the King got wind of it, there would be hell to pay. Her father was oblivious to the sideways glances, the unease in the hall. He was too consumed with rage, his face nearly purple.

"I tell you," she continued passionately, in the words Kedric had chosen for her to speak, "I would rather wed your *fool* than allow this Massid, this foreigner, to touch the smallest finger of my hand!"

For one moment she was afraid she had overreached herself—that she had gone just a little too far, that her father, who was so much more practiced in deception than she, would see through her.

But her father seized the bait like a ravenous shark. His head came up, and his eyes flashed with rage. "Oh you would, would you?" He turned to the rest of the room and thrust his fist in the air. "You have heard it! You are all my witnesses! She will not take my choice of husband, but wishes to marry the fool!"

He turned back toward her and seized her hand. Expecting this, she did not resist him as he dragged her to where Kedric sat on a stool at the back of the dais. With a wrench, he flung her at Kedric's feet. Kedric moved with amazing swiftness, somehow managing to put his lute aside and catch her before she fell.

"Take the ungrateful wretch, Fool!" her father bellowed. "She would rather be wed to you! Well, I declare it, here and now, and before witnesses!"

In an ugly parody of the peasant fisherfolk's wedding rite, he pulled off his own belt and bound their right hands together, then poured the remains of his wine on the floor in front of them, following that with the entire contents of the saltcellar. "Wed and bound I declare you! Wed and bound you two are, by fruit of the land and the fruit of the sea, and the power of the lord of the keep!"

Even though this was exactly what she had wanted, Moira felt her knees start to buckle, and with surprising strength, Kedric held her up.

"And know that if you dare to touch her carnally, Fool," Ferson growled under his breath, "I'll have your stones for fish bait."

"I understand, my lord," Kedric murmured back.

"Now take her away from my sight, and keep her out of it until she's ready to obey!" Ferson shouted. "Take her and teach her, curse you both!"

Kedric stopped only long enough to pull Ferson's belt from their joined hands, and scoop up his lute.

Then with one hand cupped under her elbow, he hurried her off the dais and across the now-silent Great Hall. Moira felt the eyes of every person there on the two of them—and with a prickling of her skin, she looked back over her shoulder to see that Massid's eyes, black and cold, bored across the expanse of the hall with that same terrible, inhuman anger she had glimpsed once before.

She was glad to have Kedric's hand at her arm, and gladder still to slip into the shadowed hallway, where Massid could no longer see her.

"You'll have to keep out of his sight for now," Kedric murmured, as they hurried down the hall to the Keep Lady's rooms. A cold draft chased them down the hall, blowing out lamps in their wake. "I'll have food brought to you."

He opened the door to her rooms, and they stumbled inside, as the last of the lamps blew out in the hall behind them.

"And if you want to avoid accident, I think that *you* had better stay out of sight of Massid," she retorted, feeling her spirits return as she closed the door of her rooms behind him hurriedly.

"I know. I felt his eyes burning into my back, and it was not just with rage," Kedric replied, catching hold of both her arms. "My lady—Moira—those words your father said—I did not plan for a marriage—"

She laughed weakly. "We plotted better than we knew. We *are* well and truly wedded, my dear Fool, not merely betrothed as was the intention. It is no sham. That is a legal and binding ceremony by the traditions of the fishing folk hereabouts. It will take the King himself to undo the knot. Although I do not think my father intends you to enjoy your wedded state. I think he means for you to berate me, torment me with your sharp tongue, and humiliate me until I would take even Massid to get away from you."

"I believe you." He put his back to the door and looked at her soberly. "My lady, I fear I may have overstepped myself with my own so-called cleverness. If Massid is indeed the magician here, as you think—"

"Then he is still at dinner, trying to undo the damage my father has done, and very much occupied with repairing the situation," she replied. "Which means that you are free to speak to your master. I very much doubt that my servant will return here before morning, so we will not be disturbed."

His somber gaze brightened. "So I am. And perhaps he will have some better news."

Fishing in the bag hanging from his belt, he brought out a piece of chalk from one of the cliffs, and bent to mark out a diagram on her hearth. It seemed to consist of six interlocking triangles, and when he had finished it, the thing seemed to pull at her eyes in a way that made her feel very uneasy. She didn't have to look at it for long, however. No sooner had he finished it than he slapped his right hand, palm down, into the middle of it, obscuring the center.

The chalked lines suddenly flared with light. She looked away for a moment, and when she looked back, she had to stifle a little scream of alarm.

There was a disembodied head made entirely of fire suspended above the flames of her hearth. It was the head of a balding man with a thick fringe of hair at about ear level encircling his pate, and a pointed chin. The eyes looked like holes in the flames of the face.

"Master!" Kedric began.

"Be still!" the head said, "I haven't much time! Have you learned Massid's purpose there?"

"Not the chief purpose, though Ferson attempted to push through a marriage to his daughter tonight—" Kedric said. "But I have learned that someone here is performing magic to create a false beacon during storms that will decoy ships onto the rocks!"

The head interrupted him. "The beacon! Have you countered the magic that is changing the beacon? Have you even discovered what it is?"

Kedric shook his head, and the head in the fireplace swore.

"Listen! The King has been forced by a crisis to sail this very day for Linessa with most of the fleet. His convoy must pass by Highclere to reach it. You must make certain no one there learns of this! If the beacon is wrong—"

"Master! You must warn him!"

"Impossible. No birds could reach him from the shore, and there are no magicians with him that can speak at a distance—it is combative magics he needs, and those are the magicians he took. Kedric, at all costs, you must see to it that no one learns that the fleet has sailed, and if a storm comes up, you *must* counter the false beacon at all costs!" The head turned, as if looking elsewhere. "I must go! Heed me! Counter that magic!"

The head vanished. The fireplace held nothing more than glowing coals with a furtive flame hovering above them. Kedric sagged.

"You won't want to hear this," Moira said hesitantly, "but it isn't a question of 'if' a storm is coming. One is on the way. It will be here by Midwinter Moon, *and* there will be a high tide at the same time."

Kedric groaned. "I suppose there's no chance you could be wrong? If the King sailed today he'll be just off this shore by Midwinter Moon."

She shook her head, and her hair fell out of its pinning, the long braid tumbling down her back. She didn't trouble to pin it back up. "It's partly the moon magic and partly sea knowledge, and no, I won't be wrong." She stopped then, and stared at the dark glass of the window for a moment. "Why would the King sail now? What kind of crisis could put him and the fleet on the water in such haste?"

He sat back on his heels and looked up at her. "I don't know. It would have to be something very serious. It's risky enough sailing in this season as it is. But Linessa is the key to the Daenae River. If it was taken, for instance, you could sail your invasion force all the way up the Daenae and into the heart of the kingdom without anyone stopping you."

"And Linessa is another sea-keep, like this one. It's next to impossible to reach during winter storms, so there's no point trying to bring the army to reinforce it." She clenched her jaw. "And what are the odds, do you think, that the message that sends the King and his navy in such haste was false? And that in fact, it came from here? I am not the only person who can read the wind and the waves. What's more, I am not certain but that Massid can summon up storms at his will when the conditions are right."

Kedric's jaw dropped as he stared up at her. "God in heaven. A man sent by Massid! One messenger—no one looks very closely at a messenger. The man wearing Linessa livery gallops in on an exhausted horse, gasps out his message, then throws himself back on a fresh horse to take the King's reply! No one would think twice about it. They've planned this all along!"

"With one storm, they eliminate the King and his navy." She nodded. "This marriage my father plans was probably never more than a distraction for the rest of the keep folk. They will keep their tongues on that and pay no attention to my father and the Prince."

"There I must differ with you," Kedric replied, getting slowly to his feet. "There is a deeper game being played here. If Massid is to somehow gain control of the coast, which is, I believe, his plan, he must have some way to appease the lords of the sea-keeps. You, my dear, are that means. He will probably play the besotted groom, believing he can deceive them and you together. They will think they can control him through you. You are meant to think the same until it is too late and the Khaleem's men are in command of all the keeps and the coastline."

She ground her teeth in anger and frustration, but nodded. "So. What do we do? What *can* we do?"

"We have a few days yet," he replied. "I will try to find the key to the magic that controls the false beacon. And you—"

"I am pent up here like a fish in a trap!" she snarled.

"No, you are not. You are supposedly isolated here, and yet, anyone who cares to can seek you out here virtually unobserved. I will search for some sort of answer, and you—" he actually smiled thinly "—you will remain here in state, and see if allies come to us. The lord may be the head of the keep, my lady, but I think you will find that *you* reign over the hands and the heart."

And Kedric, she found as soon as the first light of dawn greyed the horizon, was right. Aided by Anatha, by ones and twos the servants and workers began to come to her, or send messages via their friends. It was true enough that Massid and his men had not thus far exercised any of the cruelty or arrogance for which the men of the Khaleemates were noted—but they had not made any friends here, either. She got the sense that if she had given any sign that she welcomed this marriage, the people of the keep would have bitten their lips and kept their tongues still. But since she had very vocally and publicly voiced her objection to it, not to mention pointing out the treasonous aspects—well, it seemed that she had more help here than she would have thought.

However, that "help" brought disquieting word. Down in the shelter of the boathouse lay the Prince's ship that had brought him here. No more than a handful of men were here in the keep itself, but the servants told her that a great deal of food went down to the boathouse three times a day—and nothing came back up again. The Prince, it seemed, might not be taking the cooperation of his ally for granted.

Meanwhile the wind and the waves increased, and by midafternoon, with dark grey clouds scudding across the hard blue sky, she was getting the sense that this might be one of the worst storms the keep had ever weathered. Massid might not need the false beacon to lure the King's ships onto the rocks. If they didn't keep well out to sea and risk being lost or delayed, the storm might do all of Massid's work for him.

But the wind and the storm might be her allies, too.

That night, she huddled at the fire with two of the men who worked the docks and one of the carpenters. A set of blocks and a toy boat from the nursery stood duty as Massid's boat and the boathouse where it was being kept.

She had spent the better part of an hour being made acquainted with how the boathouse was put together. Now she was going to use that knowledge to take it apart.

"First, you need to make sure that all the ropes are untied or, at least, loose. If you can saw through the roof ties here, and here," she said, tapping the crude model with her finger. "And then, at the right moment, fling open the door to the boathouse, so the roof will fly off and the walls will be blown out."

Kedric stared at her. "How do you know that?" he demanded.

She shrugged. "Because that is what always happened to my model boathouses in a good breeze. If we can collapse the boathouse and turn the ship loose, Massid's men won't be able to get off it before it's at the mercy of the storm."

"Well, let me deal with the roof ties and the ropes," he said firmly. "We don't want Massid's little army to know what we're up to. I can make potions that will dry-rot both wood and hemp, creating in hours the damage of centuries."

She blinked. "You are a dangerous man!" she said in astonishment. "Can you do the same with iron fittings?"

He nodded. "Child's play."

She turned back to the servants. "In that case, none of you need be on that dock at all once you've used Kedric's alchemical potions. Weaken the roof ties, the hinges and hasp of the door, the ropes and anchor chain of the boat itself, and every crossbeam supporting that dock, or at least as many as you have potion for. We'll let the wind do our work for us."

She watched as the men looked solemnly at her little model, then slowly, gravely smiled, as they realized what was going to happen.

Because the moment that the doors went—and taking the brunt of the wind as they would, they would be the first of the weakened components to go—the roof would fly off, the walls collapse, and then the whole dock itself would fall apart. Even if Massid's men realized that something was wrong, they would be too late to escape their boat. Some would certainly be crushed beneath a cascade of heavy lumber, or knocked into the icy ocean. The boat itself, if it was not sunk immediately, would be hit by the storm full force and driven up on the rocks below the keep. No one could survive that.

Kedric frowned. "I don't—" he began.

The dockmen explained it to him. Moira held her tongue. No need for her to say a word at this point. The men were already turning the plan over in their minds until they could take credit for everything but the idea in the first place. And that harmed her not at all.

They left, after making arrangements to have their several gallons of potions waiting at the kitchen door. Anatha would bring them down as "dirty slop water" and complain how much Moira was making her clean. The metal-rotting ones would go first—they took longer to work. Then the ones that did for wood and hemp.

"You are a dangerous woman," Kedric said, his eyes narrowed. "I've heard worse, and less cold-blooded plans out of seasoned soldiers."

She tightened her jaw. "Is it cold-blooded to want to keep my people from having to fight Massid's beasts in the halls of their own keep?" she demanded.

His expression softened a trifle. "Put that way—no." He sighed. "But you may be the death of me as well before this is over. Buckets of potions *and* trying to find what magic Massid is doing on that beacon! I will be worn to a shred."

"At least there will be something of you left when this is over," she retorted. But despite her sharp words, she couldn't help but cast a worried eye over him. He *was* looking worn and tired, and if he had slept more than an hour or two, she would be surprised. Yet, when she yawned, or blinked to stay awake, it was he who urged her to her bed if there was nothing for her to do—or brewed her some strange herbal concoction to help her stay awake if there was.

And she resolutely turned her mind away from what Massid would do to both of them if they lost this hidden war. Likely he would not even consider the notion that she could have been the author of at least half of the mischief; none of his kind gave women the credit for having intelligence. But Kedric—she remembered all too clearly the cold ire in Massid's eyes as they escaped the Great Hall. No, Massid had likely planned something devilishly ingenious, diabolically painful, and excruciatingly prolonged for Kedric. That he would have proved himself a true King's man would only make Massid the more determined to inflict as much suffering as possible. Compared to that—

Well, there wouldn't be much comparison with what Massid planned for her.

She pulled her mind away from those unpleasant thoughts to find that Kedric was staring at her with a most peculiar expression on his face. She blinked. "What?" she demanded. "Have I got a smudge on my nose?"

"I was just thinking that—never mind." He shook his head.

"Kedric, if you believe any woman would let you begin a sentence like 'I was just thinking' and end it with 'never mind,' you truly *are* a fool," she snapped, her brows furrowing with irritation.

"All right!" He held up his hands. "I was just thinking that—this is going to sound very stupid—I was just thinking that I owe your Countess a great apology, as well as a debt of gratitude."

She raised an eyebrow, and regarded him expectantly.

"I owe her the debt of gratitude for sending you," he elaborated. "Although I confess that when I was told you, a mere slip of a child, was supposedly a Grey Lady, I was very angry and sure you would be less than useless. So I suppose I owe you an apology as well. I could never have hoped to stop this without you—I was never meant to be an assassin, and I cannot think of any other way of removing Massid."

She smiled grimly, thinking of her own training and the weapons still hidden in her chest. "You would never have gotten past his bodyguards," she replied firmly. "They *are* trained as assassins. The Khaleems require such, since treachery is so much a part of their lives. Not unless you could conjure up some subtle poison and the means to deliver it that they had never seen before."

"Alchemysts make poor poisoners," he murmured. "We do not meddle much with physic and medicine. We leave that to the healers and doctors."

She tilted her head to one side, curiously. "Why *did* you choose to become an alchemyst?" she asked.

He laughed bitterly. "Trying to transmute this—" he tapped his hunched shoulder "—since healers and doctors had so little success at it. Then, well, I was apt to it, and alchemysts *do* make good spies, the more so when they have other talents to disguise their true nature."

"Does it cause you pain?" she asked, regarding him steadily.

He gaped at her. Not surprising, it was a surpassingly rude question. But she had a reason for her bluntness.

"No—" he replied, clearly without thinking.

"Then why bother?" she retorted, with a shrug. "It makes you neither more nor less intelligent, nor healthy, nor any other thing that matters. Have you *looked* at the faces, the bodies, the hands of my people?" she continued. "Really *looked?* Or because they are merely underlings, have your eyes slid right by them? I will confess, before the Countess trained my eyes, I would have done the same."

He shook his head.

"Then when this is over, do take the time to look. See how many of them are scarred, twisted, missing fingers or toes or hands or feet." She nodded as his eyes widened. "The sea is a harsh mistress, and a harsher teacher. She often claims a tithe of flesh and blood, especially to pay for a mistake. But they carry themselves proudly, and find ways to do their duty—or find a different duty. They do not think overmuch of what they are *not*. And neither should you."

She had intended to leave it there, but her mind was tired, and what she had intended to keep to herself slipped out before she could stop it. "What you *are* is a clever and kindly man, a skilled and wise man, more noble in heart than most are by blood—altogether the sort of man I wish was my husband in truth."

He stared at her blankly. For the first time in a very long time she felt herself flushing, blushing so hotly she was sure that her cheeks rivaled the coals of the fire. "I have said too much. More than I ought. I was tired. More tired than I thought. Forgive my rudeness, my foolishness, and forget what I—" she blurted, and got up, stumbling out of the room and into the bedroom to hide herself behind the bed curtains and curse herself until she unaccountably fell asleep.

* * *

The transition from dusk to full dark on the evening of Midsummer Moon passed in the blink of an eye as Moira watched from her window. She had seen the edge of the coming storm itself just before the sun set, and as the light was sucked out of the sky, watched as it scurried across the waves toward them on a hundred legs of blue-white lightning. Then the storm came down on the keep like a shark on a herring. It roared across waves already washing over the lower terraces and hit the walls with an initial blast that shook the entire building.

She strained her ears for the one sound she was waiting for, over the screaming wind, the thunder, and the howling waves—and she strained her eyes during the lightning flashes for a glimpse of—

There! A tumble of planks and posts slammed up onto the rocks beneath the cliff face!

And there! For just one moment, farther out than she would have guessed, a glimpse of a slim fighting ship, masts stowed and sails safely stowed away belowdecks, tossing on the crest of the waves like a child's toy, whirling rudderless and out of control—

She bit her lip in grim satisfaction, and turned at the sound of a familiar step, a familiar tap upon the door. "It's—" said Kedric. He looked at her in shock.

"Yes, it is," she agreed, shifting her sword belt a little. "It's quite gone, boathouse, ship, and private army. Now it is up to us."

He continued to stare in disbelief. So, she had managed to keep one secret from him, at any rate!

"Massid knows that the King is out there somewhere," she said, waving a hand vaguely in the direction of the window. "And I have questioned every servant that has ever been around him when a storm has struck. I know where he goes, and I know he goes alone. I am going to stop him."

Strange irony that where he went was the timber room. She must have just missed encountering him there dozens of times.

"You? But—"

"If I am to succeed, I desperately need *you* to deal with my father and Massid's men," she continued. "I don't know how, but you *must* keep them occupied! Keep them from learning what just happened to Massid's ship, and keep them from going to fetch Massid!" She threw a mantle on over her armor. It looked enough like one of the loose gowns she favored, particularly in the uncertain light, that he might not notice what she wore beneath it for a few crucial moments. "You said yourself that you are not trained as an assassin. Well, I *am*."

The look on his face might have been funny under any other circumstances. She hoped that she would survive to laugh about it later.

To laugh about it with *him* later...

Please God...

"He won't be expecting a female assassin," she continued, staring into his dark, stricken eyes, willing him to believe her. "I'm going to pretend I followed him to beg his forgiveness and ask for him to take me as his wife. That should let me get close enough. Perhaps if *you* went to my father and told him you had persuaded me—?"

He swallowed hard. "That might suffice, my lady," he said, his normally melodious voice gone harsh. "I will do that—"

She ducked her head, to avoid the pain and the fear—for her!—in his eyes. "Thank you," she murmured, and started to push past him.

But he seized her before she could get out the door, and pulled her to him, holding her in an embrace that probably hurt *him,* given the armor she was wearing. He cupped one hand behind her head and crushed his mouth down on hers in a kiss that felt as if one of those lightning bolts outside the window had struck her on the lips. She couldn't breathe—couldn't think—didn't want it to end—

He let her go, and she stood, wide-eyed and swaying, staring at him.

"You *will* return to me, wife!" he grated, his eyes wild. "You will come back to me whole and unhurt, for Grey Lady or not, I shall not give you or myself up to the service of any other, nor shall I let anyone part us, even if he be the King himself! And if you do not come back to me, then by the signs and the seal, I *will* follow you, though it be to the gates of heaven or hell!"

With that, he whirled, and was gone, his footsteps,

half-running, echoing down the hall amid the noise of the storm.

She stood swaying a moment more, somehow managed to get some sort of control over herself, and walked with swift but uncertain steps to the first servants' stair that would take her where she needed to go.

It was a good thing she knew the way by heart, because most of the lanterns were out, and she fumbled her way through the darkness in a kind of daze. Half of her wanted to shout with elation, and the other half was frozen with fear, for despite her brave words, she was not even remotely certain that her ruse would work. Women *were* used as assassins all the time in the Khaleemates, though usually it was poison in the festive cup or a knife in the dark, the pillow over the face or the serpent in the bath. But there was no guarantee. And no guarantee that Massid himself was not an assassin, and had already recognized her for what she was.

She stumbled out into the open space of the timber room, looking every bit the confused and distressed maiden, she was sure, though it was not by design. The cavern echoed with the storm below and all around; strange drafts whipped her clothing tightly to her body, and the flickering and uncertain light made bewildering shadows everywhere. She could not see Massid.

"Massid?" she croaked, her voice not even carrying a foot from where she stood. She coughed and cleared her throat. "My lord Prince?" she tried again. "Massid? My lord?"

A movement that was not shadow warned her, and she half turned as Massid, clad from head to toe in black, rose up from behind a pile of masts. She could not see his face, but there was anger in his voice.

"What do you want, woman?" he growled. "This is no time for the idiocy of females! Begone!"

She stumbled toward him, deliberately trying to make it look as if she could not make out her footing. But she knew every stick and plank in this room, where it was, and how steady or unsteady it was underfoot. Her stumbles, at least, were feigned.

"My lord?" she said plaintively. "My lord, I have sinned against you and my father. I was evil, disobedient, my mind polluted by that wicked woman with whom I have lodged all these years. I know I was wrong to say what I did, I know that I never deserved the honor of being made your wife, and in spurning you, I—"

"Enough."

The unmistakable sound of a sword being unsheathed made her freeze where she stood.

"Do you think I do not know about the Countess Vrenable and her Grey Ladies? Do you think I had not guessed that you were one of that detestable creature's polluted assassins?" He took a step closer, and it was all she could do to keep from shrinking backward. "How like that weakling King of yours, to hide behind skirts and send little girls to do his work! Well, there is no dishonor to a blade in using it to spit a viper—and there will be no dishonor in using mine to rid the world of one more poison-tongued witch!"

He leaped, and that was enough to shock her into dodging, not backward, but to the side—to fling off her mantle and throw it at him in the hopes of entangling his blade while she unsheathed hers, dagger and rapier together.

A gust of wind caught it as she got her sword clear, and threw it over his head.

Her body recognized her one chance, even though her mind went blank.

Her body acted as she had trained, throwing her forward in a long, low lunge under his flailing blade, flinging her arm out in a swift strike.

Her body followed up the hit as the blade, instead of encountering the resistance of armor and a blunted tip, slid into his gut as a fish slid through water.

Her arm wrenched upward of itself, driving the blade in and up until it grated against bone, and hot wetness gushed against her hand.

And her body drove home the dagger into his throat, as he flailed at her head with the hilt of his sword, in blows already weakening, until he dropped to the floor of the cavern, taking her weapons with him.

His eyes stared up sightlessly at the ceiling; she turned and stumbled away a few paces, and fell to her knees, heaving and retching, until there was nothing left in her stomach—and weeping hysterically between each bout of gut-wrenching sickness.

Then, out of the darkness, a voice, and hands on her shoulders. "Moira? Moira! By God, if he has harmed one hair—"

She turned into his embrace, laughing and weeping at the same time, the taste of bile bitter in her mouth and her throat raw. "You'll do what? Bring him back to life so that you can beat him?"

"Fiat lux!" came the unexpected words, and the cavern blazed with light from a globe that appeared just over Kedric's head. "Oh, my love—" He wiped her mouth and chin with his soft linen sleeve, then dabbed at her eyes with the napkin someone behind him handed to him. He took her chin and tilted it up. "You'll have a black eye in the morning," he said, with calm matter-of-factness that belied the fading fear in his eyes. "And a sore stomach."

"Yes, well, I've never—" She made herself say the words. "I've never killed anyone before. I suppose— I—" She started to relax in his embrace, then pushed him away in alarm. "Father!" she exclaimed.

"Lord Ferson has met with an accident," said Kedric. "I don't know the details. Your cook tells me I do not want to know the details. There was some little to-do in the Great Hall when one of Massid's men came up with the news that the ship, the boathouse, and the dock were all gone. Unaccountably, they blamed me—and your loyal retainers rushed to my defense."

She took in his own battered face now, for the first

time. "Kedric!" she exclaimed, anger replacing the sick sourness in her stomach. "Are you hurt? Did they—"

"And you will do what? Send out men with nets to haul in what was thrown out the window?" With some difficulty, he curved his swollen lips in a smile. "I think we should both save our energy to deal with the King. He is not going to be very happy about losing his Fool and his Grey Lady—"

She brought up her chin at that, covering her wince— she thought—rather well. "He will not have a choice," she said. "I am the Keep Lady, and you are sealed and bound to me by the Keep Lord and my own will. If he does not wish to begin a revolt of the sea-keeps, he had better keep his opinions on the matter to himself!"

"Well said, my lady!" crowed someone behind Kedric, and the Fool began to laugh, shaking his head.

"Oh, you are a terrible woman, Moira of Highclere," he said, tears leaking out of his swelling eyes. "I fear for my sanity, if not my life!" But the arms that held her did not release her; in fact, he pulled her closer as some of the men behind him began to chuckle. "Come along with you."

He pulled her to her feet, though his own balance was none too steady. "Do you think it is possible in this howling gale to manage a bath for your lady?" he called over the storm.

"Eh, trust a Fool to want a bath at a time like this!" someone shouted mockingly, and everyone laughed, as they parted for the two of them to pick their way across the lumber and down into the heart of the keep again.

Yes, she thought, with warmth and a sudden feeling of contentment! *Trust a Fool. I shall certainly trust a Fool, with all my heart, for all my life.*

* * * * *

Look for
ONE GOOD KNIGHT
by Mercedes Lackey coming in
January 2006.
Don't miss this Tale of Five Hundred Kingdoms!

THE HEART OF THE MOON
Tanith Lee

Dear Reader,

The heart of the moon is, of course, the heart of a cool, strong and self-controlled woman. In this case, Clirando. She wears a "mask" because she's been hurt. And because she is tough, she challenges what hurt her, and drives it off.

But most of us know there are things that, discard or deny them as we may, leave their marks on us, like the scratches of a lion. Some fade, some scar. The *scars* are still there to be looked at long, long after.

I wanted very much to find a way to free my character from her hurt. She deserved that. But like most of the ones I write about, she, or others in this tale, told me how her freedom would come about. She needed not only new light, but the means to confront the shadows. When Zemetrios entered the story and showed his worth, the core of the narrative began to flame—the fire-heart was being refueled.

In fact, I first saw the heroine's name in a dream, written across a white moon above a dark isle. It's a kind of play on words, too, I believe. Clir-an-do: *Clear and do.*

Prologue

The moon's face is cold, but her heart is full of fire—how else could she give such light?

Lightning

The night that lightning struck the Temple of the Maiden—that was the night she found them. Clirando would never have suspected the warrior goddess Parna of such harsh melodrama. Though justice, of course, was partly her province. It seemed she had wanted Clirando to see and to know. Perhaps she had expected Clirando to behave differently after it had happened.

The narrow streets of Amnos were moon-and-torch lit, and people were shouting and running up toward the Sacred Mount, where stood the temples of the Father and Parna the Maiden. Smoke and a thin flame still sizzled from her roof, and the sea-washed air was full of the reek of scorching stone.

But by the time Clirando reached the lower terrace, men were already on the tiles, girls, too, from the various female warrior bands. Clirando saw two of her own command, Oani and Erma, busy there.

She shouted to them. "Are you safe?"

"Yes, safe, Cliro. But come up—"

One of the men, no less than the architect Pholis, swathed in his bed gown, called down, "Use the stairs! No more swarming on ropes here, the roof is damaged."

So Clirando and several others ran up the final terrace and in from the side court.

There were guest rooms off the court. Priests and others used them, if they were on duty that night at the temple.

Almost everybody had come out. They stood around the tank of crystal water under the fig tree, talking, shaking their heads, some offering prayers.

Two people were late, however, leaving a room.

As Clirando walked into the court—yawning, she afterward recalled, for the levin-bolt had woken her from sleep like most of the town—she saw them. One was Araitha, her closest friend. The other dark-haired Thestus.

Clirando knew them both so well that for a long moment it did not startle her to see them there. She was pleased, very probably. Her best friend, as well as her lover, Thestus, both of whom would be excellent at assisting on the roof.

Even with his hand slipping from Araitha's shoulder...even with the way Araitha suddenly drew aside from him, her eyes blank with far too many emotions to show.

And his rasp of guilty laugh.

"Ha—Cliro. Are you going up, too? That was a strike and no mistake. A wonder the temple withstood—"

Behind, the two of them, the curtain of the little room had been drawn back, to show a disheveled bed, narrow but still wide enough for the pair of slender and hard-muscled figures who had chosen to couch there together. A flagon of wine stood on the floor. In the grey-red moon-and-torch mixing of the light, it gleamed in a horrible way, blinking and winking at Clirando like the center of an evil eye: *Didn't you guess, girl?* it seemed to say. Didn't you *know?*

Clirando walked past the water tank and met Thestus and Araitha at the door of the cell, and pushed them both back inside. They let her do this, not resisting.

Thestus was taller than she, but Araitha was her own height. Araitha with her beer-brown eyes and long, dark golden hair. Thestus had always honestly praised that hair. And other things. Araitha's warrior skills, her musical gift with lyra and tabor. Clirando, Araitha's sister-friend since they had been six years old in the training courts of the temple, was always happy when others praised Araitha.

As for Thestus, he had come to the Father Temple, a warrior, with his own band of twenty men, only two years before. He had singled Clirando out inside three days, as she had him. Since the Spring Festival they had been lovers. Parna never minded such liaisons. Her warriors were also allowed love, and to make children, if they wished.

Clirando shook her own long brown hair over her shoulders and looked at him. Then she looked at Araitha.

Neither of them spoke.

Thestus's mouth locked shut as if a key had turned behind his lips.

It was Araitha who laughed now and said, scattering her words light as beads, "Oh, Cliro. It means nothing. We only—only for a moment. That was all."

"Liar."

"Cliro—what could it matter? We both love you. Do you—" she threw back her head, defiant "—grudge me a little pleasure?"

Always her way. Attack was defense to Araitha.

"I grudge you this."

Thestus opened his locked lips and spoke to Araitha.

"Don't try to reason with her. We both know what she can be like when she loses her self-control."

Cliro turned and slapped him stingingly across the mouth.

He swung aside with a curse, was already reaching for the dagger lying in its sheath on the floor. Araitha made a noise. Cliro kicked Thestus's hand away, then kicked Thestus full in the chest so he fell back bruisingly on his well-formed butt.

"No," said Cliro. "Soon but not yet, sweetheart."

"Cliro—" said Araitha.

Clirando no longer liked the sound of her name from her friend's beautiful mouth. The mouth was very red and swollen from Thestus's kisses tonight. Maybe that was why the name of *Cliro* sounded wrong.

"Be quiet, you bitch. Both of you. I'll issue the challenge now, so you know. In seven days at first light, before the Maiden. First you, I think, Thestus, for the shorter time I've known you—if ever I knew you at all. A little later for you, Araitha, you filthy slut."

"I am no—"

"*You are a slut*. You are a *traitor*. To me. Him I hate. But *you* I hate the most. I called you friend."

Araitha began to cry, like any soft merchant's wife.

Clirando turned, her own eyes burning. She stalked out and across the court, where the others standing there, who had seen most and heard all of it, murmured together.

She knew that anyone, other perhaps than some great sage, would have felt shocked pain and anger. But aside from her personal hurt, this very publicly witnessed betrayal showed her own judgement up poorly. No one could fail to be aware she had been in ignorance until tonight. Clirando was a commander. In no respect could she be seen to have been stupid.

She thought now, in horror, that, blind to their antics, she might well have trusted them beside her in battle—and possibly been unwise in that, too. Had their desire proved so irresistible, honor demanded they should have told her to her face. But they had deceived her as if she were some silly woman reared only for the house.

Clirando did not go up to the lightning-blasted roof.

"Forgive me," she said to the goddess, in the private shrine beside the main hall. Amber lamplight starred the goddess's calm face. Polished marble etched and dressed with gold, her eyes were two green stones. Clirando also had green eyes—Thestus had said they were green as leaves of the bay tree. "I can't help mend your roof, Maiden. I'm shaking like some fool before her first skirmish. Pardon me."

The calm face looked down at hers.

"I will meet both Araitha and Thestus individually in the war-court. Before the whole town. I think you allowed me to see what those two had done to me, to find them out. I'll punish them. Oh, not a fight to the death. But I'll shame them both. They'll lose their places in Amnos and go far away. Where I need never look at them again. Do you allow it, Lady?"

Above, there came a faint rushing—tiles dislodged—and then cries and a crash as they plummeted onto the terraces below.

"Is that disapproval, Lady?"

Parna did not answer. But Clirando had never known her to. It was a formality to ask. Clirando's human course was already set.

She had long thought, though one must respect the gods, one could not expect understanding from them. They gave favors or hurts according to some indecipherable law of their own.

And I am hurt, she thought. *Struck in the heart.*

She would make them pay, her lover, her sister. There was no other road now to peace.

Arguments among the warrior-priests of Parna and the Father were often settled in the war-court, in public duel.

Generally it was two men who fought. Women tended to settle their disagreements with only their bands to witness. Rarely did a female warrior demand satisfaction of a male in the court, though there had been cases now and then. Clirando had known that aside from the officials and certain priests bound to attend, a lot of Amnos would crowd into the public seats to see.

It had occurred to her, many people had known about Thestus's liaison with Araitha. Some even came to her, subsequent to her finding out, and confessed— among these was Erma from Clirando's own band.

"I never knew if I should tell you, Cliro—"

"You should have."

"I know. But—"

Clirando forgave Erma, who was holding back her tears. She was still young, only fifteen, five years younger that Clirando. Tuyamel, on the other hand, offered to skin Thestus for Clirando. "I wouldn't want the skin, thanks, my friend," Clirando said. Tuy had laughed. "Fair enough. I shall leave it to you then."

The morning was fine, the sun just torching the east, when Clirando stood on the war-court and faced her former lover across the clean paving.

All around, the crowd sat in respectful silence. There was none of the shouting or merriment that went on when ritual games or war exercises took place here. This was a solemn, fraught occasion.

Clirando had to steel herself, too. She had fought beside Thestus only once in battle—against pirates last fall, blood raining among red leaves at the edges of Amnos's forested shores. But often he and she had exercised together. They knew each other's moves perhaps too well.

She had thought he would try to surprise her. She judged correctly.

The instant the signal came to begin, he dropped onto the ground and came rolling at her like a human hedgehog. As she leaped aside, his short sword whipped out. It cut one of her sandal thongs. Only her reflexes had saved her from much worse.

She tore off both sandals and he, having stood up again, watched her mockingly.

There was contempt in his face. Maybe that was only a mask. Or maybe his looks of love had been the mask.

She had tried very hard not to examine why he had used her as he had, and played her false. Now certainly was not the time for analysis.

Clirando wondered if he had other tricks, and he had. Having allowed her space to undo her shoes, he lounged idly, paring his nails, so a slight amusement rippled through some of the audience, only to be shushed as improper.

He would not move again to meet her.

She stood waiting.

He stood idling. He began to whistle a popular tune of the town.

"Come on," she said. Her voice carried.

"I'm here if you want me. *You* come on."

She knew it was another trick.

Clirando moved toward him slowly, then suddenly very fast, running as if straight into him—veering at the last second. A fine pinkish powder spurted from his left hand, clouding the air between them. He must have taken it out with the paring knife. It would have been in her face, her eyes, if she had dodged less effectively. Play dirty then. A bitter smile touched her mouth. He must be scared of her.

From veering, she swung and cut him across the left shoulder. Blood burst like a flower.

With a roar he turned on her.

To her he seemed heavy now, graceless. He had not bothered to prepare for this, only his tricks. She had been practicing every day.

He was a poor warrior. Brave and strong, cunning sometimes. But his skill was not so great. She had thought more highly of him when she loved him, seeing him through lover's eyes, wanting him to shine.

Inside six minutes more, she had scored him lightly across arms and chest, thighs, and even his back as he went skidding down from a sidelong blow. She did not aim to cripple him. He would need his fighter's trade where he was going, out into the wide world far from Amnos.

But by then he was a mess, and losing blood, his face pale and congested, ugly, frantic. He was bellowing at her, oaths and blasphemies for which the priests would be setting him a penance. He told her, also, and told the crowd, why he had lost his sexual interest in her. She was too cold, he said. Cold as Moon Isle with its heartless crags. She was too masculine. She had no feminine gifts to match her male ones.

Clirando knew these things were lies, and saw that possibly, in desperation, he was trying to unnerve her that way, and so catch her off guard. She felt nothing by then, only the desire to end the fight. As he lunged she brought up her blade under his and sent it spinning—to be fair, his sword had grown slippery from his blood—then she punched him clean and square on the point of the jaw. He keeled over and fell with a crash, his already unconscious eyes staring at her all the way down.

The priest and priestess of the court approached and asked if Clirando was satisfied.

"Yes. But one more thing."

"What is it?"

"Let him be sent away."

"You know, Clirando, that he must be. You have disgraced him before the town. He will never fight for Amnos again."

They offered her an interval to rest, then.

Clirando said she would meet Araitha at once.

She believed this would be harder, but in fact when her sister-friend came out, pale and angry and lovely in the broadening rays of the sun, Clirando felt nothing still.

They fought well and without tricks for ten minutes, during which each cut the other.

Clirando thought, *This is too much like play. This is too much like times when we have done this for exercise, and to learn from each other.*

Something came to Clirando then. The terrible rage she had not wanted to feel and, so far, had avoided feeling.

When she loses her self-control, he had said.

Clirando lost it.

Some part of her stood in the air, watching in astonishment as she slashed and hacked at Araitha, who was now falling back before her.

Words tried to boil from Clirando's mouth. She held

them in, but they radiated from her eyes she believed, judging by Araitha's face.

Finally Clirando sprang. She went through the swirl of Araitha's blade—which afterward Clirando found had sliced her left arm from shoulder to elbow. As they tumbled over, she drove her knee into Araitha's midriff, exploding all breath from her body.

Clirando knelt over her vanquished opponent, plucked the sword from Araitha's loose grip and slung it clattering across the court.

"You're done," she hissed.

Araitha had no breath. She sprawled away and curled up on the paving, crowing for air, in the same posture Thestus had adopted when first attacking.

"Clirando, are you satisfied?"

"Yes."

"She too is disgraced. She too will never fight for Amnos again."

A victor might be applauded by the crowd.

The stands were applauding loudly. In the tumult Clirando could hear the battle shouts of her own band.

She did not look, did not acknowledge. She went below to one of the fighters' rooms, was bandaged, drank a pitcher of ale, and fell into a deadly sleep.

Araitha visited Clirando's house three nights later. It was the hour before Araitha's ship was to sail, taking her away to the distant city of Crentis, where she had relatives. Thestus by then was long gone.

Araitha wore a woman's dress and heavy cloak, and her hair was braided with golden ornaments.

She stood staring at Clirando.

Clirando said, "Who let you in?"

"Old Eshti. She doesn't know. She thinks we are still friends."

Above, the dusk was already full of stars over the little courtyard. A tiny fountain tickled the night with silvery sounds, and leaves rustled in the trees as the house doves settled. Through a lighted door, Eshti the servant woman was already bringing cups of fruit juice and wine.

"Thank you, Eshti," said Clirando. "Put them there."

"Something to warm you. The nights turn colder," said Eshti. "And she, our poor lady-girl, this long journey." Then Eshti went to Araitha and pressed her young hand in two old ones. "Don't fret, dear. You'll be home in Amnos before too long. I'll see the mistress doesn't forget you."

Clirando had not been startled by her servant Eshti's ignorance of what had happened—only glad Eshti, who would have been upset, and not been bothered with it. The market no doubt would have carried the gossip, but Eshti was a little deaf, and besides well known and liked. It seemed lips were tactfully sealed when she approached.

When the old woman had gone, Clirando found she had dug her sharp nails into her palms. She relaxed her fists.

"Best she doesn't know then," she said. "But tell me, before you go, what you could possibly want from me?"

"To give you something, Clirando."

"I want nothing of yours. How could you think I would?"

"This gift you must take."

"No."

"*Yes.* I've had it especially worked for you. The ancient women who live in the caves on the mountainside—they helped me fashion it."

Clirando's heart turned to stone.

Witches lived up there, and other mad and dangerous sorts.

She readied herself for one more trick—some poison or assault.

Araitha spoke softly.

"I curse you, Clirando. It's nothing much. Your life will be hollow as an emptied jar. Nothing in it but dust. Love may come and go, adventures may come and go. But they will echo in the hollow of you, and they too will become dust. And never again will you sleep. Oh, no. That respite from your thoughts will never be yours—unless some drug gives it to you. All your life, be it short or long, sleepless and empty you shall go."

Clirando shrugged. "You're a fool, Araitha."

Araitha said nothing.

Her face was like a statue's, expressionless and blind. She slipped away out of the courtyard, vanishing from dark to light to darkness in the subtle way of a ghost.

Clirando poured the juice and wine on the ground. They *had* been poisoned, by Araitha's words, her childish, horrible little bane.

Clirando was not afraid.

She spent the evening as she had planned, reading books and scrolls from her father's library. He had been both scholar and soldier, and traveled to many lands.

At the usual hour Clirando went to bed. Coolly she mused a moment on Araitha's words, but paid them no proper heed. Just as she always normally did, she fell asleep swiftly, and slumbered until morning. She had suspected it was a feeble curse.

The trading ship, the *Lion,* which was to carry Araitha to Crentis, sank in a gale off the unfriendly coasts of Sippini.

All on board were drowned, and the ship herself dragged to the bottom. Only remnants of cargo washing in to the port evidenced what had happened.

When news reached Amnos two months after, it was Tuyamel and Vlis who came in person to tell Clirando.

She heard the tidings quietly. When her girls were gone, Clirando threw a pinch of incense into the watch fire of her private shrine.

"Forgive her, Parna. Let her live well in the lands beyond death. Forgive me too for I don't know what I must feel."

That night Clirando dreamed of Araitha, not drowning, nor as she had been in life, but veiled and hidden, passing through a shadow to a light—to a shadow.

When Clirando woke with a start it was still deep night. She lay awake through the rest of it, until dawn showed in the window.

The following night, though tired from exercise, she did not sleep at all.

Her life was active and under her command. She did not think this insomnia could last. But it lasted. Night followed night, sleepless. She grew accustomed to the changing patterns of moon and cloud reflected on the ceiling. Even when, exhausted as she came to be, she lay down to rest at noon, sleep would not come. It fluttered over the room before the cinders of her eyes, brushed her with its wing, and flew far, far off.

Death it seemed had cemented the curse firmly into a place of power. Or, it was Parna's punishment.

Winter entered Amnos. Now was the time of long nights.

Clirando suffered it as best she could. When an alarm rang from the town's brazen gongs, she leaped down the streets leading her band among the other warriors. Pirates were trying their luck again, made hungry by lean weather. They were beaten back into the sea. Clirando's band did well, and sustained no casualties.

As the season moved toward spring, Clirando took herself in hand. The physician had already supplied her with an herbal medicine, which scarcely had an effect. Now she gained a stronger one. With its aid, every third or fourth night she was able to sleep two or three hours—though waking always with a heavy head and sickened stomach.

The bane will die away in its own time, like a venomous plant. I must ignore it, which will lessen its hold on me.

She pushed the burden from her, would not think of it by day, and lay reading through the nights.

Strangely, her body, young and fit, acclimatized to sleep loss, even if, on the third or fourth evening without slumber, sometimes she would see phantoms moving under trees or against walls—tricks of her tired eyes. Surely not real?

The priestess she consulted listened carefully to all Clirando told her. The priestess, who had been a warrior too in her youth, and was now middle-aged and stout, told Clirando gently, "And you have not mourned Araitha."

"No, Mother. I've made offerings to the goddess for her sake, and put flowers by the altars in Araitha's name. But I can't mourn. I—I'm angry still. *Disgusted* still."

"Yet you fought her and bested her and ruined her life in Amnos."

"Do you mean I killed her?" Clirando stared. "It was because she had to go away that she died."

"No. It wasn't you that caused her drowning. The sea and the wind did that. But you broke her spirit, Clirando. Why else did she curse you in that way?"

"She could have wished *me* dead."

"I think," said the priestess quietly, "she preferred you to live and suffer. Thestus did not curse you. He didn't care enough, or love enough. But Araitha was your sister. Measure her feeling for you by her last acts."

"What shall I do?"

"Like all of us, Clirando, you can only do what you are able. Do that."

The moon, which by now figured so vividly in Clirando's sleepless nights, began to be important to all the town—indeed to all the known world, from Crentis to Rhoia, and the burning southern deserts of Lybirica.

Every sixteen or seventeen years, through the strange blessing of the gods, there would come seven nights of midsummer when every night the moon would be full: seven nights together of the great white orb, coldly glowing as a disk of purest marble lit from within by a thousand torches.

The last such time had been in Clirando's earliest childhood. She had only the dimmest memory of it, of her mother leading her up among the family on the roof each night to see—and of all the house roofs of Amnos being similarly crowded with people, who let off Eastern firecrackers in spiraling arcs of gold and red. Among Clirando's band, only Erma and Draisis had never seen the seven full moons.

But all of them had heard of the Moon Isle. Even Thestus, come to that. He had compared Clirando to its unlovely rocks when they fought.

The Isle lay out in the Middle Sea, beyond Sippini. It was sacred and secret but, as was also well-known, on every occasion of the Seven Nights, certain persons had to go there, to honor and invoke the moon's power.

Amnos would send its delegation of priests and priestesses. Sometimes others were selected to sail to the Isle. How they were chosen was never made public, and no one was permitted to speak—or ever did so—of what took place upon the island. Nevertheless, or perhaps *because* of the silence, theories abounded. The Isle was full of dangerous and terrible beasts, also of spirits and demons. It was a spot of ultimate ordeal and test—and some of those sent there had not returned.

Clirando herself had never speculated unduly. She had been too busy, too fulfilled in her life.

The same priestess was waiting for her when she answered the temple's summons, and entered the shrine beside the main hall.

In the altar light below the statue of Parna, the dumpy older woman had gained both grace and presence.

"I have something to tell you, Clirando."

"Yes, Mother?"

"You, and the six girls of your band, have been selected for an important duty."

"Certainly, Mother. We'll be glad to see to it."

"Perhaps not." The faintest nuance went over the priestess's face. It was an unreadable expression—caused only, maybe, by the flicker of the altar lamp. "You seven are to travel to the Moon Isle."

Clirando felt her heart trip over itself. She swallowed and said, "To the Isle?"

"Yes. You will leave in ten days, in order to be there at the commencement of the Moon Month."

"Mother—this is an honor for us—but none of us have any notion of what we must do when we arrive."

"None have," said the priestess flatly.

"But then—"

"Clirando. This is both an honor for you, as you say, a reward for your valor and care in the past—and a penance. A privilege and a trial. You'll have heard disturbing things of the place, yes?"

"Yes, Mother. I thought most of them fanciful."

"Forget that impression. The Isle is supernatural and may produce anything. It is a place half in this world and half elsewhere. In spots, they say, it opens on the country of the moon itself. For philosophers have decided the moon is not what it appears, a disk, but rather a world, an unlike mirror to our own. Therefore anticipate magic, and great danger. Sacrifice is common on the Isle. So is death. But too the land is mystical and profound, and from death life may spring. There is a saying, a closed eye may sometimes see more there than one which stares. Do you consent to go?"

"Mother—*I* consent. But my girls—"

"Have no fear for them. They will be safer than you. *You,* Clirando, are the one the Isle requires. Human presence on it invokes the power of the moon, her cold fire. But sometimes pain is needed in the process, but not from all."

Clirando felt a shadow fall on her, like a heavy cloak for traveling. Her sleep-starved eyes half glimpsed Araitha suddenly, standing there in the shade behind the goddess's statue, motionless, with face averted.

"This is my true punishment, then."

"You may see it as such," said the priestess. "Or as a chance at salvation. The seas at this time of year are calm as honey. The voyage will last no longer than nineteen days, and perhaps rather less. Go now and tell you band. Pack anything you may need, for battle or for mere existence."

Landscape

Across night and water, in darkness: the island.

There was no moon tonight. Tomorrow was the moon's First Night.

"Clirando, do you see?"

"I see. The beacons are burning."

High up, the coastal cliffs were gemmed with them, drops of brilliant fire, each one separated from the next by many miles.

They were like eyes, watching, as the boat came in. Nothing else was to be seen, but the luminous rollers of the surf on the shore.

The galley had put them off as soon as the sun set in the Middle Sea. The Isle was visible, a black dot far away. The captain told Clirando the water there was too shallow for his ship, but also no man or woman, unless called or ordered to the Isle, might go in any nearer.

Strong, and aching for action after the slow voyage, the band was quite eager to take up oars and row.

Gradually the sea dulled to a leaden blue and the sky faded like an autumn rose. Great darkness came, scattered with stars. The galley had drawn away.

Briefly the younger girls chattered, excited or unnerved. Then they fell silent as the rest.

The hump of the island grew from the night, always still blacker, and then the beacons burned out above.

Clirando had been given by the captain a rudimentary map, which showed a way in. They found the entry soon enough. A narrow defile sliced between and below the steep surfaces of the cliffs.

They followed the sea channel and soon the beacons were left behind them. Only starlight then shone like steel on the water.

For perhaps a further quarter of an hour they rowed under the cliff stacks, until the channel opened again into an inner bay.

They drew the boat up across pale shingle.

A statue of an unknown goddess stood there, guarding the beach, her eyes glittering grey zircons.

"Who is she?" whispered Draisis.

Seleti said, "Maut, I think."

"A goddess of the East?" asked Tuyamel. "Do *you* think it's Maut, Cliro?"

Clirando bowed to the goddess. "Maybe. But whoever she is, this is her place. We'll offer some wine when we uncork the skin."

After they had set their fire, the ordinary sounds of arrival and domestic preparation ended. Then each of the women heard, Clirando thought, the vast stillness close about them. It was intense and fur-soft, and fearful, this silence. It had in it a kind of tinsel quivering—noiseless yet always in the ears. They spoke, the women, in hushed tones, eating the cold meats and apples from home, drinking the wine.

Clirando observed them. They were good girls, awed and probably nervous, yet staying cool and contained. This was not like fighting. What war asked of you was quite different. What the Isle asked... Only the gods knew.

Presently Clirando, who had not yet drunk, took some wine in a bowl along the shingle and poured out a proper measure for the goddess who seemed to be Maut, Haunter of Waters.

"Let all go well for them, Lady. Protect them and allow them to win honor. For myself, I won't ask you. Nor for sleep. I know, even if you'd grant it, I'd be unable to receive your gift."

Firelight made the zircon eyes sparkle—but only the firelight.

When she went back, they were saying that games were celebrated at a town on the island, deep in its interior, to mark the Seven Nights, and a great fair was held as well, full of wonders, with goods and animals on show that came from remote lands. She wondered where they had heard this. All Clirando had ever heard of the Isle, even on the galley, had been mysterious, uncanny and troubling.

Someone yawned—Vlis. Clirando said, "I'll take the watch."

"Yes, Clirando." They nodded solemnly. They believed that their leader had trained herself to need little if any sleep on duty. None of them, even Tuy, knew Clirando now seldom slept at all. Why worry them? They boasted of her talent for wakefulness.

As they settled down, Clirando again went off a short way. She sat on a boulder jutting from the stones and sand, about forty paces along the beach. From here she could see all the long curve of the shingle and, beside, a cliff path that slipped suddenly up along the rock face. It looked to be rough going, but they would use it in the morning.

Would they find other people here quickly? The beacon-lighters perhaps, if no one else.

The sea sighed and crinkled to and fro, lit by phosphorescent runners of foam. Like a lullaby—for some.

In the red circle of firelight, the others had curled up. Already they were all sleeping, heads on rolled cloaks, long legs and folded arms relaxed as the limbs of sleeping cats. Only Tuyamel softly snored, just audible in the quiet. But Clirando was aware the snoring would stop once Tuy was properly asleep.

How well I know them.

I know them better than I know myself.

Clirando regarded the act of sleep. Sometimes it had seemed to her, wandering up to the roof of her own house, she had seen all Amnos sleeping, all the world, with only she herself awake forever.

A pebble, loosened by something or nothing and tumbling down the cliff side, jolted her into a tremendous jump.

Clirando started to her feet, dazzled and alarmed. What had happened? She had *slept—she had slept?* For how long? Her trained eye scanned the stars. From their positions she worked out that all of an hour must have passed.

She did not sleep. She had been watching for hours, now and then prowling up and down along the edge of the sea...and then.

A deadly chill washed through her, and slowly she turned her head. The campfire burned low, and in its smoky glare she saw that no one now lay curled about it. Every one of her band had vanished.

Clirando ran forward. She kicked the fire up in a blaze, drew out a flaming stick and held it high. Where had they gone—and *why*—without waking her?

All around, the rolled cloaks, undisturbed, the impressions of sleeping heads still pillowed into them. The last baked apples sat along the fire's rim. Nothing else was there, apart from a bit of wood Seleti had been carving, and the wineskin.

Clirando drew her sword. If some enemy were about, he, she or it must be confronted. It was too late for subterfuge. "Here!" she called. And then she gave the ululating battle cry of the band. It echoed wildly off the cliffs.

She hoped against hope for some answering call. When her own yell died, none came. Nothing did. Only the sigh of the waves and the thick glimmering sound of the silence.

She could not help herself, a kind of terror was in her. She who could not sleep had slept, and her brave girls—none of them a weakling and all six together— had been taken—or had gone—away.

A weird gleam shone out across the water now. For a moment she could not think what it was. But it was the dawn beginning.

Clirando walked to the sea and plunged in her hands and her feet. The water was night-cold, shocking her back to some sanity.

She was alone, as all were when it came down to it. She must rely on herself.

Whatever had lured or forced her girls away, Clirando would find it and them.

While the light strengthened in the east. Clirando gathered her few belongings together. As the last stars winked out, she was already on the tortuous path that wound upward from the beach to the high places above.

* * *

Just as predicted, it was hard going. When she at last broke out of the thin clinging shrubs onto the plateau of the cliff top, the sun was two hands' width above the sea. Behind and below her the beach and the water. But ahead—Clirando looked inland.

Shoulders and walls of rock palisaded the headland, grey and white and grown with sea ivies and wild peculiar flowers. Quite some way off, the plateau tipped over and down into what seemed to be thick forest of pine and larch, the dark evergreen trees sacred to night and the gods of hidden things. Far in the distance, other heights rose from the forest and stood on the sky.

Nearby a narrow stream of clear water emerged from the natural stonework. Thankfully Clirando drank from it, cupping the water in her hands. It was sour and salty here, too near the sea, but it quenched her thirst.

When she raised her head, a creature was there among the rocks, staring at her. The wildflowers framed it oddly. It was a kind of lion or large lynx, yellow eyed, with a dappled creamy hide.

Clirando pulled the knife free of her belt. She had hunted where she had to, for food or protection. Though she had never seen an animal quite like this one, she could deal with it if necessary.

The beast fixed its eyes. Against the lean flanks a long tail lashed.

Generally they did not meet your gaze this long.

Was it magical?

Clirando said, very low, "What do you want?"

The lion creature flung up its head, eyes narrowed and jaws open to reveal lines of white fangs. This gave the irresistibly unsettling impression it laughed. Then, with a final lash of its tail, it sprang around and bounded away between the stands of rock. It had been a male, and obviously not hungry.

Clirando walked toward the plateau's dip and the forest.

By day, the Isle was not so silent. From the shore the cries of seabirds sometimes lifted, and from the forest occasionally other notes. However these sounds were sparse and intermittent.

For this reason the faint shuffling and skittering that started to accompany her progress, and which had nothing to do with her own light footfalls, seemed at first an illusion, some obtuse echo stirred up from the aisles of rock as she moved. But in the end Clirando knew her instinct that something followed her must be addressed.

She turned slightly, still going forward—and caught a flash of vague darkness darting behind a rock.

Paying no apparent heed, Clirando strode on, but again she drew her knife.

She could not be sure what tracked her. She did not think it was human. Yet she had not seen enough to judge what sort of animal it might be.

By then she had reached an area where the cliff plateau bulked upward to a stone hill, on the top of which was built one of the great beacons. Unlike the others along the outer coast, this had not been set alight, though a thin smell of old fires clung here. The beacon itself, she saw, was built as a round cauldron of stones, the kindling stacked ready inside and covered by oiled skins, pegged into sockets in the hill. This emblem of human activity both gladdened and disconcerted her.

As she was looking up, the skittery soft scuffle came again at her back, definitely not an echo of her own movements.

Clirando spun round.

She froze.

Three things poised on the rock in a curious huddle—almost as if they were chained together by some invisible rope. They were unlike anything she had ever seen—yet mostly piggish in shape, large pigs covered in an ashy black skin, from which stuck out spines like those of some Lybirican cactus. Their heads were misshapen, with tusks or horns pointing from their jaws, the sides of their faces, and above their small, flat, greenish eyes. Horrible things. Monsters. The very stuff of the legends of Moon Isle.

They made no move to attack.

Clirando took half a step toward them—they neither ran at her nor backed away.

Stooping swiftly, she plucked up a handful of loose stones and hurled them at the creatures.

They shied a little at the impact, tossing their ugly heads. That was all.

Were they the beasts of some local god?

Abruptly all three peeled back their upper lips. Unlike the lion beast earlier, their teeth were blunt and yellow, but even so not an encouraging sight.

Clirando rasped her sword out of its sheath. She would not turn her back on these things again, she thought.

Exactly then a voice called down from the beacon above.

"Who is there?"

It was the voice of a woman, and not young.

"Stay where you are, Mother," Clirando shouted, "till I deal with these pigs."

The old voice broke into a cackle of laughter. "Pigs? Is that what you see? Deal with them? I doubt you can."

Something came slithering and bouncing down the stone hill behind Clirando.

She turned, affronted but not amazed to be attacked from both sides, and saw a large wedge of dark wet bread falling. It shot past her, landing between her and the pig things.

"Let them have that, whatever they are, a morsel of comfort," called the old woman from the beacon. "And you come up here to me."

Clirando could see the pigs were sniffing after the bread, creeping forward to it, more interested apparently in that than in the warrior girl.

So Clirando jumped at the hill and ran up it, leaping over the loose stones and tufts of lichen.

At the top she looked back down. The pig things were eating the bread, sharing it in an unusually well-mannered way among them. It had been soaked in wine or beer, and obviously pleased them. One animal raised its head, and from its snout came the strangest sound, a kind of jeering whine—nearly human.

"So it's pigs, is it?" said the old woman. Clirando turned again and saw her. She was sitting around the far side of the beacon, weaving on a little upright frame, a cloth of grey and red. "Pigs for you," she said.

"What are they?" Clirando asked.

"Yours," said the woman.

Clirando let out a bark of mirth. "They're nothing to do with *me*."

"Oh, you think not?"

The woman herself wore a mantle that was grey and bordered by red. She looked ancient as the rock, but her eyes were still black and bright.

"Mother," said Clirando, "thanks for your help. Now perhaps you'll tell me, did a band of girls come by this way, warrior women of Amnos going to the festival of the Seven Nights?"

"Warriors?" asked the old woman. Clirando thought she had a clever, wicked face. "They'd be all in their fighting garb, with swords and such, walking proud?"

Clirando nodded.

"Nothing like that," said the old one.

"Then—Mother—if they went by you, *how* were they?"

"Oh, I saw no one," said the woman. "I was asleep. I lie up in that hut over there, while I tend the beacon. Tonight I must light it for the moon. Fire, to tempt the moon to shine full."

I'll get nothing helpful from her, thought Clirando. The old one had the look she had seen on the faces of certain grannies in the town, who found everything the young did funny, enjoying scorning and misleading them.

"Well, my thanks in any case."

Clirando moved off over the hill. She passed the leaning hut—it looked as if no one had stayed there for ten years or more. Glancing over her shoulder, she noted the old woman had disappeared around a jut of rock. Had *she* been real?

This is a place of demons and shadows.

At least the pigs were not now on her track. Clirando reached the beacon hill's foot and broke into a fast lope.

She came to the descent and the edge of the forest just before noon. Picking her way down, she found a trail, now and then carved to earthen steps at the steeper spots.

An altar stood by the path side, just in under the trees. A black formless stone was there, with a wooden cup in front of it, holding dregs of honey, from the smell.

Prudently Clirando took out a sweet wafer from her food store and dropped it into the cup.

"I don't know you, but I respect you," she said, bowing to the altar and the stone. Then she went down into the depths of the forest, dark green at noon as the heart of a malachite.

Story

The pig creatures came back that night, with the dusk.

She had thought she was free of them.

All day Clirando had trekked through the forest. It was dark as a cellar in parts. In others long aisles opened, lit by filtered sunlight. Here and there the conifers gave way to oaks, and even beeches, about whose roots drifts of flowers sometimes lay. But the flowers were small and pale and the leafy cloudbursts of the canopy seemed full of cores of blackness. In areas the trunks of the pines massed thick as an army, closing off not only all light, but any view or path.

Now and then Clirando heard birdsong. Once—only once—a single grey pigeon sped across from tree to tree. She saw tracks of deer and foxes, once of a wolf, and twice of boar—but none of the animals were ever to be seen. Elusive as the wildlife, her comrades from the band.

Nowhere did she detect any evidence of their passing, either freely or as captives.

Little streams went through the forest, often falling down over tall rocks into some pool below.

By such a pool she decided to make her camp that night, and arranged it in the sunset hour.

Clirando took from her pack a handful of oat flour and mixed it with water and raisins, putting the cake to bake in the fire. She sat with her back to the rock, the waterfall splashing softly to her left.

Long shadows gathered as the peachy glimpses of the sky cooled.

Well. There was no fear she would sleep again tonight. Clirando had considered what had happened on the beach. Since she only slept now if drugged, then she *had* been, and her band with her. They had talked quite a while over the food, so probably that was not at fault. Very likely the wine they had brought was the culprit. Clirando, who drank it the last, slept the last. She had left the skin today on the shore, because it was too cumbersome to carry. But who had done it? Who had put the sleeping draft into the wine, and why? Some new enemy?

Tonight was the First Night of Full Moon.

The old woman would be lighting her beacon, and all the other beacons would also beam out again along the coasts. And somewhere the island celebrated like the rest of the world—but where?

Here in these trees she would see the moon, threading through the boughs, clear at the center of the glade, and over there in that gap.

Clirando ate her oat bread and drank water from the pool. She tried not to think of pirates stealing up the beach to take her drugged girls for slaves. After all, there had been no marks of them anywhere inland. It seemed but too likely now they had been stolen away by ship. Why then did the robbers leave Clirando? Not tempting enough, perhaps, she thought ironically. Thestus had praised her looks, comparing her to a young lion. But Araitha was the beautiful one. And besides Clirando was "cold" and had no feminine talents—

In a sudden rage Clirando hurled the husk of her bread into the fire. A splash of flame rose there.

"I am not *cold*. I have passion. I showed you that, Thestus, but best I showed you when I beat you in the war-court."

Her voice rang hard on the silence, as if it hit the darkening sky.

And in that moment, from out of the noiseless forest where not even the birds had sung a farewell to the sun, surged up a piercing, wailing, jeering cry.

Clirando was on her feet, weapons ready.

But after the jeer, silence.

The forest *breathed* as the sea did, leaves touched by

faint night breezes. Not a bird or animal had reacted to the unnerving noise.

She had the rock behind her, the fire and the pool in front. A reasonable defensive position. She waited, tense as the sword in her hand.

Minutes went by, three or four, maybe longer.

Nothing stirred beyond the pool among the columns of the pines.

The cry—some night bird, perhaps, some animal hunting? No, she had never heard such a screech from any animal or bird, or been told of one. But then again, Moon Isle was—

Scalding her ears and brain, searing her heart and blood, the awful wail went up again. *Now* it had three voices.

Human—it was like the jeering of some insane and evil crowd.

She saw them trot, the three of them, from among the trees and the folding cloak of night. The pig monsters from the cliff top.

Clirando bent and drew from her fire a long branch ripe with flames. She held it aloft in her left hand.

Then purposely she walked by the fire, skirting the pool, taking measured steps.

They stood together in a looser formation than before. The beast in the middle lifted its lip, and out came the mocking cry, full blast.

She would move slowly, then sprint straight at them. Fire for the one most to the left, the sword through the neck of the middle one. Then around to take the third with whatever she had.

She was shaking inside herself, but also lit with fury.

What happened then seemed like the childish joke of some cruel god.

Something *else,* rushing like a whirlwind, bowled directly into Clirando, sending her headlong and sprawling. It leaped over her back as she went down—she felt it go, hot as fire.

Pushing herself up, the burning branch lost, the sword juggled back into her grip, she checked in astonishment.

What had knocked her down was the other animal she had met on the cliffs, the lion with the dappled pelt. Either that, or one exactly of the same species. It had jumped over her and gone plunging at the three pig things, just as she had planned to do. As she stood there gasping, she saw how it plummeted straight into all three, angling its leonine body as it did so, the large paws thrashing.

Squealing now, all three pigs jumbled away from it. They went galloping back among the trees, the cat in hot pursuit.

The last she saw of the incredible scene was the lion's creamy tail lashing in darkness like a snake. Then everything was as it had been, and silent once more.

Clirando retrieved the burning branch from the ground and stamped out the scorches it had made. Uneasily, confused, she turned to retrace her way to her fire.

Something else was there.

The reflection of it, fire limned, went down into the pool.

Clirando straightened and raised her sword. Her green eyes were wide, and burning like the flames.

"That is my place. Come away from it."

"But you left your place," he said casually.

"Did you see why?"

"I saw something running off through the wood."

Clirando said, "Move over there, away from my fire. I shan't ask you again."

"Were you *asking?* Very well then. As you like."

When he moved along the poolside and out onto the apron of turf, she never took her eyes from him. He too was a fighter—she could tell from the way he stalked forward, the coordination of his movements. But he had a beauty not often seen among mortal things, found more commonly in well-made statues of young male gods. His hair was so fair it seemed white as mountain snow. White as the moon.

This one also is some illusion or demon.

He stood now about twelve paces from her. Backlit by the fire, she could see a thin scar high on his right cheekbone, and how the muscles flexed in his arms as he slid the knife he had held back into its sheath. There were darns and recent tears in his clothing, and on one of his boots the silvery trail of a tiny snail that still slid along there, then descended to the grass.

If a facsimile, he was a good one. He looked real.

"We don't have to quarrel, do we?" he inquired pleasantly. "We can share provisions, perhaps. I have some bread and cheese and a little alcohol."

"Who are you? What are you doing here?"

"My name is Zemetrios—Zemetrios of Rhoia. I was told to come here. You too I imagine. Unless this sacred and terrible place is your home."

The sword weighed heavy on her hand. She thrust it back into the sheath, almost startling herself. Tiredness droned in her head and up her spine.

"Very well. I accept your words."

"Then I may share your fire?"

"If you like. It's the oldest law of the gods, isn't it? To welcome the stranger."

"But how unconvinced you sound," he said.

He waited for her to seat herself, but she waved him down first. They sat at opposite sides. Around them the night was now noiseless and, beyond the range of the light, impenetrable.

"The moon will rise in about two hours," he said.

He set out his provisions, the cheese and loaf, the flask. Clirando had eaten, but since she had accepted the terms of hospitality, she created another of the oatcakes and handed him an apple. She waited until he had swallowed a bit of the cheese before she would try it.

She saw he noted this, but he said nothing.

She wished he was not here.

They did not speak beyond the barest civilities. After

he had drunk from the flask, he offered it to her, having first wiped the lip of the vessel.

Clirando took one sip, for politeness. It was some raw spirit of Rhoia, not really to her taste.

"Since we're two now," he said, "perhaps we should set a watch."

"You speak like a soldier," she said.

"I am—I was. I've fought in the king's legions. Traveled quite a distance, seen the wonders of the world. But that's done now."

His eyes, a clear deep blue, looked away into his past. Clirando could see he beheld something there, bleak and unforgiving.

What else? This place was for testing and penance. For punishment probably.

She wondered what he had done, then chided herself for being at all interested. He might be dangerous, that was enough to know.

"Well," she said, "I'll take the whole watch. I've already slept my fill." The lie was practiced, ready.

He lifted an eyebrow at her. "You don't trust me, then."

Clirando smiled. "Of course not. Why should I? But I'll take the watch anyway. If anything occurs, I will wake you."

"Wake me when the moon rises," he said. "I want to see it. The last time I saw the Seven Nights I was only eight." He stretched out with no pretence or air of feeling vulnerable. His movements were both masculine and graceful, a pleasure for anyone to observe, she thought sourly; a pity they should be wasted on her. "I wonder how it is," he murmured, "she can renew herself these seven times together. Scholars have written," he added dreamily, "there's more than one moon involved in these nights—our own, and six of her sisters she calls from other spheres...." He turned his head a little and fell, apparently, instantly into sleep.

It might be an act. But Clirando thought not. The gods knew, she had in recent months had endless opportunities to study the sleep of others.

And for a stupid instant she felt jealous of his ability to sleep so simply. To her, now, it was an alien concept.

When the moon rose he woke anyway, the way in fact Clirando herself had often done, sleeping in the open. They said, if the full moon touched your face with her white hand, you roused. In the past of course, Clirando had then gone back to sleep.

"There she is," said the man called Zemetrios. He lay still, looking up.

Together they stared awhile at the bright disk passing over the glade, reflecting like pearl in the pool.

"The moon looks as it always does at full," he remarked.

"What did you expect?"

"Something more—as these are the Seven Nights."

He sat up abruptly, stretching so she heard the strong

muscles crack in his arms. "I'll take the watch now, if you like."

"No need," she said.

"Come on, girl. You're a trained fighter. You'd know in a split second if I was trying anything—doubtless you'd kill me."

"Doubtless I would. But I have no difficulty in keeping the watch myself."

He said, "You look tired to your bones."

Clirando blinked, affronted and defensive.

"That's for me to judge."

"Then I'll say no more. But at least, will you tell me your name? You have mine."

It was true, in courtesy she owed him that. "Clirando, one of the warrior women of Amnos," she said shortly.

"Yes, I thought you'd be from there. Your bands are highly spoken of." He paused, looking now down into the moon-shining pool. "Clirando, in fairness, I'd like to tell you something of myself. Of what sent me here."

"I ask to know nothing."

"Or you'd *prefer* to stay ignorant of me? Well and good, but this island is no place for human secrecy or deception. Nor do I think it the best place to travel alone."

Scornfully she said to him, her heart beating too fast, "So you're afraid of the Isle? My regrets. But I'm no companion for you. I have my band to think of—" and broke off, aware that she had lost her band and very likely would never find them again. A wide grief swept through her and a sense of shame. She had failed her girls.

He said, "Do me the kindness then, Clirando, of letting me tell you of my crime. In the temples of the Father, anyone may go and tell his worst sins to a priest, if the burden becomes too great. And I know, in Amnos, there is also a priestess tradition among the female warriors."

Clirando lifted her eyes from her own emotions, and looked at him levelly.

He took this as his cue. Clirando did not know if she had meant it to be one.

"I killed a man," Zemetrios said woodenly. He began to gaze again into the pool. "Fair and square, you might say, in a duel outside my father's house. Or my house, since my father died last year."

Clirando watched him.

The moon lighted his face, but his eyes were shadowed, looking down at the water.

Zemetrios of Rhoia told her how the man he had slain had been his best friend. "We'd fought as comrades in the legions since both of us were seventeen. He was a fine soldier, loyal and trustworthy and clever. We were like brothers from the first. We've fought side by side in enough battles...been promoted to the rank of leader at the same time. I was at his wedding. A pretty girl, a sweet girl. I don't know where she's gone now. She ran away from him, you see. That was after he changed into another man."

A silence.

"What do you mean?" Clirando heard her voice. It had a sound of awe. Zemetrios had caught her with his storytelling. She must be on guard.

Zemetrios said, "He turned into a drunkard. Oh, there had been times in the past—you fight hard, you take leave and drink hard. But those sessions are occasional. Then, with Yazon, they became habitual."

Zemetrios spoke briefly, in terse sentences, of drunk brawls, meaningless and savage fights with citizens of the town that Yazon, deranged with wine, would pick. "He was a trained fighter. You see what that would mean. They hadn't a chance. He broke their legs and arms and knocked them senseless like cold stones. I and others dragged him off, doused him in the horse trough. Sometimes we would have to chain him up like a mad dog till he sobered."

Yazon began to beat his young wife also. She fled to her parents' house on the hills, and later, after Yazon pursued her there, firstly with gifts, then with threats, to some other land.

"They cast him out of the legions in dishonor. He had only his soldier's pension then, much reduced since he was young and had ruined his own career."

Yazon, Zemetrios said, went to live in an old fisherman's hut near the quay. He begged for his living, or committed acts of robbery—twice ending in the jail-pit for a public whipping. All he could get in money went on wine—bad wine, now, the dross of the water-front taverns.

"I tried my best to help him, Clirando. I'd paid off his debts three times, I'd begged the legion to give him a second chance—twice I did that, but the second time a second chance was refused. He didn't know me mostly anyway, said he thought me some enemy. By then he was never sober. My father was sick by then, too. I had other difficulties, and soon enough the duties of burial and mourning."

Zemetrios paused again.

Clirando said nothing. The tale disturbed her. She empathized with this unknown man and, not daring to trust him—Thestus had won her trust, and Araitha had always *had* her trust—would not speak.

In the end Zemetrios told her that he came from the house one morning to find Yazon lying across the threshold. "He was filthy, covered in sores and fleas, half-dead. I took him in. He had been my friend. What else could I do?"

Cleaned up, fed, and doctored by a physician, Yazon was surly and irritable. Refused more than three cups of wine, he stole it from the cellars, and broke the pitchers in the courtyard when he was done. On a morning when Zemetrios needed to report to the town fort, Yazon attacked two of the kitchen girls. He raped one, and beat them both with a stick, and when someone came running to the fort, Zemetrios raced to his house and pulled the yowling drunkard out into the square. Before a crowd of citizens and soldiers, Zemetrios punched his former friend to the ground, threw him a sword and told him to get up and fight.

"It lasted less than the tenth of an hour. I never meant to kill him, or believed not. But he was no longer Yazon and I perhaps was no longer much myself, either. I'd seen the girls crying. My father had kept a kind and worthy house. The sword pierced him through cleanly enough. He fell over and was dead. Yazon. Dead. I remember," said Zemetrios, "one time in the deserts, marching east, he and I sat looking at the stars and talked about what we wished for ourselves. Both of us wanted only good things. Nothing to anger the gods. But he died on the street and I left my legion, and sold my father's house. And now the priests have sent me here."

Clirando had been holding her breath. She let it go carefully, so he should not hear her sigh.

The full moon reached the perimeter of the trees. It slipped behind the canopy, looking for a moment broken in silver pieces, before darkness closed the view.

In the morning Clirando forced herself to alertness. This now was her fifth night without sleep—aside from the deadly drugged hour on the beach. She had not taken much of the herbal medicine on the galley, not wanting her band to guess her predicament, or herself to be unready for any demand the voyage might make. On Moon Isle, she had always realized, she could not risk it at all. Parna's temple had supplied instead a cordial to help her keep her energy and a clear mind. Clirando drank from the vial.

Zemetrios, after he had made his "confession" to her, had lain back and slept again, but not, she then saw, so well. His slumbers were disturbed. She felt a mean amusement at it. But what if this too were some act?

I can never trust him. He may be a liar and felon. Or—he may not be real at all.

Was such a thing possible? Yes. There were demons here, she had encountered them, for what else were the pig things but some type of animal demon? A man demon might also be feasible. And he had appeared by her fire—as if from nowhere.

She thought grimly, *And enough demoniac men already exist in the human world.*

They shared bread and oatcakes for breakfast. They drank water from the pool.

He told her then that the priests in Rhoia had assured him a large village lay at the heart of the Isle, deep in the forest and below the mountains. This was where the Seven Nights were celebrated.

"We should make for there."

Was this a lie, too? Or a trap?

But she could think of nothing else to do. Against all common sense she had a wild hope the girls of her band might be at this village, part of the celebration they themselves had discussed.

Journey

They both moved at a steady lope along the continuing track that ran through the trees. Everything was as
it had been, a hot day burning up behind the leaves and
pine needles, freckled sun-shafts, cool shadows, little
wayside streams, rocks, and the rare sound or sight of
a bird, and once a yellowish fox trotting over their path.

Near noon they came into another glade, without
water, but the turf covered with drifts of the pale flowers. Vines hung from the trees like nets, jeweled by
fast-ripening grapes.

They paused here, picking and eating the fruit.

From behind the walls of the pines, there came suddenly a jeering, eerie whoop.

He heard it too she thought.

Transfixed, Clirando saw a dark huddle of shapes

ruffling along behind the curtains of the vines. There were more of them now. A whole pig herd of these demons of hers.

Last night she had yearned that the lion cat would catch and devour them. But obviously, even if it had, other members of the tribe existed.

"What is it?" Zemetrios said to her.

They had, until then, spoken very little, and of nothing beyond their own advance, the grapes, and the mooted village.

Shaken again, Clirando said, "Animals."

He stared over where she did.

"Or," he said, "supernatural things."

"Can you see them?" The question burst from her before she could decide to withhold it.

"Something…but the island is full of such stuff. They trouble you?" he asked, turning his blue eyes full on her.

Angrily Clirando said, "What business is it of yours?"

"Only this—I too am tormented by creatures or images that roam through the trees. Not animal in that sense. They call to me in drunken voices…insubstantial. An army of drunken ghosts."

As he said this, clear as if drawn in paint, Clirando saw Araitha standing between two pines. She wore her traveler's cloak, and her golden hair with its ornaments caught the sunlight. Her face had no expression.

Clirando began to tremble. She told herself dizzily that it was only her sleepless eyes that played the trick.

She shut them, which was a mistake, and felt Zemetrios catch hold of her, lifting her clear of some abyss into which she had been about to fall.

She pushed him away. His strength and quickness alarmed her. She was humiliated by her own weakness.

But he would not let her push him off. He held her up and put the flask against her mouth.

"Take some."

"No."

"It's only water. I drank the last of the spirits last night."

Clirando drank. The water was still cold, and despite his words, kept the tang of alcohol. It steadied her."

"My thanks. Let go of me now. I'm well."

"You're not. But yes, I'll let go. There."

She could smell him, the health of his young body, the clean aroma of his hair and breath.

Clirando glanced at the pines.

The ghost was gone.

"Did you kill her?" Zemetrios asked.

"What?"

"You spoke a name, two in fact. A man's name and a woman's. You spoke *his* name with utter scorn. And hers with—forgive me, warrior girl, with *fear*."

Clirando dropped herself down to her knees, and sat back. She no longer felt faint, but drained and—what Araitha had promised—*empty*.

This man *was* real. She had disgraced herself by nearly fainting in front of him like some pampered lady. What did the truth matter now?

"I killed her. Not directly. But she died because of what I did."

"Because she lay down with your lover? Oh, Clirando, it isn't hard to guess. You spoke two names, remember?"

"She lay down with my lover. She'd been my friend. Him I beat in fair fight and he was sent away. She also. She went to Crentis but the ship sank. She's dead, as you say. Through me."

"By the Father," said Zemetrios softly.

"She cursed me, too," Clirando gave a small rasp of laughter. "I can't sleep. A slight curse, you might think."

"No, I don't think that."

"Well," said Clirando, "let's get on."

She stood up again.

The forest was silent and black beyond the sunlight of the vine glade. Like all her life surely now, beyond that night when lightning struck Parna's Temple.

Why did I trust him? Stupid, to blab it all out to him. Are you a child, or what? Well. He knows now.

Clirando ran lightly beside Zemetrios, through the glints and shades, angry with herself, lamenting, full of pain.

Nothing had importance, only to go on, to find her band. Or if not, respectfully to complete this awful and

weird penance set her by the priestesses of the Maiden.
And then be done with all of it.

*I too will go away. Into the East perhaps, where peo-
ple lose themselves. Because already I'm lost. Who is Clirando? Clirando would never have blurted out her secret
to some stranger.*

But as they loped shoulder to shoulder, glancing up
at the "stranger," from time to time she saw the twitch
behind his eyes, and once his head turning, then snapping around again. He too heard and saw devils in the
forest as he had said, that fact alone was certain.

And she—she came to hear sometimes an unearthly
low sound that filtered through the trees like wind,
though the leaves never moved. It had for her no noise
of drunken voices—the multiplied voice of Yazon in all
the moods of his insanity. If she detected anything it
was the jeering cry of the pig things—but now never
too close.

Possibly he had been right. To travel together might
provide a little distance for both of them from their
haunts. Even the ghost of Araitha had not drawn near.

Had it *been* she? For sure?

Clirando frowned as she ran. *They are my devils. They
come for me. Out of my heart and mind. It's only that the
forest makes them real. But how real? Could I have gone
to her and seized her, run her through with a knife?*

Clouds massed across Clirando's eyes. She half stumbled, and he turned and looked at her. His face was
concerned, curious.

"A root," she said.

And pushed memory and idle surmise to the edges of her brain.

The trees began to thin out near sunfall.

The downward slopes were more gradual, and oak trees and wild olive predominated. Here the track ended abruptly. Another altar place stood there, this one with a whitish stone roughly carved and pocked, a sort of uneven globe.

He and she halted beside it. In the bronzy light now slanting sidelong through the trees, the globe seemed to pulse with uncanny inner light.

Clirando took the last honey wafer from her pack, and laid it by the stone. "I do not know you, but I reverence you."

Zemetrios, rather sheepishly, she thought, put the final sliver of cheese on the altar. It was mostly rind. Any god would disdain it—or perhaps not, since they would otherwise have eaten it.

"Look," he said quietly.

A hare bounded among the olives, its long ears brushed with light and glowing red.

They could have brought the hare down for supper, either of them, she was certain. But in this place neither had wished to, or though it wise.

Did they in some ways then, think alike?

No.

Remember Thestus, the arch deceiver. Though

Thestus, she believed, would have wanted to throw his knife or a rock at the hare, and she would have had to stop him.

As they turned from the altar, Clirando saw an old man sitting about fifty paces away under a broad-leaved tree. His hands were busy with something that sparkled—and she was positive he had not been there in the preceding moments.

"Do you see him?"

"Yes," Zemetrios said.

Slowly they walked forward, making no attempt at caution. The old man did not look up. But when they were almost within arm's length of him, he raised his aged face. His eyes were black and keen in the pleated paper of his skin.

"You're going to the village," he told them, "the Moon Town."

"It exists then," said Clirando.

"Perhaps," said the old man.

What spangled through his hands was a threaded skein of brilliant stones—like Eastern rubies and diamonds they looked. He seemed only to be playing with them and suddenly he cast them down.

Zemetrios but not Clirando sucked in breath.

Meeting the ground, the sparkly web changed instantly to a long and coiling snake, marked along its back with points of red and silver.

"Oh," said the old man, sarcastically polite, "did I make you jump, bold soldier?"

"Yes, Father," said Zemetrios. Good-naturedly he laughed. "You're a magician, then."

"Sometimes a magician. Sometimes other things. Sometimes I am a tree."

They regarded him wordlessly. The burnished snake poured itself away and up the narrow trunk of a nearby olive.

"Things come, and also they go," said the old man.

"How great a distance to the village now, Father?"

"Not far. Be there before sunset ends. They close the gates at first dark."

"A wise precaution," said Clirando.

She guessed Zemetrios, as she did, tried to draw the old man out, provoke him into some revealing word or action.

But he did not reply now, only took from the inner folds of his garments another skein of beads. Moving it to and fro between gnarled hands, he crooned what must have been the spell to make a serpent out of it.

"Well, good evening to you," said Zemetrios.

He and Clirando walked on.

About twenty steps farther along, both of them turned as one. Only shadows sat under the broad-leaved tree.

"The snake-maker, I shall call him that," said Zemetrios.

"It was a trick, an illusion."

"Maybe. Did you see how he did it?"

"No. But then often you never can—that is the idea of it."

"I met an old woman, too," Zemetrios said, "the first day, when I'd climbed up from the beach. There was an unlit beacon there. She wove only cloth, not snakes. She said she lived in a hut."

"I met her also. The hut hadn't been used for years."

"What are they?" he said softly, as they paced on again. "Are they demons, too? If so, I don't recognize them."

"Not all demons are recognizable."

"You're sensible, Clirando."

She shrugged.

The ground sloped up now. The trees were much fewer in number, long stretches of grass and weeds between them, and no path anywhere, as if, though many walked through the forest, none ever came as far as this.

The sun, which they could see now, hung low in the sky, a red ball in a curdling of gold and scarlet cloud.

They had reached the top of the hill. They looked down into the small basin of a valley.

Impending sunset described it exactly. Fields and groves, vineyards and orchards clustered there. And from them protruded high walls of dressed stone, above which showed tiled roofs, and one tall slim tower. The village. Behind everything, mountains rose, three peaks, one behind another, and touched sidelong with flame by the dying sun.

The way down to the valley was easy. The slope was broken now by another pathway, itself of laid stone, and broad enough for three men to walk together.

"At first dark the gates shut," he repeated.

They broke into a racer's run, leaping down the roadway into the valley.

4

Village

Shadows are called
By the ending of the day
Night unfolds her wings
With the white moon in her hair...

Clirando shuddered. The fragment of song had
sounded inside her skull, words clear as the plinking
of the lyra which accompanied them—*so* clear, for a
moment she thought a voice had actually sung aloud,
a hand actually plucked the chords. Araitha's voice
and Araitha's hand. It had been a favourite song of
hers to play after supper.

Zemetrios this time did not seem to notice Clirando's lapse.

He said, "There are no lights in this village."

Clirando said, "Nor any lights anywhere among the fields and orchards. Not one torch burning. Not a single dog to bark."

The sun was just now down over the horizon, leaving a solitary rift of gold. Darkness was claiming the landscape. But not a lamp shone out anywhere, and over the stubble of the fields, where already the grain must have been scythed, not one figure walked. The orchards too had been stripped of fruit, which surely would not have been ripe.

"What's happened here?" Zemetrios asked.

The walls of the village-town lay ahead of them, and in them two tall wooden gates stood wide. A street of tamped earth ran in from there, and buildings lined the way. But there also—no movement, and no illumination.

"We must go and see," she said.

The thought of her girls as in her mind. They had vanished—and now this deserted village.

They hurried to the gates, and reached them as the final golden wash faded on the sky's edge and darkness bloomed like a long sigh over the earth.

"*Look!* The gates are *closing—*"

Together, not thinking, caught by some primal instinct, they bolted between the slowly joining gates. Clirando cursed herself even as she did so—to pelt into this unknown enclosure that might contain anything—and heard Zemetrios curse louder.

But by then they were in.

The gates padded together at their backs.

And, in a fiery chorus, at once every lamp, torch and candle in the village was, or began to be, lit.

The village street, the houses and other buildings, blushed to sudden life. Faces appeared at windows and figures emerged on terraces. Others came strolling along the thoroughfare. Two men, that neither she nor Zemetrios, she thought, had previously seen, were securing the gates with bars.

"Just in time, travelers," one of the men remarked to them.

Then down the street came striding a giant creature, tall as the roofs, her black hair swinging as she swung her impossibly long legs, a lighted brand in her grasp with which she brought alive the last torches leaning from house walls.

Zemetrios laughed. Clirando glared at him. Had he gone crazy?

"A stilt-walker, Clirando," he said.

And looking back, Clirando saw the woman, who was dark skinned as a Lybirican, was perched on two long poles, each swathed in her abnormally long white skirt.

A child ran up then. She carried a basket of apples and dates, and offered it to them.

Zemetrios reached out at once.

Clirando said, "Be wary."

"I'm hungry, Clirando."

"Yes, but if you eat that you may also be dead."

"Or," he conceded, "this is magic food."

But the child waited there, smiling and holding up the basket, which had been lined with vine leaves.

Before either of them could decide, a man rode by on a brown horse and called the child to him. Bending from the saddle, he took a fruit and bit into it.

"Are these truly people?" Zemetrios asked, "that one there on the horse, the child—or are they another sort of demon—illusions—even figments come from our own heads?"

"We both see the same things here," said Clirando, "men with snakes, lamps lit, a horseman and a child. A basket of fruit."

"Yes. But suppose—"

Another man tapped Zemetrios on the shoulder. Zemetrios shot around to find the fellow bowing low. He wore the leather apron of tavern staff.

"Come to our inn-house, warriors. It is a fine house. The best wine on the Isle. Good meat and new-baked bread. Our rooms are of the nicest—though we're full for the celebration of the Seven Nights, still one or two choice chambers remain. We also boast a bathhouse, and water always hot from a steamy spring. Come to our house, warriors."

"He sounds like any tavern tout from Rhoia to Ashalat," murmured Zemetrios.

The man swayed, beaming and bowing.

All through the village circulated the usual evening

street sounds, laced now with rills of laughter and notes of music.

Above, a woman called across from one balcony to its neighbor, and in another window another woman appeared with a little pet dog on her shoulder.

The scene was normal. Perplexingly so. As he had said, Rhoia—or anywhere thriving in the civilized world—would parade like this after sundown. Even Amnos.

Clirando said to the taverner, "What's the name of your inn?"

"The Moon in Glory."

Zemetrios added, "And why does your village hide until the gates are shut? And why is there no one out in the fields and not a single light?"

"Oh, master, it's our custom on the Seven Nights. Soon as the sun starts to sink, we sit in quiet and not a candle's lit till the last ray's gone. Then we shut the gates and every light is kindled. As for the country about, why—everyone's here. Of course they are. Where else to see and salute the great moon?"

Zemetrios turned to Clirando. "Do we believe him?"

"Oh, *believe* me, master—" The taverner had a round face that now grew anxious. "The innkeeper will be displeased if I lose him custom." Sidling nearer, the man whispered, "He's a skinflint, and he loves to make money."

"Ah, *money*. Then I reckon this is real enough."

Clirando looked about her. Her weariness pushed

against her back and shoulders. Who cared if it was a trap or an illusion… She should not think this way. But she said, "We can see for ourselves."

The man skipped before them up the street and along an alley to a blue-plastered wall, out of which a lemon tree grew, its hard green fruit scenting the air.

A boy, all smiles as well, whisked open a gate into a yard. Torches blazed on walls, night-perfumed flowers spilled luxuriously from urns. There was additionally the smell of good bread and roasting joints, and over the low wall steam puffed from the domed roof of a little bathhouse, just as promised.

"Oh, Clirando—forgive me. I can't resist." Zemetrios sounded both amused and charming.

"Nor I," she admitted, but with chilly reserve.

Yet from nowhere the oddest feeling fled through her. What in the Maiden's name was it? In dismay, Clirando accepted it had been a moment's natural pleasure. As if her life was quite natural too, and the town her friend, and Zemetrios, this unknown fighter from another country, someone she trusted, liked, and perhaps much more…

Night unfolds her wings
With the white moon in her hair
And love rises from her bed of dreams
To waken all the sleeping earth.

"What is it, Cliro?"
She gazed at him, stricken. "I can hear a song—"

"I can hear it, too. About night and the moon and love. I've heard it in Rhoia. It's an old tune."

Something loosened in her. She thought, *Even if this is fakery, we both see and hear the same things now. Something in that. And besides, that voice singing is a boy's. Not hers—not Araitha's—*

It was only after they had parted to seek the male and female sections of the bath that she recalled Zemetrios had called her *Cliro.* As if long familiar with her, and close.

Despite the taverner's boast, the inn seemed not that full—or certainly not the bathhouse. Clirando had the three narrow rooms to herself. She washed in the first under the tepid fountain, and then soaked in the second in a pool of delicious heat that blanketed her up to the chin. An attendant in the first room washed her hair. Now it spread about her in the hot pool, scented like the perfumed shrubs outside. Finally she sprang into the last cold pool, with a hiss of anguish that quickly disappeared as the water toned her muscles, closed her pores and awarded her a feeling of vigor. She might have slept a whole night through. It seemed to her there must be special salts in the spring that fed the bathhouse, which was often the case. She felt literally renewed, her eyes clear and well focused, her blood moving like waves of light.

Unnerving her less now, the feeling of pleasure, almost of happiness and anticipation, continued and grew stronger.

She thought of Tuyamel tilting her head doubtfully, and Vlis chuckling, and young Draisis enthusiastically vindicating happiness at all costs.

I'll find them, Clirando thought, kicking her feet in the cold water as a child might. *I shall find them here. This village, tonight—or tomorrow. I'll ask, and I'll look for them.*

But she knew her exhilaration had to do also with Zemetrios.

She felt lenient with herself. Why should she not be glad at the company of an apparently decent and highly attractive man?

Every reason.

But as that warning voice stirred at the back of her mind, Clirando kicked it up in the air with the sprays of cold water. Then she climbed out and dried herself, shaking her hair like a dog.

He had already commandeered a table for them and two benches, tucked into a wall nook. He had ordered beer, which generally Clirando preferred to wine. She thought he himself did not care that greatly for wine— understandable, if he had seen its ill effect on Yazon.

They talked to each other now freely, again as if well-known to each other and quite at ease. But the subjects of the conversation were only the excellence of the hot water, the types of food the inn offered. All around, a crowd massed at the tables, and serving girls and men went to and fro. Clirando saw no one else she knew.

"I have hopes my band of girls reached this village," she said at last. "I was separated from them after we brought in the boat."

He looked at her, consideringly. It was like a question, and reluctantly, after a few seconds, she heard herself say, "They vanished from the beach. They'd been sleeping—and I too—I fell asleep, which now I never can, unaided. There was some drug in the wine."

Before she knew it would happen he put his hand briefly, and warm, over hers. "I'm sorry, Clirando. I've heard so many tales like that about Moon Isle. It will come right. You'll make it so."

His touch chimed upward through her flesh. She stared resentful at her own hand, as if waiting to see a burn or scald appear where his fingers had rested. Gruffly she said, "I mean to walk about the village, to see if I can learn anything."

"Don't ask any of them here," he said, surprising her. "I'd guess you'll learn nothing that way."

"I thought you believed this inn—this village—trustworthy."

"Did I say that? No. I said it was all irresistible."

She saw he too was looking intently at her hand. Suddenly he said, "I like your hand, Clirando of Amnos. Forgive me, but the firmness, and the callus there from a warrior's knife. My first love, I have to tell you, was a warrior woman. Even before that, my mother had belonged to a band. But then she wed my father and gave it up."

Clirando frowned. "Did he force her to?"

"No. He was an honorable man. It was her choice. She never lost her edge though. She would wrestle the other girls for practice, and she could ride as well as any man, better than many. She was the one who taught me horses."

The food came, and they ate, dipping the warm bread among the sauces, tearing off chunks of the succulent roast.

Around and about, the inn went on as inns did everywhere in the known world. Clatter of dishes, clink of metal cups, mirth and singing, the occasional quarrel roused and calmed. Abruptly a long, high call went through the room. "The moon! She's risen!"

Not one person kept their seat. Even the servers went out. They all stood on a high open terrace above the yard. There on the wall balanced the moon, round and blazing white.

"Yes," said Zemetrios, "something new after all. She looks whiter here, don't you think. Clean and cold."

A man spoke behind them. "It is the snows that cover her."

Clirando turned.

A merchant, well dressed and well groomed, wiping his ringed, dinner-greasy hands on a napkin.

"Snow?" Zemetrios queried. He smiled.

"Indeed. So our sages tell us. At midsummer in this, our world, up there midwinter comes. The snows fall thickly. And so the moon shines so white."

"The moon is also a world, then?" Clirando asked innocently. It was what the priestess had said. But she thought of Zemetrios's stricture: to ask anything here would be profitless. Perhaps something so esoteric would not matter.

"Do you see that mountain?" The merchant pointed back over the roof of the inn, the other roofs of the village, and up into the sky where all three peaks showed, as if faintly drawn on by a brush. "The central height is known as Moon's Stair. There is, they say, an entrance up there that leads between the worlds and out onto the surface of the moon. Sleepers often travel to the moon, as do sorcerers, or priests in a trance. But physically there's only one way, and that is by climbing the mountain called Moon's Stair."

Zemetrios said, "I've heard of an entrance to the lands beyond death. That's in the East."

"Like that, then," said the merchant. "Or maybe it's all lies." His grin was crafty, knowing. It seemed he understood quite well what Zemetrios had said to Clirando earlier.

Down in the yard, servants were lighting the tails of firecrackers. Now they dived upward on flights of glittering topaz.

Clirando thought, *Surely they would have done this*

last night, too—we should have heard something of it, seen it even, far above the forest....

She was unable to feel alarm at this, not even suspicion.

When she glanced back, the merchant had gone in, returning apparently to his meal.

Others were jostling down the terrace steps and across the courtyard.

"Come watch the magicians!" came the cry now.

"Shall we go and see the fun?" he said.

"Perhaps."

"If your girls are here, no doubt they'd go to see. Isn't that the best chance?"

Clirando thought of Draisis and fifteen-year-old Erma. She nodded.

As they followed the rest of the people out of the alley and along one of the wider village streets, Zemetrios said in her ear, "One further thing, Clirando. The inn's so full the taverner could offer us only a single apartment—I mean it has only one bed. He seemed to reckon us partners, but I assured him you would use the room and I would take a place in the common area."

Clirando was jolted. She did not know why, then thought she did. "No, Zemetrios. You take the room. You know I never sleep. A place on a bench is less trouble for me."

"No, Cliro. You must have the bed. It's more comfortable, particularly if sleep eludes you."

"What?" She scowled at him. "You think me some

soft little lady? Even when I could sleep, I managed as well on a rock as a couch."

Zemetrios burst out laughing.

For an instant her annoyance increased—then melted. Clirando began to laugh, too. "Excuse me," she said. "Of course you'd think of nothing of the sort."

"Of course not."

"It was only your fairness, offering me the bed. I thank you, but no need. You take it."

Still following the crowd, they were turning now into an open square.

"We'll argue it later," he said.

The moon fired white arrows through the garden vines that overhung the square. The tall narrow tower, seen previously, rose from one corner, and nearby was a temple to the Father, its crimson-painted columns gilded with torchlight. A grove of trees grew in the center of the space. They were clearly sacred, carefully shaped conifers, strung with baubles and little masks made from fine Lybirican paper. A line of four men sat cross-legged on the ground before the grove. They wore vivid clothing sewn with glinting beads, red, yellow, green, and blue.

The people elsewhere in the square had also sat down except for latecomers at the back, among whom were Clirando and Zemetrios. Behind them was only the high wall of a house.

To begin with, the four magicians acted out a short play. They were traveling performers, Clirando thought. But during the drama, a burlesque that concerned a runaway servant, a harsh master and a mischievous god, magical effects abounded. At first they were of the sort that Clirando had watched many times from such troupes at Amnos: birds flying out of sleeves, coins found in ears, objects disappearing and then reappearing somewhere unexpected. Bit by bit however, the magic became more miraculous, and much stranger. The man in the yellow robe, who played the servant, opened wide his mouth—and out darted a silver frog, swiftly pursued by six other silver frogs from the same spot. All these bounced about the square, finally leaping together and becoming a silver ball, which rolled away under the blue robe of another man, he who played the god. The actor who played the master meanwhile lit a fire on the bare earth by sneezing—or pretending to sneeze—directly at it. The fourth mage-actor, who had taken all the other parts, suddenly assumed the head of an ass. Clirando could not see how he managed this. One moment he was man-headed and the next not. The ass-head was also extremely convincing, waggling its ears and letting out mad brayings through wrinkling lips.

The play ended with the cruel master punished and the servant rich. All four then danced a maniacal stamping dance to the twanging accompaniment of entirely invisible musicians.

Laughter had rumbled through the crowd, shouts of approval, encouragement or chagrin at the plight of the characters. Clirando and Zemetrios were not immune. They had laughed and shouted, too.

The fourth magician now reached into the fire, and drew out two handfuls of it.

Flames burned and flickered in both hands, matching his red robe and lighting up his face. Then the fires froze. It happened slowly and completely. *Then* he held up before them two dully glowing bunches of steaming orange ice. These were passed into the audience, which in turn passed them around.

When they had reached the back of the crowd, both Zemetrios and Clirando were able to examine these ice-flames. They certainly were ice-cold, sweating at the warmth of the night—as ice would have done. After she had handed them on to her neighbour, she rubbed her frozen fingers and thought, *These mages are very great.*

Next thing, the magicians pointed up into the sky. Above, the moon was lifting toward the zenith. Only the most engorged stars gleamed strongly enough to be seen against her extravagant light.

The magicians started to wave their arms and call up at the heavens. "Stars! Stars come down and visit us! No one will miss you up there, on such a moon-white night."

And the stars came.

They detached themselves from the black sky, circling, *swarming* like diamond bees down toward the island.

Clirando heard Zemetrios murmur beside her. She too was astounded, and filled by the wildest happiness. Why should stars *not* fall from heaven? If they did, what else wonderful might not be able to occur? The laws of the gods were often so harsh. Did this magic signify such laws might be broken?

Scintillant, in drifts, the stars began to festoon the trees. Some were large as a platter, others small as a brooch. They lit up the square with a pure, bluish radiance.

Others fell into the hands of the magicians, who began, carelessly, to juggle with them. Arcs and fire-bursts dazzled as these tinier orbs dashed from hand to hand.

The show went on, hypnotically, until a far-off note sounded from above, musical as any lyra.

"She calls them back!" the crowd bellowed. "The moon wants her children home again."

And the mages let go the spangled stars, which swirled together, while others swooped from the trees to join them. A vortex of white fire spun above the square, then flew upward.

The great light faded. Each star must be fitting itself back into its place. Clirando thought she saw several do this, settling in unseen sockets in the velvet dark.

The four mages stepped forward, brushing off their palms—as if the stars had left a slight stella pollen on them.

What now?

Clirando realized he and she stood so close their shoulders and arms were in continual contact. His right arm—sworn arm. Her left. She had not noticed before, as if this were quite natural.

The magicians were reaching out now toward the grove of sacred trees. Also as if *this* were natural, they were drawing down the boughs, drawing them outward and over. Like tall cloaks of thick black-green fur, the trees unraveled, bringing their baubles and decorative masks with them, and wrapped all four figures round.

The men vanished into the mantle of the trees. Then the trees *smoked*. The whole square of people breathed as the mass of men and conifers coiled and spiraled up into the sky—up to where the stars had gone, and the white mask of the moon.

But where men and trees had been—

A creamy lion prowled the center of the square beside a patterned lynx with emerald eyes, an antlered deer black as ebony, a tusked elephantus from the East, heavy with long grey hair—which, providing its own fanfare, trumpeted.

The crowd shrieked, applauded, scrambled to its feet in a mixture of fright and pleasure.

"Illusions," Clirando murmured.

"Dreams," said Zemetrios.

But the animals too sprang upward now. Like the rest, they surged away into the air.

Smaller and smaller they became. At the last moment four flashes like miniature lightnings occurred.

Each creature became one last star, just visible against the brilliance of the moon.

"I've heard all men," Zemetrios said, "have a spirit animal that lives inside their soul. Perhaps…"

Perhaps.

Zemetrios escorted Clirando up the inn stair to the allotted room. It lay deep in the house, behind winding corridors and countless other chambers, from most of which eddied quiet voices, and now and then unstifled cries of delight.

The whole village had become flagrantly amorous. Returning from the display in the square, they passed through laughing, kissing groups, couples dancing with linked hands to the music of flutes, their eyes fixed only on each other. By shadowy walls, under courtyard trees, embraces. Arms about each other, mouths fused, lost only in the world of love—two becoming one.

A sadness had stirred in Clirando. She shook it from her. She would not become one of those who grudged other women the joy of lovemaking. After all, Oani and Seleti among her girls had both had lovers.

There had been no sign of the band anywhere. Surely they would have come to see the magicians, as almost all the village had seemed to. She believed she had not taken enough notice of their absence as she should.

If they were not here, then— Then tomorrow she must search.

Let me fret about that, not give in to pointless jealousy.

She kept her mind on the problem as she and Zemetrios walked through the inn to the room they were not to share.

The door was of old wood, carved with a sort of tree, a tree of fruit, but the carving was rough and had faded away, sanded off by time. Even so, it was a splendid room when once they had opened the door. The window had been shuttered though the night remained close and warm. Clirando undid the shutters. Outside, the village curled away into the dark, hardly a light anywhere aside from a few last smoldering torches.

They lit the room's two candles. Despite the low ceiling, the chamber was large, and clean. The bed too was large, heaped with covers and furs as if for the cold months.

He said, "Maybe after all you'll sleep tonight." She said nothing, knowing she would not. "I'll look forward to seeing you again, in the morning. Rest well."

"Wait."

"Yes, Cliro?"

Her back to him still, she said crisply, "This is a great cave of a room. Why not stay? There's space for both of us, and enough pillows and covers for an army—enough therefore to spare if one of us sleeps on the floor."

When he did not reply, she turned and looked at him. In the dull light she could not read his face, saw only the slight scar on his cheekbone, the lucent steadiness of his eyes.

"If you trust me," he said.

"I trusted you in the forest," she answered flatly. "Or rather, Zem, I trusted *myself* if you were *not* to be trusted."

I too have now called him by a familiar name—did I mean to?

He lowered his head. It was a meek gesture belied by his tall, muscular frame, and for a second she did *not* trust him. But then he said, "You *can* rely on me, Cliro. Don't insult me by making out I'm a mannerless oaf. I won't lay a finger on you. However much—"

She waited. What had he meant to say? However much he would *like* to?

The excitement of the night still fizzed in her blood like strong-spiced wine. Be careful!

She pointed at the bed.

"This is a wide couch." He did not speak. Clirando drew her sword. "Do you know the custom?"

"Yes. A woman and a man who must sleep in the same bed put a sword between them, and so keep chaste."

"Here's mine then," she said. "We'll both lie down here. Neither of us is a baby, let alone a dishonorable fool. What do you say?"

Another sword rasped, and candlelight slid down it as it in turn was drawn from his scabbard. He placed it in reverse, head to toe with hers, the hilt under the tip of her blade, her hilt upon his point.

"Agreed."

Either side the bed, looking down at the swords which already lay and slept there, she and he.

"Well," she said.

"Do you prefer I sleep clothed?" he said.

Something flamed at Clirando's center. No use to deny it. None at all. Nor to deny—she had *not* been careful.

"Only if you prefer. We've pledged faith. Strip if you want. I'll turn my back."

So she turned again, honorably enough.

Behind her she heard the click and rustle of his garments undone and coming off. And—there, on the wall, Clirando saw his shadow reflection, clear in every detail, drawing the tunic over his heard, unbuckling his belt.

Did she dare look around at him?

She wanted to.

Her core was full of fire, leaping and alive—no longer frozen flame, defrosted by desire—

Abruptly he cursed.

At the signal, irresistibly, Clirando spun about.

"What is it?" she lamely demanded, hardly knowing what she said, her eyes full only of Zemetrios, standing naked before her.

"A sharp bramble from the wood caught in my boot—it had a sting—" he said, explaining the curse, breaking off.

His body was tanned and beautifully made, as it had promised to be. Again she thought of statues of gods, but this one was living. From the width of his shoulders to the narrowness of his hips, the coordination of arms, the long legs—perfect—aside from the scars of old wounds that marked him. Yes, he was soldier and warrior. So much was obvious.

"What caused that scar?"

"This? Oh, that was at Ashalat three years ago. A spear. He lived just long enough to regret it."

"And that one, over your ribs?"

"A knife. I can't recall—Disbuthiem, I think, in the Northern Isles. Or was it Bas Bara?"

"That one, then, on your stomach?"

"Oh, *that* one. My first year as a soldier. My own fault. I managed to stab myself at practice. Shameful." He laughed. His laugh was golden, like his body and his beauty. Unselfconscious—no, flaunting himself, yet in such a still, couth way.

He gave however no sign of wanting her. Judging from evidence already clearly before her, that would have been a proud show, too.

Did she dare go over and touch him—that slender final long-healed wound on his thigh…? Would he recoil?

He did not want her? Maybe it was only that. He liked her, respected her, maybe. She was a warrior woman, like his "first love" and like his mother. She meant nothing else.

"I count four—no, five scars. I include the little scar on your cheek." She paused. "Is that your total?"

"You mean my back, do you, Cliro? By the Father, no, I haven't one on my back."

Her gaze left the alluring playground of his body and fastened on his blue eyes.

"Nor I."

"I didn't think so."

"I have more scars than you, Zem. Perhaps this shows me to have also lesser skill in battle."

"Or to be more brave? How many scars, then?"

"Seven."

One candle flickered, as if a spirit had breathed on it.

Neither of them looked at the candle.

He said in a low voice, "Show me."

And at his own words, his *thought,* Clirando beheld on him all the arousal any woman could ever have required.

It matched, she conceded, her own hidden want.

Her hands flew over her garments. She was bold, also flaunting. Her slim and tawny shape came from its concealment, the tips of her breasts already woken and hard.

In silence she pointed out the seven narrow scars— one on the right shoulder, three at her stomach and waist, two on her right leg, tiny as small coins, and the longest, deepest scar on her left arm, made by a blow that, in the moment it happened, she scarcely noted. It had been Araitha's in the war-court.

The bed still lay between them. Divided by two swords.

"Cliro," he said, "be sure. If you have doubts, I'll take myself off into the inn. I do warn you though, I shall then get myself very drunk."

"Stay sober. Stay with me."

As they moved about the bed to meet each other, each of them saw in a sudden glimpse one more magic, stranger and less strange than the sorcery of sex—

"The swords—"

Both blades had twined together, roping each other round like vines.

"Is that because we—?"

But he reached her then.

He took her face in his hands. His body gathered hers in. His mouth was familiar to her. She *knew* it, as if many times before—

All the inebriated power of sexual hunger coursed through her.

Her hands moved over his smooth and unmarked back. She gripped him against her.

In moments the entwined blades were thrust from the bed, and furs and coverlets in heaps across the floor.

His lips on her breasts were like a rain of warm honey, his teeth grazed her with shivering darts. At the flaming center of her flesh he woke her fire into a conflagration.

They raced quickly along the road of lust, unable, either of them, to delay another minute.

As he filled her, her body sprang to amalgamate with his. The struggle of ecstasy began, and exploded like every firecracker ever loosed on a night of full moon. Blind and moaning, they clung, the crescendo bursting them in an infinity of stopped time. Until, cradling each other, rocking, sighing, they fell back into the hollow of the night.

"We went too fast," he said.

"What else? I have waited."

"You waited for me. Did you know that?"

"But now you're here."

"Cliro," he said into her hair, as he lay on her, heavy, blissful, one cover she did not wish to push away.

They stayed like this for a short while, until she felt him stir again.

"Now we go more slowly," he said gravely.

And with his hands and mouth he played her, exquisite as any master musician, the strings of her body flowing with boundless notes. In an agony of joy she held herself away from the brink. They rolled, still connected, and lying over him she now began to search out the melody of *his* flesh, tuning and waking him, torturing him to the peak of pleasure, casting herself over into the roiling sea only when she saw she had mastered him. The vast wave hurled them up again high as the moon, and over and slowly downward into the second valley of aftermath.

Winter

Clirando was cold. Winter—it was winter and she lay outdoors. Where was she? Thestus lay by her, she could hear his deep sleeper's breathing. But she had slept as heavily, and now her skin seemed rimed with frost—

Clirando flung herself off the bed, panic-stricken, feral.

This was not Thestus. She was not on campaign. It was summer not winter.

She did not sleep.

Night's darkness was done with. A pallid, livid dawn was beginning over the village, and Clirando could make out how the sky was somberly whitened, for she had left the shutters open. But this white sky was far *too* white. The roofs around were also *far too white*.

She went to the window. A blast of freezing air met her naked body like pain.

Small wonder. Heavy snow had fallen in the night. It covered everything—trees, buildings, and on the narrow alley below, undisturbed, it made a flawless marble paving.

Not a sound rose from the village, either. Not a trickle of smoke from any hastily stoked hearth. No bird flew. No human thing was visible. Under the deadly blossom of the snow and ice, only an intermittent conifer showed any growing covering. The rest of the trees were bare as bones, and on a nearby wall, an Eastern rose-briar snaggled, skeletal black and white. Last night it had been smothered in red flowers.

She heard Zemetrios erupt from the bed behind her.

"In the name of all—"

They wrapped themselves in the formerly redundant furs, and both stood in the window.

"The village is empty," he said. "Deserted."

"The village is *ruinous*," Clirando added.

It was true. The more she peered at the icy vista, the more she noticed the holes in the plaster, fallen stones, and gaps where roofs had given way, not the previous night, but long ago. The snowy trees had not all been cultivated in gardens and yards, but had rooted in the houses, and out of streets and alleyways.

Even in this room—that crack along the wall, the broken stool she had not seen yesterday. The balding furs were musty with age.

Looking across the room, she dismally noted the old carven door was half off its hinges.

"The snow," he said with irony, "must have fallen down from the moon, if the moon's covered in snow as the man said."

"Perhaps it did. This place is a demonic trap. It's accursed, as we are."

He drew her around to face him.

"No longer. You and I are no more one alone to face the dangers and dirt of this world. Two together. Yes, Clirando?"

It did not go easy with her, even now, emotionally to bond with him so quickly. If a summer morning had woken them, very likely she would have felt otherwise. But now once more she was not sure she could trust Zemetrios, her beautiful and mesmerizing lover, the one she had "waited" for, her equal and her beloved.

Nevertheless, she nodded. And saw in his eyes he knew she put him off that way. For a moment his mouth thinned. Turning from her brusquely, he gathered up his gear and began to dress.

No longer twined, their two swords lay among the quilts, separate.

Around and below, the inn was as void as suspected. In the long main room, under a now partly broken staircase, bushes clawed from the floor and icicles hung where the onions and green herbs once had. The

smoke chimney had fallen into the cooking hearth—
a hundred years ago from the look of it.

They exchanged very few words. Brief comments on
the wreck, warnings about treacherous places in the
floor, and in the snowy hollows of the streets and al-
leys outside, when once they got there.

The village was desolate, and desolating.

She—and he, she had believed—had been happy
here, nearly carefree. The good food, the well-mannered crowds, and the music, magic, friendship, the
potent law-breaking of the four magicians in the
square—all of it lies. Hallucinations.

Traps.

Nothing to do with life or enjoyment had gone on in
this winter village for ten decades or more, nothing
but loneliness and decay. Not even any animal laired
here.

And the snow. The snow. Could it had fallen from the
snow-covered midsummer moon? Was that likely—of
course not. But then, neither was all the rest.

*We were lovers. This demonstrates we were fools after
all. Or I was a fool. And he, trustless, one more chancer
and traitor.*

For once a kinder inner voice, perhaps more rational—or less guilt-ridden, less *involved*—murmured
within her: Do you react too harshly? What, after all,
has he done that you should call him by such names?

But winter had shown her, with its unseasonal cruelty, that she must not soften. She had trusted before. Now she must raise her shield if not her blade. She must be forearmed.

They emerged from the village at another gate. In fact out of a hole in the wall.

Looking back, Clirando saw the remains of the slender tower, leaning like a smashed tooth on the sky.

Beyond the "gateway" was only a waste of white, in which groups of dead orchard trees huddled like black cages draped with ice.

The mountains rose ahead. They were solid now in snow, and the white land ran up to them. Pine forest still grew thickly at their bases.

"Moon's Stair," Zemetrios said. His voice was bleak.

Clirando scanned the middle peak.

It was not so high as she had thought, only a frigid hump. Who would want to go up there?

"Everything was deception," she said. "The merchant lied, too. How can there be some supernatural doorway on that mountain that allows men to pass through, and walk on the moon's globe—if a globe it truly even is. The moon is a lamp, that's all, like the stars. The gods made them simply to give light."

"In Rhoia," he said, "we call the moon most often *she*. She's frozen. She's cold. Unjust. A bringer of regret."

Clirando flung about. Before she could make some hard rejoinder, she thought confusedly, *He spoke of the moon. He was not Thestus taunting me.*

A wind woke suddenly from the island's edges, where, invisible, the sea still coiled, its rim perhaps now layered with ice.

"What's that sound?" he said.

"The wind blowing."

"No."

He pointed.

Along the snow, out of the nearest bundle of pine trees, something came striding with huge steps. On all the white it was night-dark. And it was giant-tall but narrow, a black banner blowing like a black flame from its top.

"The woman on stilts," Clirando exclaimed.

"So it is."

They waited.

Such was her speed, the striding stilt-walker reached them in less than a minute.

Last night she had lit torches in a ruin that had looked whole and living.

Now, passing them, the apparition bent her head to regard them.

"Moon's Stair," said the black woman in a remote tone. "That's your path."

"Why?" Zemetrios shouted up at her.

"Why else?" the woman nonsensically said.

She grinned. Her teeth were white as winter. On she strode, around the crumbled village wall. She vanished from sight.

"A sign," he said. "Guidance."

"Only if you're insane enough to think it so. I'm making back the other way toward the coast. My band of women was abducted by pirates, that's what I must suppose. At Amnos, to be a female warrior is to be a priestess, too. I owe them more than mere comrade-ship—they were in my charge. So damn the Isle and the Seven Nights. I'll build a beacon of my own and hail some ship. I must find them."

"Clirando," he said, "don't you see, you and I—*we* must go up the mountain."

"Why should I see something so absurd."

"Our penance. Didn't your temple speak to you of a sacrifice?"

Clirando stared at nothingness. "Yes. They said too that there was less danger for my girls than for me."

"I'd swear your band is safe. They're valiant and strong. You've trained and led them. So you must trust them, even if you can never trust me. As for this—don't you feel the tug of that place—whatever it is—up there?"

She licked her lips. The chill wind was biting through her clothing and the molting furs in which she, as he, had wrapped herself.

Unwillingly she accepted that it was true enough, the mountain pulled at her. It was not so high. It would be no awful task for either of them to scale it.

Instantly on the wind then, she heard a many-voiced and horrible jeering wail. As her head jerked up in re-membering fear and distaste, she saw Zemetrios too was glaring along the snows, his eyes searching. Their demons had returned.

There had been a sip of happiness for them at the phantom inn. Now they were due to pay.

"Then, let's go," he said. "What choice?"

"None."

He broke into the fast steady lope before she did, running toward the skirt of pines.

It would not matter, she thought, despite any prior notion or hope, whether they went together or apart. Both of them must face the individual punishment the Isle had in store.

Yet she too jogged forward. Increasing her speed, she caught him up. They advanced again shoulder to shoulder, up the rising slope.

Moon

All that day they climbed. Once they were through the hedge of pines, the mountain was not itself irksome, but the slides of impacted snow and translucent ice sometimes presented blocks to swift progress.

They began, inadvertently, to work as a team.

Bittersweet, this. Clirando had never met a man so sane in his judgment of obstacles or so decided in solving them. Nor, where she detected the solution, so willing to agree. She had found many men in the past, even some of the best, obstreporous as it were on principle. Thestus primarily. She would have understood this if she had been a house-reared woman, but she was educated, trained, fit, and canny.

Where necessary, they assisted each other.

They took only short breaks from the ascent. Neither had any food, and only a little water, which they drank sparingly.

Once he remarked that the previous evening's dinner had seemed to nourish them, even if it had been sorcerous and nonexistent.

At this she recalled again the other feast—the sexual and emotional feast of their lovemaking.

She saw that he did, too.

He said, looking at her, "My name you know. It was never Thestus."

Rage boiled in her, then died.

"I know. But let that be for now."

And silence returned to divide them as two swords had not.

Twilight, after the unseen sun went down, found them high on the shelves of Moon's Stair.

A broad cave, one of many, yawned in the mountain. They ducked in, and made a fire.

"Who watches?" he asked.

"I."

"Last night you slept."

"That was some spell. I shan't tonight."

"Do you think so?"

Presently they portioned the watch, in the acceptable way, between them, lying or sitting far across the fire from each other.

The full moon of the Third Night swam up the sky, only partly tearing the veil of snow-cloud. Later more snow fluttered down.

How beautiful he was, asleep.

A rift of tenderness opened in her heart. She slammed a mental door against it.

Clirando did not slumber. When he took the watch, she lay static as a log, her back to him.

Outside, at frequent intervals, and as she had heard it during the slog up the mountain, there echoed the dim jeering yodels of the pig things, her personal demons. He presumably heard the abusive shouts of his dead friend and brother, Yazon.

It was not that she dreamed, but she had one brief almost-vision of Araitha. Clirando's own friend and sister floated through the depths of a dark sea, a corpse with golden hair furling and unfurling.

Next morning they drank the last water, some of which was by then ice, and went out.

Inside an hour of traveling, the way flattened to a craggy, endless-seeming plateau. They had gained the top of Moon's Stair.

They paused. Snow armored the crag. Outcrops thrust white into the dead sky. Boulders lay everywhere. There was nothing unusual, but also nothing comfortable up here. It was a place of the known earth, yet *alien*—as only the things of the earth could be.

"There was after all no purpose in climbing here."

"Nevertheless, we climbed," he said. "Everything in life is like that, surely. It's our choice and talent to make a purpose from such chaos."

The wind lifted and fell, cutting about itself with sharp blades.

Into the lea of one of the outcrops they went, for shelter.

Below, far off, slopes, forest, the lost village. It was just possible too she thought, even in the wan daylight, to imagine the mighty outer circle of ocean ringing the island.

By nightfall they had trekked some way over the mountaintop. They sought a crevice between rocks for the night's bivouac.

Tomorrow they would descend. There was nothing else to do.

The moon came up in the dark. This evening it was unclouded, shining on the snow.

It was the Fourth Night. The middle night of the seven.

Clirando again took first watch.

In order this time not to gaze at him in his sleep, she stared rigidly out across the fire.

An hour later, in the moonlight and with no warning, Araitha came walking toward Clirando over the mountain.

Clirando got up. She drew her knife—pointlessly.

Araitha wore her traveling cloak, and in her hair were the ornaments she had put there for safekeeping during her voyage to Crentis. No doubt in reality they lay with her on the sea's floor.

Lovely, strong, brave—how proud you could be of her, this ghost. *Comrade—friend—sister—*

"Stay back, dead thing," rasped Clirando. "Only say what you want from me."

Araitha did not slow her pace. She sighed, and her ghost-breath, clean as when she had lived, touched Clirando's face.

Clirando thought the ghost would keep going until it walked right through her. She gripped her knife and braced herself—but at the last second Araitha dissolved like colored steam.

Yet, in the open area beyond the rocks, everything now was changed.

The mountain plateau was no longer there.

A vast blank alabaster whiteness loomed and curved away. It was not snow, but level, even, and icy *cold* with a burnishlike freezing fire. While above, contrastingly, the sky was an inky-black Clirando had never witnessed on any other night. Stars *seared* on this black like volcanic embers, and of all shades—purple, russet, amber, jade. But the moon itself had disappeared. Instead, hanging low over a distant jumble of countless spiked mountains—as unlike those of the Isle as was possible—*another* moon shone. In colour *it* was greenish turquoise. It cast an underwater light, and formed peculiar shadows. Soon Clirando did not think it *was* a moon. It was some other—lamp? *world?*—or was it in fact the earth, hung in the sky off the moon itself?

She found she had stolen forward. She felt no star-tlement, only a dull terror when, turning, she saw even the rocks from which she had just emerged were now no longer behind her. All the mountain was gone now. On every side, the white sheer surface ran to its horizon.

She took a breath. Very oddly, it seemed to her the air here was not air at all—and still her lungs expanded. She thought, *I am on the moon's world now. Or some part of me*— She did not know which part, nor how she breathed that which was not air. But she did. For she was not meant to perish yet, oh no. Araitha, vindictive, had undone the barrier between the worlds, and Clirando had been sucked through.

The shadows though—they moved.

They slithered forward, growing solid as they did so—be ready!

They are not shadows.

How many of them were there? It was a herd, a *battalion* of the blackish pig creatures, tusked and spined, their misshapen heads lolling, glassy little eyes riveted on her.

Before she could do anything at all, they had pressed inward, forming a circle about her. She was surrounded. Two or three animals deep, the live cordon wobbled on narrow feet, grunting, snuffling. Until at last the familiar hideous jeering screams broke from them, deafening now and no-longer weirdly synchronized, but all out of rhythm.

Clirando hissed in fury. It thrust out her fear.

Knife in hand, she flew at her tormentors. She raked and slashed them. She felt the blows strike home. She saw the blood spurt burningly red in the uncanny light. They did not resist, nor did they attack—but the jeering cacophony never ceased.

All around the circle she pelted, and around again. Still not one of the black pigs retaliated. None harmed her. She stopped all at once, panting, somehow disabled— Each blow had lessened her.

And only then the circle gradually fell quiet.

After the unbearable horror of the noise, the *un*-air of this second world congealed inside her ears. It was as if she had gone deaf—

And *now* they must close in. She had hurt them. They would trample her and kill her. Eat her alive.

Clirando straightened. She could sell her life expensively, even if she must sacrifice it in the end.

And so she saw.

It was like a blindfold dropping from her eyes.

The creatures stood there quite motionless and still making no sound. They were striped and running with blood. Much worse that this, from their greenish eyes enormous glittering tears poured down like rain.

Crying, they clustered in their circle, and they looked at her. And as Clirando stared into their weeping eyes, she saw through to the backs of these eyes, as if through polished mirrors, and then straight down to some other thing, repeating, amplifying, which she could not make out.

"Why do you do this?" she whispered.

They only wept.

Clirando took now a few tentative steps. She approached the nearest of them.

It lifted its head. It was ugly, terrible, piteable. The crying seemed to have made its eyes much larger. They were deeply green, like the leaves of a bay tree.

Memory flashed in Clirando's brain. Her mother was picking her up from the courtyard, where she had fallen, a Clirando then about four years old. "Don't cry, my love."

"Don't cry, my love," Clirando murmured.

She found she had dropped the knife. She put out both her hands and touched the pig's nightmare face quite gently. "Don't cry. It will be better soon."

To her bewilderment, the pig at once nuzzled in close to her. It was warm. It smelled healthy and wholesome, but not really animal. Her hands slid over it. It had no spines after all. It was smooth. Under her fingers, the wetness of the blood, the wounds she had caused, healed like seams sewn together.

Now the next animal was nudging at her. Eagerly?

"Come here," said Clirando.

She had shut her eyes.

She took the second pig into her arms.

She took all of them into her arms, one by one. She

stroked them. She kissed their bizarre faces, she kissed the tears away and their wounds healed.

All this, with her eyes shut.

She too was crying, she discovered. And then, softly laughing. And from the pigs as she went around to them, embracing them, soft laughter, too.

She knew when she had reached the end of her ministrations and closed the fateful circle. That was when she opened her eyes.

Twenty or thirty other Clirandos stood all about her. They were her age, and her height and weight, clothed as she was under the furs, in summer garments, tanned and fit, shaking back brown hair.

The pig-creature had been—herself? No, no—*facets* of herself. Her *self*.

Jeering, tormenting—*ugly.*

Was this then what she really was? Or what, deep in her mind, her heart, she had *believed* she was?

If so, then she had mocked herself, and driven herself, *hurt* herself, made herself *weep* if not actual tears, then *symbolic* tears. To lose love was a very terrible thing. To lose affection for one's own self—this must be worse. For you could, at least in your mind, move far off from others. But from yourself you never could, until death released you.

She regarded the other Clirandos, and they her. Clear-eyed, these looks, and mouths that did not laugh, calm mouths, quiet.

They were separated from her, her other selves. Her

anger, and her attempt to suppress anger, both, had done this. And her pain and her denial of that pain. For pain and anger needed to be felt and to be expressed—and then let go.

She tried to count them, the other Clirandos. Twenty—thirty—ten—she could not get the number to come out.

But she had split herself into these pieces. She thought of a mirror made of glass, as they formed them in the East—shattered.

Clirando bowed her head. Anger was spoken. Pain acknowledged. Both now must begin their journey away from her. She visualized a glass mirror, mending...

Did she feel her other selves return? Perhaps—perhaps. When she raised her head, they were gone. Only she remained. But all of her now, she thought all mended and in one piece.

And so when, next moment, she saw rushing across the moon's long vista, the dappled lion-beast she had first seen on the cliffs of the Isle, she did not draw her knife. Now, she *knew*.

As it sprang, she too sprang forward.

In space they met. The collision was instantaneous and had no impact, only a brilliant lightning that coursed through her, cold then hot, then warm.

Landing in a warrior's practiced crouch, Clirando knew herself for one moment to be a dappled lynx-lion, tail lashing, claws ready, eyes of fire. And then the beast sank back into her spirit, accustomed as a fine knife in a sheath of velvet.

The male lion also had been—was—hers. It was a part of her. She had no need to dread it, only to know and guide it—and permit it, at the correct times, to guide her.

A joy beyond all joys filled Clirando. She ran about the moon plain, jumped high, whirled through the air, light as a feather, playing.

Never had she known such liberation. But even as she experienced it, intuitively she recognized it could not and must not last. Mortals had their duties in the world. Only before and after death could such freedom deservedly be theirs.

She sat thinking this for a while, there on the surface of the moon, quite calm. Until something altered in her mind, and suddenly she began to see instead her ridiculous predicament. For she knew no route back. If a psychic gate had been opened for her, where was it now? She did not think the ghost of Araitha could conduct her home into the world.

The surreal euphoria had left her. Perplexed, Clirando stood and looked away to all the white horizons.

Vaguely then, she heard a distant shouting. It was no longer any nightmare of her own.

"Zemetrios...?"

Had he too been pulled through to this other place, to contend with his past?

At this thought Clirando became fully herself, or reckoned she did. In the heat of battle you could not always carefully plan.

It took her some hours to walk across the long curving of the moon's back, and the fish-bone spikes of the mountains were much nearer when she halted in astonishment.

Before her lay a fine house, that would have fitted well in the upper streets of Amnos. It was surrounded by a grove of trees, winter bare and thick with icicles. The house seemed to think an ordinary earthly night had fallen, for lamplight burned in the visible windows and over the gate of the courtyard. The gate itself was ajar, as if to invite Clirando in.

She hesitated. But then the strident shouting came again. She had heard it many times as she traveled; it had guided her here.

She pushed wide the gate and crossed the yard, between ranks of frozen urns and shrubs.

The door of the house too was open.

Clirando entered, sword in hand, and reached the threshold of a graciously furnished room now rather spoilt. A chair had gone over. Broken pitchers lay on the floor. Two men were there also, one of them stumbling, shouting. It was this awful voice she had heard before. Then, in the moment before the shouting stumbler fell, the other man caught him back. "Yazon, listen to me. This would have been your twenty-ninth day without drunkenness. Think what you had achieved."

"And lost," the other grated. "I have ruined it. Besides, what do I care? Give it me back, the wine—" But Yazon's voice dropped away into sobs. He sank down on a couch. And Zemetrios seated himself beside him. "No, my friend. No wine. You'll have to kill me first."

Zemetrios. His face was weary as that of a man who had been entirely sleepless for months, yet also hard and resolute. Yazon—he could be no one else—was speaking now of horrible secrets of drunkenness. But his eyes at last were growing sane and sad.

As if some god had told her—Sattu, perhaps, the little god of domestic things—Clirando seemed to know it all.

This naturally was not what had taken place in the world, at Rhoia. Instead, the house of Zemetrios's father had been magically rebuilt here on the slopes of the moon, by some spirit or spell. And now, in this new reality, Zemetrios—having given up his post in the king's legions and sent all his servants, women and men both, away to safety—cared for Yazon, striving to cure him, to make him whole.

That then must have been in Zemetrios's hidden mind. Not that he had killed Yazon in rage—but that he had not devoted his life, however briefly or lengthily, to helping Yazon. Not with money or shelter, but with the comradeship and dedication they had each shown the other in war. Now Zemetrios wished to atone.

It was very plain that Zemetrios believed utterly this situation truly existed.

Clirando did not know if she could, or should, have any part in such a scenario. But the previous bliss of her own liberation now filled her with the desire to assist in whatever way was possible. To assist, that was, Zemetrios.

She spoke his name. Could he hear her?

Yes. He looked across at her instantly. His face, which had seemed older than its twenty-four years, was suddenly as she recalled. A smile lit his mouth and eyes.

"And here is my beautiful wife, Clirando."

The other man—ghost—illusion—whatever he might be—also looked up at her. And he too gave her a smile. It was not corrupt, only distant. Some half-forgotten good-manners from an earlier time when he had been himself. And she wondered then if perhaps really this was Yazon, come back from death to undo this knot of pain and anger, as needful for his phantasmal life as it was for Zemetrios's mortal one.

"And I warn you, Yazon," said Zemetrios, with amused lightness, "try nothing stupid with her. She'll kill you and have your skin sewn up as a sunshade."

His *wife*.

In his fantasy, this dream of righting wrongs and making all good, I am his wife…

Zemetrios got up, came to her and kissed her gently on the lips. "Things will be better now you're here."

* * *

Only Clirando marked accurately the passing of the last three nights of full moon. Though perhaps she did not do it as accurately as she meant to, because she had to get her bearings from the rise and fall of the blue-green earth-world above.

In the house, apparently, months went by.

She herself was not conscious of these. Her time frame functioned very differently, and the scenes that were enacted, and in which she sometimes took a small part, were fragments of some vaster drama, played clearly for Zemetrios alone.

She went along with everything, knowing he did what he must. His penance and self-examination were longer than hers, deeper and darker though less savage.

In the segments of events that Clirando witnessed, Zemetrios hauled Yazon back to sober health. Zemetrios was by turns dominant and consoling, as appropriate. He never gave up, and gradually the physical ghost-image of Yazon responded. Then Clirando would find the two of them at friendly, noisy practice with swords or bows, or wrestling, eating, talking. They played Lybirican chess. They would discuss the army days, and reminisced away the nights that somehow came and went inside the outer time which she alone observed. They would look up at the blue orb in the sky, and call it the moon.

Of course, Zemetrios never separately sought her. It

seemed she was tucked away somewhere in his illusory life in the house. Mainly, she was peripheral to his task. Sometimes he did not even see or hear her as she entered a room only a few paces from him. He only ever fully saw Yazon, the one in fact who probably was not there.

She began to think Yazon was not a ghost, working out the dilemma of its life. No, he was solely a conjuring of Zemetrios's mind. And of Moon Isle.

She came to believe all this would end at the finish of the moon's Seventh Night. Till then she could do nothing but be present, offering her slight participation—a touch, a cup filled from the well in the courtyard. Every illusory thing seemed real, as in the village. Therefore, how would this saga be resolved?

She pondered too with the winter snow in her heart, if Zemetrios would have been driven mad by the finish of it.

The ultimate problem was their return to the world, which still she had not solved. Maybe they must stay here, despite all expiation. And maybe too they would be segregated here from each other.

Do I love him?

Even in that extremity and strangeness, this question was paramount, and unanswered.

Sometimes she sat alone in the winter yard of the simulated Rhoian house, gazing up at the multicolored stars. Indoors the men talked rationally, remembering old campaigns.

The food and drink she had found in the kitchens had nourished her, and them. Even the rug bed she had made herself was comfortable. She could sleep now. Anywhere therefore would have been comfortable.

Perhaps madness has taken all of us.

But the lion lashed its tail in her spirit, and she herself quieted it. *Be patient.*

When next the blue orb rose, that would be the Seventh Night, as far as she knew. She could do nothing but wait.

In sleep, she heard Zemetrios speaking to her very softly. "It's done, Cliro. He has gone."

Instantly she was fully awake.

"Where?"

"Away. Away where he must."

He spoke of Yazon. Who, it seemed, had gone back to the lands beyond death.

Zemetrios said, "This has been a dream." She thought, *Thank all gods, he knows.* "But it was a dream I needed to be dreaming. Oh, Clirando, I should have given him that, no matter how he was. I should have tried so much harder to save him, in the true world, while he lived. Not dragged him into my house and shunned and treated him like a sinful baby, despised and left him always to himself, busy with my own affairs. I should not either have gone out, and left my servants at his mercy—afraid of him, afraid to offend *me*.

I've done what I should have done, but here. It's—freed me. But I shall never cease to be sorry." He leaned close to her, resting his forehead on hers. "How long has all this gone on? It seemed a year— But he was my friend, my brother—oh, Cliro—if only I'd done this *then,* as I should."

She held him. They lay wrapped among the rugs, like two children in the dark. "Hush, my love," she said. "If only any of us had done what we should. We see it clearly when it has passed by. Yet we must try to see, and try to do. That's all the gods ask. That we try."

And she thought, *And is he my love, then?*

And she thought, *Yes, he is my love.*

They curled together. Beyond the narrow window the blue disk gemmed the sky.

He had survived the test, and was not deranged. Each of them had paid their debt to themselves. They slept exhausted in each other's arms.

The next time they woke, it was together, and they lay on the bare plains of the moon. The house with all its lamps and groves, its rooms and well and yard, was gone. Only those mountains like spines scratched along the horizon.

The earth hung above, and all the stars.

"There was a way that led us here, beyond the rocks," he said. "But how do we find it?"

Clirando stared into her mind. There were visions

there still, things which came from the magic not only of this place, but from the sorcery of the Isle.

Slowly she said, "There's home," nodding at the disk above.

"But the *way* to it?"

Clirando's brain showed her the magicians in the square who had called the stars.

Instinctively she raised her arms.

Up in the inky black, the exquisite jewelry shivered. One by one, stars—*stars*—detached from their moorings. They began to float down, not a swarm now, a snowfall—

If it was a dream, you might do anything. And if not, still you might attempt it.

The stars wove around one another in slow, sparkling tidal surges. She thought of the old woman weaving on the headland, the old man who made snakes at the forest's end, and of the stilt-walker lighting torches.

High in air, a bridge began to form in a wide, swooping arc. It was laid with coruscating stella stones—emeralds, rubies, amethysts—it curved down toward the surface where they stood, making a hill-road for them to climb. While the rest of the arc soared away like the curve of a bow. Infinities up in the air, the earth disk had received the far point of this incredible bridge, without the tiniest ripple.

They neither debated nor held back. Both he and she ran at the bridge of stars, this extraordinary path that led toward the ordinary, and the mortal.

Simultaneously they leaped, landed. Clirando felt the faceted paving under her feet. Ethereal colors washed them like high waters, now copper, now bronzy, now golden.

Not to sleep so long—it had been worth it, to know a dream like this one.

Both of them laughed. Children laughed like that, innocent, and prepared to credit that dreams came true.

As so often on the Isle, shoulder to shoulder, Clirando and Zemetrios broke into their companionable, well-trained, mile-eating lope. Over the night, over the heavens, running home through the spatial outer dark which, for them, was full of a rich sweet air, mild breezes, summery scents, branches of static stars, rainbows and light, wild music, half-seen winged beings.

Clirando knew no fear, no doubt, and no reticence. She thought idly, as she bounded earthward, *This is the truth.*

But somewhere, something—oh, it was like a vagrant cloud, feathery and adrift. It bloomed out from nowhere. It poured around her. Zemetrios was concealed. She half turned, missing him, and then a delicate nothingness enveloped her. That too brought no alarm. It was also too good, too *true*.

And after only a second anyway it was done.

And then—

"Clirando!"

This known female face bending to hers, someone well liked, familiar—

"Tuyamel?"

Clirando's eyes were clearing. She stared into six faces now, all known, all in their way loved. Her girls, the women of her band.

"Lie still, Cliro," said Tuy firmly. "You've flown such a great way off, and had such a long journey back."

They were sworn to secrecy, they assured her, all of them. No one who came here must ever afterward speak of the secrets of Moon Isle. Besides, they knew very little.

"Certain persons—they go to certain places. The priests—and the gods—direct them. Some even go—so we heard—to the moon itself. And you went somewhere, Cliro. That's what they said."

Her band told her how, the morning after they had beached their boat on the strand of the Isle, they had found her unconscious, and had not been able to rouse her. Though she breathed, she seemed all but dead. And so they picked her up on a litter improvised from cloaks, and bore her inland.

An ancient priestess by a beacon on the cliff top declared Clirando had suffered no awful harm. "She has not slept a while," the priestess said. "Now she must."

So Clirando's loyal girls carried her, with much care and attention, to one of the seven inland villages of the island.

"Every night of the full moon you lay here," lamented Seleti.

"We tried to wake you—the moon *was* full for seven nights!"—Draisis—"But you never stirred."

"And the old priest, the one with the pet snakes he names after jewels—he said we must let you slumber. You were so young, he said," affrontedly added Erma, "you would certainly see in your lifetime several more such seasons of seven moons."

"You missed all the festivities," elaborated Oani.

"Jugglers—magicians—" Vlis.

"One of them made a bridge over the sky, all like precious stones—green, red, mauve, yellow—" Tuyamel. "Though *I* knew it was all a trick."

Clirando lay on the narrow pallet, in the cell of the temple in Seventh Village.

Her heart beat leadenly.

It had been—*all* of it—a dream?

And yet, she had been enabled to throw away the negative and hateful things. Only proper grief and regret remained. Except... Zemetrios.

If all this had been a dream—including even, as it had, transcripts of actual external things—what had *Zemetrios* been? His thoughts, his personality—his mouth, his arms?

She lay a few days in the little Temple of the Maiden. Then, when she had recovered enough, Clirando roamed through its courts, admiring columns and the flowering vines on its walls—for summer had continued uninterrupted in the world. Here and there, meeting others, she mentioned a particular name. "Zemetrios?" they asked, the mild priestesses. "Warrior," they said to her, not un-kindly, "no one may be told anything more than the min-imum of any other here. This is Moon Isle. For those like yourself, or the man you mention, what each does and experiences is a private matter. Only they and the gods can know."

So they would tell her nothing. And was there any-thing to learn?

Everything else had been her dream, so why not this golden man? She had wanted a lover. Tranced or asleep she had had one.

And now she knew for sure she loved him? Well then. She loved a figment of her dreams. She would not be the first or last.

Two days following the celebration of the Seven Nights, which all of them repeatedly reminded her she had missed, Clirando walked around the village.

It was not at all like the one she had seen when asleep. The buildings were clean and garishly painted. The three or four temples were garlanded, and that of the Maiden had walls of deep red patterned with silver crescents.

Just as she had heard, priests and priestesses thronged the Isle, and lingering warrior bands were there too traders and performers, but now the proces-sions and shows were over. A great packing up was going on. A great leave-taking.

And neither was it any use to question these people, let alone the villagers, who seemed educated in coy evasions. There seemed too a polite, unspoken wish that visitors should go. It began to make her band uneasy, and soon enough Clirando, as well.

I threw off my guilt. I must throw off this also.

She slept always soundly at night. She did not dream, she thought, at all, as if she had used all her dreaming up. Would she ever see the ghost of Araitha again? Or him—would she ever see Zemetrios again? No. Never.

On the fourth day they set off along the forest track. It was rather as Clirando had visualized it, but then her girls had carried her this way. Now animals and birds abounded. A statue marked either end of the road, island gods, nicely carved. Clirando thrust her introspection from her. She acted out being her ordinary self, calling it back to her. It came.

Meanwhile her girls were so attentive and careful of her that Clirando eventually lost her temper. "Leave off treating me like some fragile shard of ancient pottery! What will you do on the boat? Wrap a shawl over my legs and pat me on the head?"

There under the sun-sparkling pines, she wrestled Tuyamel and Vlis, and threw them both, and hugged them all. They danced about there, laughing, embracing, loud and boisterous as eleven-year-olds.

Next day they reached the shore and rowed out to the galley. By sunfall they were on the way to Amnos, and life as they remembered it.

Epilogue

Paper

The windblown sky was full of birds that morning.

Summer had stayed late in Amnos, giving way at last to a harsh, bleached winter.

Now spring tides freshened the coast, and men and beasts were casting the torpor of the cold months.

Clirando had been with Eshti, her old servant woman, to the fish market, and coming back Eshti bolted straight to the kitchen with her prizes. Clirando climbed up to the roof of her house. She was watching the antics of the house doves circling over the courtyard trees.

And out of her inner eyes, from nowhere, Araitha came, and stood silent in her mind. Clirando recalled how she had stood in the yard too laying her curse, then turning away from shadow to light to shadow— or had it been light to shadow to light....

Unlike her companion, her dream lover, Clirando had had no dialogue with her dead friend to set anything right between them.

Araitha therefore might always haunt her. No longer injurious, only bitter. It could not be helped. At least her curse was spent.

All winter Clirando had carried on her life as she had in the past. If her mood was sometimes uneven, she hid it. Mourning the loss of a dead comrade was one thing, but to mourn the loss of someone who had not been *real* was wretched and bewildering. Sometimes she even mocked herself. But now—now it was spring.

Clirando turned. Eshti had come up on the roof, puffing from the steps, wiping fish scales off on her apron.

"What now?" Clirando inquired. "Has dinner swum away?"

"No, lady. The priestesses of Parna have sent for you."

Clirando's thoughts scattered apart and back together in concern. She sprang downstairs to fetch her cloak.

In the shrine by the main temple hall, one of the two priestesses who received Clirando was the middle-aged woman who had dispatched her to the Isle.

Clirando saluted both of them. She said, "Have I committed some error, Mothers?"

The two of them gazed at Clirando. Only the older priestess smiled. "Not at all. There are matters which have just come to our attention. Now spring has driven the ice from the harbors, ships are moving, and letters have arrived in Amnos."

Clirando nodded. Though familiar with books, she had seldom seen a letter. Next moment she saw two. Normally they would be of folded cloth, written on, then waxed, Both of these letters were of fine paper, made from Lybirican reeds.

"A ship's captain brought them here this morning," said the other priestess. "One is for you, Clirando. The other—"

"The other was sent to us by one of the Wise Women of Moon Isle. She is over a hundred years of age, but she lives sometimes in a hut on a headland, and still she weaves cloth, for her eyes stay clear and her fingers agile."

"I met her," said Clirando. She checked. "Or thought I did."

"The Wise Woman—she has no other name—says that something has come to her notice about a warrior girl, Clirando she is called, who was sent to the Isle to work out some inner tussel. The gods allowed her the trance of profound sleep which the Isle can give, and in the sleep various adventures, by means of which her trouble was healed. However," the priestess paused. And Clirando's heart paused within her. "It seems, during this time, Clirando showed strong evidence of being herself a healer and a spiritual guide."

Shocked, Clirando interrupted. "*No,* Mother—I did nothing like that—"

Ignoring her, gently the priestess went on, "Although personal experiences on the Isle are not generally spoken of, there are two exceptions to this rule. Firstly, as perhaps you will guess, anyone may speak in secret to a priest of their own experience. This recital may naturally include mention of others who have—or who have seemed to have—been part of it. The priests, though they will answer no direct question, will nevertheless, should it be needful, afterwards pass on any insight to those others who have shared the event, providing, and this is the second exception, the insight is sufficiently profound. And so: A man, a soldier formerly with the Rhoian legions, reported the events to the Temple of the Father on the Isle. He too had been sent there to work out some penance and guilt and sorrow, and he too had the god's trance fall on him. The priests cared for him in this sleep, as it is always done, just as the priestesses cared for you, Clirando. But when he woke, he had an unusual story to tell. It seems he found himself in a forest, and there he met a young woman, who engaged his interest at once, being, he freely says, for him the perfect type of woman, both a warrior and a girl of great grace." The priestess smiled again, peered into one of the paper letters, and read aloud: "'Also blessed with a passionate clear mindedness.'" The priestess allowed the letter to fall closed once more. "It seems too, that in this dream he had, and which apparently he shared with her, the woman he describes so admiringly—and whose name he gives as Clirando—that she gave him to understand she was not averse to his person. At the conclusion of their journey, she assisted him further, guiding him forward, as he describes, through a magical gateway, and so on to the mystic plains of the moon itself. Here his own difficulty was resolved, but once again Clirando remained at his side, helping him always. Now, we hear of visits to the moon, which may happen on the Isle— how else did it come by its name?—but they are rare. He insists that, had it not been for the woman, he himself would never have got there, and so never confronted what he must. Finally, when all was done, she—" the priestess again consulted the paper "—summoned a path of stars and led him home by that route to the world. But—to his horror—he lost her on the way." The priestess folded the paper into her sleeve. She looked at Clirando. "Do you know anything of this?"

Clirando could not speak.

Then words came. "He is called Zemetrios?"

"So he is. I note your heart is full of love for him. That is the Maiden's gift to you, then. But it takes much more than love alone to work the magic you have done, my girl. And so it transpires the Maiden gave you another gift, too. For you are a healer and guide, as he has said. No, don't shake your head. Of course you have made mistakes and blunders on this occasion. It was your first excursion into such realms. You will need training, as tough and demanding as any you've known in the fighter's art. You stumbled on your gift, which till now you never knew you had. But this man Zemetrios is no fool. He insists you possess psychic powers. He has convinced the Wise Women. That's enough for us. Such talents must never be denied."

"Then—"

"Then, as I've said, you shall be taught. You will still be a warrior, but to one trade will be added another."

"But—Mother—I—"

"Now, sit on the bench there and read this second letter, which has come only for you. The ship's captain has said he wishes a moment with you then. He's in the Little Fountain Courtyard. No doubt he expects to be rewarded for bringing such costly paper all this distance."

Clirando found she had sat down. She sat with the second letter unopened. All she could see or think was filled only by one face, one name. He was real, he lived, and knew her. She had guided him unknowing through forest and mountain and otherworld, her lover, her beloved, Zemetrios. And their lovemaking—though experienced in a dream—had in some manner taken place, for both. Yet now—he mentioned nothing of meeting her again—

The flame flicked before the statue of the goddess.

Her green eyes blinked, or it was only a trick of the light.

Clirando broke the wax seal on the second letter, her mind blank as a paper never written on.

And read this:

They will have told you I'm dead. But I did not drown when the *Lion* sank. The waves and wind dragged me to shore with two or three others from the ship, and washed us up senseless at a little fisher village. Most of a year I stayed there, making a slow recovery, but a complete one. At last I set out and reached Sippini. From the port there I write to you now. I am in good health and strong again, and have engaged with a warrior band to fight honorably for the town. My former disgrace I confessed, but they have overlooked it, saying both you, and the gods, had given me a beating and let me off. Now I might turn to better things.

Clirando, be aware that I acknowledge now the miserable wrong I did you. I hadn't any need to lie down with Thestus, and should have resisted myself and him. For this mean act I lost your friendship always. Nor do I plead that you will change your mind, for I deserve nothing else. But the other crime I worked against you— Oh, Clirando, I regret that almost worse. To curse you—you that *I* wronged. At least I know that such a petty thing

would never stick—it can never have harmed you, you are so strong. But I am ashamed. Forgive me, Clirando, if you are ever able, for both my faults. And think sometimes one kind thought, in tribute to our happier past, of me—
Once your sister and comrade,
Araitha

The letter fluttered from Clirando's fingers. The motion reminded her of a dove's wings.

Araitha lived. Araitha lived and was herself again. A hot blameless joy burned through Clirando. Standing up, she cried aloud, there in the shrine, naming the gods. It was not blasphemy, but a paean of gratitude. As such, it seemed, the goddess Parna at least received it.

When she went out to the fountain courtyard, she had all her money left from the market wrapped ready in a cloth to tip the captain. He had brought her such news.

The man was standing by the little fountain, looking down at the golden fish swimming about in the tank. For a ship's captain he was well dressed and very well groomed, his blond hair gleaming with cleanness in the spring sunshine.

When he looked up, she saw that he had grown as pale as she had.

Clirando mastered herself.

"So, you're a liar after all."

"No lies. By the gods, Cliro, trance or waking, I never lied to you once. And if I never wrote any love words upon the moon, I scarcely had time, did I? Or are you angry I delayed in finding you? For a while I could hardly even be certain you were real. By the hour I'd convinced myself, winter had closed the seas."

"I mean, Zem," she said, "you lied today, when you told them you were the captain of a ship."

"But I am. I'd sold my father's house, remember, and given up my legion. So. I bought a ship. What better means to come here? I've worked on ships before in my soldier's travels, I know them well enough. This one's a fine one. She's called the *Brown Warrior.* I named her after you with your tan skin and your acorn hair."

Clirando felt the yard, the town and the world draw far off from her. She stood in space, somewhere between sky and earth, and he stood facing her there, and they were alone together.

"Well," he said, "you helped save my mind and my soul on the Isle. But if I only *dreamed* you liked me, you must tell me to go. I warn you though—"

"You'll get drunk. Stay sober, Zemetrios. Stay with me."

He crossed the court in three strides and took her in his arms as she took him in hers.

They muttered into each other's mouths and necks and hair what lovers mutter at such times.

It had been an irony, he said, that as he set off to

seek her in Amnos, being one of the first ships out, it was he who ended up carrying with him the report of his own letter of her healing skills. As for her letter from Araitha, he was amazed when Clirando told him what it was.

He did not ask if she would ever seek for Araitha in the future. Nor did Clirando ask herself. The gods who had, it seemed, allowed all this, might one day advise her by some sign.

Four giggling novice priestesses, coming to feed the fish, dislodged the couple in the court.

So then they walked to her house down the winding streets.

Eshti showed great approval at the houseguest.

"We shall have the best candles," she told them, "and the glass goblets from the chest."

"Eshti decides these things," said Clirando.

"So I see. That's good. It will leave you more time to concentrate on me."

"But when must you sail?"

"When I want. I'm my own man."

She thought, *He'll ride his ship across those treacherous seas, those waters of gales and drowning.* She thought, *We are both fighters. Neither can curb the other's life. The gods brought us together. Perhaps they will keep us together, now.*

The spring dusk came early. Up in the yard trees, the house doves were already arranging their nests. Which signified it would be a forward spring and summer.

When the candles were lit, the polished glasses filled, she sat with him and they ate supper as if they had done so for twenty years. Tonight they would share the bed in her chamber. Where she had watched, sleepless, the unsleeping moon, now she would see him, and herself reflected in his gaze. Now she would see a future.

The sea wind tapped at the shutters, and the lamps before the household shrines dimmed and brightened. All the jewel-eyed gods there winked at Clirando and Zemetrios.

A trick of the light?

BANSHEE CRIES

C.E. Murphy

This one's for my mom, Rosie Murphy,
who wanted to know what the story with *Jo's* mom was

Dear Reader,

In September of 2004 I got an e-mail from my agent, the incomparable Jennifer Jackson, saying she'd just spoken with my equally incomparable editor, Mary-Theresa Hussey, who wanted to know if I'd be interested in participating in a LUNA Books anthology as one of three contributing authors. The other two authors were to be (need I say the incomparable?) Tanith Lee and Mercedes Lackey.

Not being a great fool, I said yes.

A month of frenzied thought was interspersed with me singing, "One of these things is not like the others," followed by a flurry of frenzied writing. The result is "Banshee Cries," Book 1.5 of the Walker Papers. It fits chronologically between book one, *Urban Shaman,* which came out in June 2005, and book two, *Thunderbird Falls,* due out in May 2006.

I hope you enjoy the story!

C. E. Murphy

Sunday March 20th, 2:55 p.m.

Cell phones are the most detestable objects on the face of the earth. Worse than those ocean-variety pill bugs that grow bigger than your head, which were on my personal top ten list of Things To Avoid.

My life had been a lovely, cell-free zone until nine weeks, six days, and four hours ago. Not that I was counting. On that fateful day I got an official business phone to go with my bulletproof vest and billy stick. I'd even been given a gun to go with my shiny new badge.

I wanted those things about as much as I'd wanted to bonk my head on the engine block I'd sat up beneath when the phone rang. I rubbed my forehead and glared at the engine, then felt horribly guilty. It wasn't Petite's fault I'd hurt myself, and she'd been through enough lately that she didn't need me scowling on top of it all.

The phone kept ringing. I rolled out from under the Mustang and crawled to her open door, digging the phone out from under the driver's seat. "What?"

Only one person outside of work had the phone number. As soon as I spoke I realized that a politer pickup might have been kosher. The resounding silence from the other end of the line confirmed my suspicion. Eventually a male voice said, "Walker?"

I turned around to hook my arm over the bottom of the car's door frame and did my best to stifle a groan. "Captain."

"I need you—"

These were words that another woman might be pleased to hear from Captain Michael Morrison of the Seattle Police Department. Then again, if he was saying them to another woman, there probably wouldn't have been the slight tension in his voice that suggested his mouth was pressed into a thin line and his nostrils flared with irritation at having the conversation. He had a good voice, nice and low. I imagined it could carry reassuring softness, the kind that would calm a scared kid. Unfortunately, the only softness I ever heard in it was the kind that said, *This is the calm before the storm,* which happened to be how he sounded right now. I crushed my eyes closed, face wrinkling up, and prodded the bump on my forehead.

"—to come in to work."

"It's my weekend, Morrison." As if this would make any difference. I could hear his ears turning red.

"I wouldn't be calling you in—"

"Yeah." I bit the word off and wrapped my hand around the bottom of Petite's frame. "What's going on?"

Silence. "I'd rather not tell you."

"Jesus, Morrison." I straightened up, feeling the blood return to the line across my back where I'd been leaning on the car. "Is anybody dead? Is Billy okay?"

"Holliday's fine. Can you get over to Woodland Park?"

"Yeah, I—" I tilted my head back, looking at the Mustang's roof. Truth was, I'd been futzing around under the engine block because I couldn't stand to look at the damage done to my baby's roof anymore. A twenty-nine-inch gash, not that I'd measured or anything, ran from the windshield's top edge almost all the way to the back window. From my vantage, thin stuffing and fabric on the inside ceiling shredded and dangled like a teddy bear who'd seen better days. Beyond that, soldered edges of steel, not yet sanded down, looked like somebody'd dragged an ax through it.

Which was precisely what had happened.

A little knot of agony tied itself around my heart and squeezed, just like it did every time I looked at my poor car. The war wounds were almost three months old and killing me, but the insurance company was dragging its feet. Full coverage *did* cover acts of God—or in my case, acts of gods—but I'd only said she'd been hit by vandals, because who would believe the truth? In the meantime, I'd already spent my meager savings replacing the gas tank that somebody'd shot an arrow through.

My life had gotten unpleasantly weird in the past few months.

I forced myself to find something else to look at— the opposite garage wall had a calendar with a mostly naked woman on it, which was sort of an improve-ment—and sighed. "Yeah," I said again, into the phone. "I'm gonna have to take a cab."

"Fine. Just get here. North entrance. Wear boots." Morrison hung up and I threw the phone over my shoulder into the car again. Then I said a word nice girls shouldn't and scrambled after the phone, propping my-self in the bucket seat with one leg out the door. Be-draggled as she was, just sitting in Petite made me feel better. I patted her steering wheel and murmured a re-assurance to her as I dialed the phone. A voice that had smoked too many cigarettes answered and I grinned, sliding down in Petite's leather seat.

"Still working?"

"Y'know, in my day, when somebody made a phone call, they said hello and gave their name before any-thing else."

"Gary, in your day they didn't have telephones. Are you still working?"

"Depends. Is this the crazy broad who hires cabbies to drive her to crime scenes?"

I snorted a laugh. "Yeah."

"Is she gonna cook me dinner if I'm still workin'?"

"Sure," I said brightly. "I'll whip you up the best microwave dinner you ever had."

"Okay. I want one of them chicken fettuccine ones. Where you at?"

"Chelsea's Garage."

Gary groaned, a rumble that came all the way from his toes and reverberated in my ear. "You still over there mooning over that car, Jo?"

"I am not mooning!" I was mooning. "She needs work."

"You need money. And snow tires. And more than six inches of clearance. You ain't gonna drive it till spring, Jo, even if you do get it fixed up."

"Her," I said, sounding like a petulant child. "Petite's a *her*, not an *it,* aren't you, baby," I added, addressing the last part to the steering wheel. "Look, are you gonna come get me or not? It's even a paying gig. Morrison called and wants me to go over to Woodland Park."

"Arright." Gary's voice brightened considerably. "Maybe there'll be a body."

Morrison glared magnificently when I arrived with Gary in tow. The two of them facing off was wonderful to behold: Morrison was pushing forty and good-looking in a superhero-going-to-seed way, with graying hair and sharp blue eyes. Gary, at seventy-three, had Hemingway wrinkles and a Connery build that made him look dependable and solid instead of old, and his gray eyes were every bit as sharp as Morrison's. For a few seconds I thought they might start butting heads.

But Morrison pointed at Gary and barked, "You stay here." Gary looked as crestfallen as a wet kitten. I actually said, "Aw, c'mon, Morrison," and got his glare turned on me. Oops.

"It's arright, Jo." Gary gave me a sly look that from a man a few decades younger would've had my heart doing flip-flops. "I bet there's a body. You can tell me about it at dinner. You need a ride home?"

"I'll take care of it," Morrison said in a sharp voice. Gary winked at me, shoved his hands in his pockets, and sauntered back to his cab, whistling. I choked on a laugh and turned to follow Morrison, tromping through a truly unbelievable amount of snow. It had started snowing in mid-January and, as far as Seattle was concerned, hadn't stopped in the two months since. Even the weathermen merely looked stunned and resigned, mumbling excuses about hurricane patterns in the South having unexpected consequences in the Pacific Northwest.

"What is it with you two?"

"So what's going on, Captain?" We spoke at the same time, leaving me blinking at Morrison's shoul-

ders and starting to grin. "What *is* it with us? Me and Gary? Are you serious?"

"He answers your phone." Morrison was talking to the footprints in the snow in front of him, not me. My grin got noticeably bigger.

"Only the once. That was like six weeks ago, Morrison. And who told you that, anyway?" I wanted to laugh.

"I'm just saying he's a little old for you, isn't he?" Morrison's shoulders were hunched, as if he was trying to warm his ears up with them. I grinned openly at his back and lowered my voice so it only just barely carried over the squeak and crunch of snow as we walked through it.

"All I'll say is, you know how they say old dogs can't learn new tricks? Turns out old dogs have some pretty good tricks of their own."

Morrison's shoulders jerked another inch higher and I laughed out loud, the sound bouncing off tree branches black with winter cold. Snow shimmered and fell off one, making a soft puff and a dent in the snow below it. Morrison flinched at the sound, head snapping toward it as his hand dropped to his belt, like he'd pull a weapon. My laughter drained away and I followed him the rest of the way to a park baseball diamond in silence.

He climbed up snow-covered bleachers, making distinct footprints in the already walked on snow, compacting it further. I put my feet in precisely the same

places he'd stepped, fitting my sole print to his exactly. We had the same size feet, and in police-issue boots his prints were indistinguishable from mine, at least to the naked eye. A forensics officer could probably tell there was a weight difference between the two of us—in Morrison's favor, thank God—but for the moment I enjoyed the idea of stealing along behind the captain, invisible to anybody trying to track me.

Morrison stopped on the step above me and turned so abruptly I nearly walked into him. I rocked back on my heels, one step below him, my nose at his chest height as I frowned up at him. "Thanks for the warning." I hated looking up, physically, to Morrison: we were the same height, down to the half inch that put us both just below six feet, and any situation that made me look up to him made me uncomfortable.

Of course, the reverse was also true, and I'd been known to wear heels just so I'd be taller than he was. No one said I was a good person.

"Tell me what you see."

Assuming he didn't want me to describe him— which, had he not been so antsy about the snow falling from the tree a few moments ago, I'd have probably done just to annoy him—I turned away, looking over the baseball diamond.

It was buried beneath two feet of the wet, heavy snow that had made my jeans damp from tromping through it. I shook one foot absently, knocking snow

off my boot. I'd lived in Wisconsin for a winter, so snow wasn't entirely new to me, but this was ridiculous for Seattle, and I said so. Morrison huffed out a breath like an annoyed bull and I puffed my cheeks, muttering, "Okay, fine. I see snow."

Well, duh. Clearly Morrison wanted more than that. "Snowmobile tracks. I didn't even know people in Seattle owned snowmobiles. Um. Footprints around the diamond, like people've been playing snowball." I thought that was pretty clever. Snowball, like baseball, only with snow, right? Morrison didn't laugh. I sighed. Poor, poor put-upon me.

"There are cops, there's some teenagers over there, there's—" Actually, there were a lot of cops, now that I was looking. Picked out in dull blue under the gray sky, they worked their way around the baseball diamond and stumped their way through the outfield. "There's, um." I frowned. "I don't hear anything, either. There aren't any people around. Dead trees…"

"No," Morrison growled, full of so much tension that I looked over my shoulder at him, feeling my expression turning worried. "What do you *see,*" he repeated, and suddenly I got it. A drop of ice formed inside my throat and spilled down into my stomach, like drinking cold water on an empty belly. I folded my arms around myself defensively, shaking my head.

"Shit, Morrison, it doesn't—it doesn't work like that.

I mean, I'm not, like, good enough to make it work, I don't know how, I don't *want* to—"

"God damn it, Walker, what do you *see!*"

I turned back to the field, stiff as an automaton, my lower lip sucked between my teeth. One of my arms unfolded from around me completely of its own will, hand drifting to rub my sternum through my winter jacket.

There was no hole in my breastbone, no scar to suggest there'd ever been one. But I found myself pulling in a very deep breath, trying to rid myself of the memory of a silver blade shoved through my lung and the bubbling, coppery taste of blood at the back of my throat. I'd nearly died eleven weeks ago, and instead found that buried within me was the power to heal myself, and maybe a great deal more. More than one person had called me a shaman since then. I didn't like it at all.

"I'm not any good at this, Morrison. I don't know if I can do it on purpose." My voice was strained and thin, full of reluctance. Morrison didn't say anything. Once upon a time—not that long ago—the only thing he and I had had in common was a complete disdain for the paranormal and people who believed there were things that went bump in the night. I'd been struggling for the past three months to get back to that place. Back to a world that made sense, where I didn't feel a coil of bright power burbling in the core of me, waiting to be used. I desperately wanted to believe it had been some kind of peculiar dream. Most days I was able to cling to that.

Morrison was not helping me cling. I could feel the tension in him, not with any extrasensory perception, but with how still he was holding himself, and the deliberate steadiness of his breathing. He wasn't any happier than I was about asking, which perversely made me willing to play ball. I put my teeth together, muttering, "Only you could get me to do this."

That struck me as being alarmingly accurate. I found myself abruptly eager to do it, so I didn't have to think about what I'd just said.

Unfortunately, I was at a complete loss as to how to proceed. I'd pulled denial over my head like a blanket the past several weeks. Now that someone was asking me to use my impossible new gifts, I didn't know where to start.

Just thinking about it made the power inside me flutter like a new life, full of hope and possibility. I swallowed against nausea that was as unpleasantly familiar as the idea of life inside me, and tentatively reached for the bubble of power.

A spirit guide called Coyote had suggested to me I work through the medium I knew best: cars. In reaching for that bubble of energy, I tried to do that. Morrison wanted me to *see*. Well, if I wasn't seeing clearly, then the windshields needed washing.

Power spurted up through me, a sudden warm wash

that felt startling against the cold winter afternoon. A silver-blue spray swished over my vision, just like wiper fluid. I closed my eyes against the brightness and a perceived sting and, without really meaning to, envisioned windshield wipers swooping the liquid away, leaving my vision clear. The sting faded and I opened my eyes again.

The world was beautiful. Even the gray sky glimmered with light, sparks of water shimmering above me. As I brought my gaze down, trees whose branches were weighted with snow flickered with the greenness of waiting life, only cold and dead to the mundane eye. Sap waited to rise, leaves prepared to bud, all a promise of explosive activity the moment winter let go its hold. The chain-link fences that surrounded the ball field had their own resolute purpose, created and placed to do a specific thing. A distinct sensation of pride in doing the job emanated from them.

The people on the field radiated different energy, swirling colors that bespoke worry or fear or determination, the rough shapes of their personalities hammering into me and leaving nothing taken for granted. I wanted to turn and look at Morrison, to get a sense of him with this other sight I'd called up, but I was afraid if I moved, I'd lose it again. I dropped my gaze to the field itself, still not knowing what I was looking for—

And a wave of maliciousness slammed into me like a tornado. It whipped around the core of power inside me and dug claws in, sharp knife-edges of pain cramping my belly. It sucked the heat out of me, draining the coil of energy in sudden throbs, faster than a heartbeat. My knees crumpled, light-headedness sweeping over me.

Morrison caught me under the arms so easily he might have been waiting for me to fall. I twisted toward him, grabbing his coat as he slid an arm around me more firmly.

"You're all right." His voice sounded like it was coming from unreasonably far away, given that I knew he was right behind my ear. "I've got you."

I didn't want to move, desperately glad for the support he offered, both physical and other. His presence was solid and comforting, a wall of commitment and strength in deep, reassuring purples and blues. I doubted he knew he was projecting his own personal energy in a way that let me borrow some, but I was incredibly grateful for it.

I managed a shaky nod, hanging on to the flow of strength he offered, using it to shore up my own depleted silvers and blues. After a few seconds I was able to get my legs under me again, though Morrison didn't quite let me go. I locked my knees and made myself turn to look at the field again.

Crimson lines, bleeding with pain and rage, flowed up from the field, following the lines of the baseball diamond. Points of vicious black stabbed behind my eyes, making marks that seemed to shoot up into the sky and fade somewhere beyond the stars. Looking at the field felt like someone was digging talons into my innards, trying to pull them out and bind me to the death that had already been wrought there.

Gary was wrong. There wasn't a body.

There were three.

2

"C'mon, Walker. Tell me what you see. Talk to me, Walker."

"How many have you found?" My voice was groggy, as if I was talking through pea soup. Morrison let out a breath that sounded like it meant to be a curse.

"Just the one. What're we missing?"

"Two more." I slid out of his grasp and to the snow-covered bleachers. My jacket wasn't nearly long enough for sitting on, and cold started seeping through my jeans immediately. "All women. There and there and there." I pointed blindly at the field, unable to convince myself to lift my eyes and study it again. Not that it would've helped: the snow was only snow again, not breathing with its own chaotic pattern of lights. I was just as glad that I couldn't hang on to the second sight for long. "What the hell made you call me in for this?"

"Holliday."

That explained a lot. Billy Holliday—besides having one of the more unfortunate names I'd ever encountered—was the department's number-one Believer. I'd played a mocking Scully to his Mulder until my own sensible world turned upside down. He'd been remarkably kind, all things considered, in not giving me too much shit since then. If something struck him as genuinely abnormal about the murders, it made a certain amount of sense for him to think of me.

God, how I wished he hadn't. I slumped down, forehead against my knees, which reminded me that I'd smacked my head earlier. I pressed my palm against it, trying—not very hard—to call up just enough of that energy inside me to smooth the bump away. It didn't work. I was almost grateful. It suggested I wasn't as completely weird as the past couple of minutes proved me to be. My silence drew on long enough to prompt my boss to keep talking, something I hadn't intended but for which I was also grateful.

"Some teenagers found the first body. Holliday was on call and when they dug her free—you should probably see for yourself."

"Do I have to?" My voice was still thin. "I'm a beat cop, Morrison, not a homicide detective." I'd never wanted to be either, despite having attended the academy. I'd been a mechanic, and the short version was Morrison'd hired my replacement when I had to go overseas for a while. But thanks to my mixed ethnic heritage—I was half Cherokee—I looked too good on the roster to actually fire. Instead, I'd gotten an upgrade from mechanic to actual living breathing cop. Morrison figured—hoped—I'd spit in his face and quit.

I couldn't stand to give him the satisfaction. Which left me sitting in the snow, whining and praying he'd give me a break.

"You have to."

So much for praying. I got up, brushed snow off my cold bottom, and stumped down the bleachers.

Billy'd obviously been on duty when the kids called in about the body, because he was wearing sensible shoes. Typically, when he got called unexpectedly he came in wearing a pair of great heels, which I still noticed because he had better taste in shoes than I did. I'd never heard anybody tease him about cross-dressing, partly because he was a hell of a detective, and partly because he was something over six feet tall and looked like he could break you in half. It didn't hurt that his wife could've been Salma Hayek's slightly more gorgeous sister. At the moment, though, he was wearing regulation boots and crouched over a frozen woman whose insides were no longer in. I stopped several feet back and said, "Jesus," by way of announcing my arrival.

The woman's intestines stretched out of her belly and into the snow, ropy frozen lines of blackness buried in the cold. Her stomach had been cut open in an efficient X, and judging from the rictus her face was frozen in, she'd probably been alive when it happened. If it'd been summertime, I probably would have lost my lunch, but the icy strands and beads of cold on her face looked so surreal I couldn't quite wrap my mind around it having been a person once. She looked like a prop on a sound stage for a movie set in the Arctic.

"Hey, Joanie." Billy was watching the guys from forensics brush snow away from the woman's body, careful detailed work that gave lie to the fact that the weather had almost certainly destroyed any available evidence. "Glad you could make it." He pursed his lips and shrugged. "Well."

"I know what you mean." I edged a few steps closer, staring down at the woman reluctantly. "Why'd you want me?"

"Look at her." He shrugged again. "Got ritual murder all over it."

"Did the dead lady tell you that?"

Billy gave me a dirty look that I deserved. I'd only learned recently that some of his intuitive leaps in homicide cases were courtesy of an occasional ability to converse with ghosts. It was not the kind of thing I was comfortable with, even though—or particularly because—I could now do it myself. "No," he said. "The physical evidence did. Can you not make jokes right now, Joanie? This woman deserves some respect."

"These women." I let out a long exhalation, looking at my feet. "There's two more. I...saw them."

Satisfaction showed in Billy's voice for just an instant. "I knew bringing you in was the right thing to do. You get anything else?"

Creepy-crawlies shivered over my skin, making me even more uncomfortable than a wet butt and dead bodies did by themselves. Billy was much, much easier with weird shit than I was. The shamanic gift that I hated having would have been far better off residing in him. "No. I'm sorry." I forbore to mention I didn't have a clue *how* to get anything else. He looked disappointed enough as it was. I lowered my voice, feeling like a member of a Sekrit Brotherhood that dared not voice its name. "Did you get anything?"

Billy shook his head. "Been dead too long. I never get anything from people who've been dead more than forty-eight hours. They lose their connection with the world."

I nodded, then frowned. "I thought you said your sister visited you three years after she died."

"I guess blood's thicker than ether."

The wind picked up as he spoke, a hair-raising keen that had no business anywhere outside of a holler. I instinctively lifted my shoulders against it, then felt a scowl crinkling my forehead so hard it ached. There was no new chill in the air, no cutting cold through my coat, despite the shriek of sound. A shadow came down over the world, making me look up at the sky, as if the sun wasn't already hidden beneath doomfully gray clouds.

There were no clouds. A window framed the section of sky I could see, scattered stars valiantly struggling against the light of a brilliantly full moon. Irish lace curtains caught at the moon's edges, making it whimsical and delicate in the clear black sky. Seattle's snowbound chill was driven from my skin, and the breath I took was full of warm air and the scent of tea.

Recognition jolted through me like needles under my fingernails. I knew the window; I knew the curtains, and I knew that if I looked to my left I would see a near stranger, lying beneath a handmade quilt and dying of nothing more than her own determination to do so.

I turned my head, for all that I didn't want to look at the woman on the bed. She had black hair, worn much longer than mine. It lay in soft-looking waves against her white pillow, stark contrast in the moonlight. Even in the blue-white light, her eyes were very green, and her skin was nearly as pale as the pillowcase. I heard myself say, "Mirror, mirror, on the wall," which I certainly hadn't said in real life. I wouldn't have let myself, even if I'd dared.

I was a wildly imperfect reflection of the woman on the bed. Where her skin was uniformly smooth and pale, mine was marked with a handful of freckles scattered across my nose; where her features were fine, mine seemed too sharp or too blunt. She was tall, although not as tall as I was, and had a degree of elegance to her that my long limbs and mechanic's hands could never emulate.

Her skin changed color, a horrid sallowness creeping in. I looked back at the moon to see blood draining over it. Fear scampered through me, the pure childish terror of the unknown. My voice broke as I said, "Sheila?" but when I turned to her, the woman was gone.

"Joanie?" Billy's hand on my elbow, big and warm, brought me back to the field with a start. I looked at his hand, then up at his worried frown. "You all right?"

"Yeah. I just…kind of spaced out. Sorry. I don't know what that was. Did you say something?" The wet chill of Seattle winter settled back into my bones, leaving me scowling at nothing. The moon had been full the night my mother died, but we hadn't spoken. We hadn't had much to say to one another, not from the time she'd called me out of the blue to say she was dying and she'd like to meet the daughter she abandoned twenty-six years earlier. I'd gone out of a mixed sense of duty and curiosity, and spent four uncomfortable months that culminated in her death on the winter solstice, almost three months ago to the day.

"I said, do you think there's anything else you can pick up? You've got more mojo than I do." His grin suggested he was biting his tongue to not ride me harder than that.

"I'll, um…shit." The last word wasn't meant to be heard, but Billy laughed anyway. I curled a lip and waved it off, perversely glad that he was teasing me a little. "I'll try." I wanted to try about as much as I wanted to stick red-hot pokers against my feet, but I couldn't quite bring myself to say that to the one person who didn't think I was at all crazy.

Granted, he was nuts himself by any normal standards, but I wasn't in a position to be throwing stones. "Is the morning soon enough?"

Billy turned a sad smile on the woman's body, then made a gesture to encompass the rest of the field. "There's a lot to do here, and I don't think another night is going to make this any harder on anybody. You work tomorrow?"

"Yeah. I'll give you anything I've got before I go out on patrol." I admired the weary confidence in my voice, as if I actually expected to come up with anything.

The problem was that I was afraid I might.

"All right. Thanks, Joanie." Billy hesitated a moment before adding, "I know you don't like this."

"So I'm a great sport for going along with it. I know. Tomorrow, Billy."

It was more than not liking it. It was like fingernails on chalkboards combined with dentist drills on unnumbed teeth. My world was a sensible, straightforward place. Checking out ritual murders on a psychic level simply did not belong. I kicked clumps of snow as I slogged back to Morrison to bum a ride home. He was driving his personal vehicle, a gold Toyota Avalon XLS—which I thought of as the American version of "boxy, but safe!"—so he hadn't been on duty when he'd called me. I didn't envy him his job.

Neither of us spoke during the whole drive, both wrapped up in our individual discomfort of what I was doing there. I didn't even say thanks when I got out, just thumped the top of his car and watched him drive off. Only after he disappeared down the Ave did I go into my building, taking the steps up to my fifth-floor apartment two at a time.

Gary, to whom I was practically certain I had not given a key, was hanging out in my apartment playing Tetris on my computer. "Thought you never touched the things," I said as I unlaced my boots.

"You didn't leave any entertainment rags. What was I supposed to do?"

"Cook dinner?" I put the boots on the carpet where all the melting snow would be absorbed and slid into the kitchen in my stocking feet.

"Nothin' to cook. I looked."

"Details, details. Besides, there is, too. I've got at least three different frozen dinners in here." I heard the telltale musical bloop that said he'd died horribly in the game, and a moment later he appeared in the door frame, making it look ridiculously small with his bulk. Even in his eighth decade he retained the build of the linebacker he'd once been, a fact that he took no small amount of pride in.

"So. Was there a body?"

I pulled two microwave dinners out of the freezer. "Do you remember calling *me* a bloodhound when we first met?"

"Nope." Gary gave me a disarming smile. "So there was a body."

"There were three. And..." I really didn't want to say anything else. I busied myself stabbing holes in the plastic tops of the dinners, then mumbled, as fast as I could, "And I said I'd maybe do a little checking out of what was going on in the astral realm sort of thing I don't suppose you'd hang around and bang a drum after dinner."

"Eh?" Gary cupped a hand behind his ear, leaning forward a little and wearing a cocky grin that would do James Garner's Maverick proud. "What'd you say? I'm an old man, lady. Can't hear when you don't speak up."

"I hate you, Gary."

He beamed at me. "Now, that's no way to talk to an old man, Joanne Walkingstick."

"Augh! Gary! No! Stop that!" I'd dropped my last name along with the rest of my Cherokee heritage when I graduated from high school, and a compulsive slip of the tongue—was there such a thing? It had felt like it at the time—had caused me to mention the long-since-abandoned name to Gary the day we'd met. "It's Walker. Don't do that, Gary." The humor I'd started with fell away into discomfort and I shrugged my shoulders unhappily as I put the first meal into the microwave. "Please."

"Hey." He came into the kitchen to put a hand on my shoulder and turn me around. "No harm meant, Jo. You arright?"

"I just…" I summarized the experience at the park, staring alternately at his feet and my own, not wanting to meet his eyes. "I just hate this shit. And the thing with remembering my mother all of a sudden just freaked me out." The microwave beeped and I turned back to it, my stomach grumbling. Gary put a hand on the door, keeping me from opening it.

"Let's hit the voodoo stuff first, darlin'. Food grounds you, you know that. You're shooting yourself in the foot by eating first." He lifted a bushy eyebrow. "Or is that on purpose?"

I squirmed, feeling like I'd been caught being naughty. Gary grinned, bright flash of white teeth that looked like he'd never smoked a cigarette in his life, and steered me into the living room. "Where's your drum?"

"Bedroom." I dragged a cushion off the couch and stuffed it against the front door, cutting off the draft that circled from beneath it. Gary went into my bedroom like he belonged there and got my drum.

It was the only thing I owned of any intrinsic value. It'd been a gift from one of the elders out in Qualla Boundary, not long after my father and I moved back there. It was painted with a raven whose wings sheltered a wolf and a rattlesnake, and had a drumstick with a soft rabbit-fur end dyed raspberry red, and a knotted leather end that made sharp rich pangs of sound against the taut leather. Even fourteen years after having been gifted with it, I was still amazed anyone would make something like it for me. Gary knew it, and carried it as if it was fragile, a gesture that made my nose sting with embarrassing emotion.

I settled down on the floor as he came out of the bedroom with the drum and a closed fist. "I thought you might want this."

I turned my hand up and he dropped a silver choker into my palm. Made of tube links intersected by triskelions, it had an Irish cross—a simple quartered circle, identical to the Cherokee power circle—as its pendant. "What—?"

"Your mom gave it to you, didn't she?"

"Yeah, I…" She'd given it to me the day she died. I'd worn it for two weeks, gradually getting used to the peculiar feeling of having something resting in the hollow of my throat, until the day I'd been stabbed through the lung and the necklace had been blackened with my blood. It'd taken days to get the stains out, and I hadn't brought myself to put it back on in the intervening weeks. "Yeah, all right." I swallowed nervously and fastened the choker with fingers that suddenly felt thick and clumsy. "You're all Mr. Insightful tonight, aren't you?"

Gary sat down on the couch cushion that hadn't been scavenged, grinning. "Somebody's gotta be. You ready?"

I nodded, fighting the urge to curl my fingers around the necklace and pull it away from my throat to alleviate the alien pressure of jewelry against my skin. "I'll wake up thirty seconds after you stop drumming." We'd only done this a few times, but establishing the time felt like ritual. Gary started knocking out a heartbeat rhythm, and I let my eyes drift shut, waiting to follow the sound of the drum out of my own body.

I had a deep dark secret. The world I saw through shamanic eyes—the one in which every thing on earth, be it animal, mineral or vegetable, sparked with the essence of life—was a world I dreamed about even when I was dead set against its reality. The world I saw with my spirit eyes was one where I could see Gary's big rumbly presence like a V-8 engine that a girl could rely on. It was one where I could slide through the ceiling and get an alarming look at my neighbors' sexual proclivities—although this time I went through the window when I separated from my body, because I *can* be taught, and I really didn't need another eyeful of somebody else's sex life.

Except for the glimpse that afternoon, I hadn't looked at the world from a spirit's perspective since January, when my life got turned upside down in the first place. There was something off-kilter as I slid into the Seattle night. Winter had come on too hard, and the life in the city that sped below me felt strained, like the world was being pushed in a direction it wasn't prepared to go in. The blues I'd seen a few months ago seemed darker, the electricity of life dammed up in some way. Streets seemed more congested, as if their purpose had been forgotten. It hadn't been like this a few months ago, and the feel of it made my skin prickle. There was a lingering feeling of familiarity below the wrongness, but when I reached for it, it slipped away.

I spun through the air, weightless and silent, watching sudden flashes of red and orange erupt in backed-up traffic, countered by calm waves of blue that I tried to encourage, clumsily. I passed a stretch of road where a woman's astrally projected spirit hovered above her car, looking down at traffic much like I did. Pure boredom emanated from her, as if driving home had been so dull it'd flung her out of her own body. She didn't seem to sense my presence, and I whisked past her, not knowing how to stop and say hello.

I left the city behind without having a destination in mind, moving as fast as thought itself. Color, vivid and strong, streaked with the coldness of winter, shot past me, sometimes forming into recognizable images, but more often staying abstract. I wondered if the abstraction was due to my lack of direction, but with the thought came a clear pathway that I recognized with a startled shiver.

A bower of trees arched over a single-track path, white flowers all but glowing under a source of light I couldn't pinpoint. The path was smooth, as if it had been often walked on. I tumbled from flight to run along it, great huge strides so I felt I was still flying. There was a presence in front of me, somewhere buried in the depths of the earth. It carried its own weight, its own gravity well, drawing me toward it. I careened around a corner, pretending I was driving Petite, and came up against a cave, its mouth blocked off with boulders.

The presence beyond the cave mouth had a genial feeling to it, as if it were amused at my audacity and youth.

I hated feeling like people were laughing at me. I glowered at the boulders and reached for the smallest stone I could find, trying to wriggle it out of its lodged position in the ranks of larger stones.

A vise clamp fastened itself around my wrist, hauled me back, and did something that put my feet over my head and my head against the ground. I lay on my face with a mouthful of dirt, not entirely sure how I'd gotten there but pretty certain that any moment now I was going to start to hurt.

"And what is it," a woman's voice above me asked, "that you think you're doing, Siobhán Walkingstick?"

The lilt of Ireland was strong in her voice, almost masking the sarcasm with which the question was delivered.

I was pretty sure she didn't want an answer. I had comparatively little experience with mothers, but the tone suggested to me that she knew perfectly well *what* I was doing, and that the real question was *why* was I doing something she obviously regarded as unbelievably stupid.

The physical pain I was expecting didn't seem to be coming, so I rolled onto my back and stared up at her. She looked remarkably tall from this vantage, and somewhat bustier than I thought of her as being. She also wore an expression of exasperation that was both more vivid than any expression I could remember seeing on her in life, and which, although strictly speaking was entirely new to me, I had felt on my own face any number of times. Distress settled over me. It didn't seem fair that I was turning into my mother when I'd barely even known the woman.

Eventually one of the numerous things crowding my mind and vying to be said won out: "I asked you not to call me that." It seemed, even at the moment, an awfully calm response to the appearance of a woman I believed to be dead.

I was treated to a second new expression: dismay, which was wiped out almost instantly by the thoughtful, examining gaze that was all I'd really ever seen of her. "Very well, then. Joanne." Her tone spoke volumes about what she thought of my Anglicized name, but I was almost entirely overwhelmed with not caring. I got to my feet somewhat stiffly, although I suspected any injuries I'd sustained were in my own mind.

Of course they were. That's what happens when you travel on the astral plane. Moving on, then. I looked back to the wall of rocks, eyeing the one I'd initially grabbed. "Joanne," my mother said in a remarkably good "don't you dare test my patience one more time, young lady" voice. I dropped my hand and turned to face her, making a point of looking around rather dramatically.

"I'm sorry," I said. "Did you think you had something to say to me that I might listen to? Is there some burning reason that I should pay attention to, I don't know, what are you, a banshee or something? You're dead, Mother. We didn't much like each other when you weren't dead. Why don't we just leave it at that and you can go do whatever it is dead people do? I'm busy."

"Busy."

"Yes." I went to work on my rock again, tugging it a few millimeters out of the wall. She clamped her hand around my wrist again. Her fingers were tremendously cold, not just like the dead, but as if she was emitting cold the way a living body emits heat.

"You don't understand what you're doing, Joanne." I hated the warm lilt of her voice, a low alto that I wanted to instinctively trust. I couldn't possibly have recognized it. She'd abandoned me with my father when I was three months old, but from the moment she'd called me, seven months ago, I'd fought against wanting to curl up in the warmth and safety of that voice and letting myself forget about the world.

"Like you could possibly know what I'm doing. I don't even know what you're doing here. Go *away*." I yanked my wrist, trying to escape her grasp. I failed in that, but I did manage to loosen the rock I held. The entire wall shifted ominously, deep scrapes of stone bumping down a few inches against one another. My mother hissed, a sound like an angry cat, then lifted her voice in a high keen that made me jerk away again, this time succeeding and clamping my hands over my ears.

"You will not pass this barrier, Siobhán Walking-stick." Her voice thundered inside my head, making me equal parts angry and dizzy. I set my teeth together and stomped forward, grabbing my stone again.

They always say, "I never knew what hit me." Technically, I knew what hit me: it was my mother. Beyond that, I really don't know what happened, except one second I had the stone in my hands and the next I was about forty feet away, lying on my back in the dirt, and she was standing over me like one of God's avenging angels in a blouse and long skirt. My lip was bleeding. I lifted the back of my hand to it, staring up at her. She crouched, putting a hand on my shoulder. It seemed to carry the weight of the world behind it, as profoundly heavy as the draw that had pulled me toward the cave mouth in the first place.

"You are not yet ready to face what lies beyond that wall, daughter. I haven't much time to act, and less time still to tell you about it. Get yourself home. I've no energy for wasting on sullen little girls who refuse to listen to their mothers."

Her will hit me like a wall itself, reaching right for the core of energy inside me as if it was her own. She shoved me into the earth with the hand on my shoulder, using my own stored power as her focus point.

I popped out the other side and into my body so hard I fell over backward. Gary stopped drumming and jumped to his feet while I stared at the ceiling and tried to determine if all my parts were where I thought they should be. They were. After a few seconds I said, "Ow," and thought I'd leave it at that.

There was no part of me that didn't hurt. It wasn't the god-awful pain of having a sword driven through me, but I ached, like someone had...well, shoved me through solid ground. I said, "Ow," again, for good measure, and pushed myself up slowly. Gary hovered over me, nervous but kind enough not to ask.

"What the hell happened?"

All right, kind enough not to ask for a few seconds, at least. I shook my head, exhaustion sweeping over me without warning. The bubble of energy inside me that I spent so much time trying to ignore was depleted again. I felt like I'd been depending on it without knowing about it. "I need food."

I got up, largely to see if I could, and wobbled to the kitchen door. When I'd reached the frame without mishap, I turned my head to answer Gary's question. "I don't think my mother is as dead as I thought she was."

I refused to say anything else until I'd eaten. Gary finally stopped asking, "Zombie? Vampire? Wraith?" and ate his own dinner, watching me with the eagerness of a kid at Christmastime. I swear, anybody on the planet— except possibly Morrison—would have been better suited to my insane new world than I was. Billy had already lived with something like it his whole life. Gary thought it was cool. I wanted it to all go away so I could sleep in peace at night, and work on Petite by day.

"There's something out there," I finally said. Gary gave an evocative snort that made me aim a kick at him under the table. To both our surprise, it connected, and he yelped, looking injured.

"Sorry. I mean, something that wants me to go check it out. My mother was standing sentinel over it tonight. She wasn't there last time."

"Last time?"

"I saw it in January. Look, that doesn't matter. She kicked my ass."

Gary put a bite of spaghetti—the closest thing I had

in the freezer to chicken fettuccine—in his mouth to hide a smirk. I drew my foot back for another kick, then remembered I'd managed to hit him once already and felt guilty. He looked smug, making me annoyed for feeling guilty, so I swung at him again. I missed. "So obviously," I said through gritted teeth, "she thinks whatever's behind door number one is dangerous."

"Then you should stay away from it," Gary said wisely.

"I don't even know what it is!"

"Mothers are always right. Don't you know that?" He wrinkled his eyes into nonexistence as I scowled at him. "Right. I forgot. Sorry." He paused. "Mothers are always right. You don't wanna find out what's behind that door."

"Gary!"

He lifted his hands defensively. "I'm just sayin'."

"Well, dammit, I want to know what's back there." I hesitated. "She said I wasn't ready for it."

Gary's bushy eyebrows rose. "If you'll excuse me for coppin' a phrase from today, *duh*. You really think you're ready for the monster in the closet?"

"No, but I'd like to know what it is! Knowledge is half the battle, or something."

"Look." Gary pointed his fork at me. "What'd you go in there looking for?"

I shrugged, uncomfortable. "I don't know. Nothing specific."

"Okay. There's your problem. You got no focus. You

need to go in there and talk to somebody who knows what's going on. Your buddy the coyote."

"Coyote never gives me a straight answer." I sounded just like the sullen kid my mother had accused me of being.

"Yeah, that's kinda what the whole trickster thing is all about, Jo."

I flung my hands in the air. "Why do you know that? Why does everybody on the whole planet know this stuff that I don't? Why didn't somebody else get this stupid talent? You can have it. You'd be a lot better at it than I am!"

Gary huffed. "Probably."

My rant cut off as my jaw dropped. Gary's gray eyes sparked good humor with a steely undercut. "You done?"

"Uh." I cleared my throat. "Um. Yes. Thank you."

"You got something special, kid. You're gonna have to learn to suck it up and live with it, or walk away. Right now there's some dead ladies out there that maybe you can help, if you stop your whining and bitching and get on with it. Are you gonna do that, or what?"

"Okay." I sounded very small and pathetic. And embarrassed.

"Arright." Gary got up, his plastic spaghetti dish in one hand. "Let's go try this again, then." He stalked into the living room, leaving his muttered, "Jeez. Dames," lingering on the air.

* * *

It took longer to go under this time, in part because of chagrin and in part because of the microwaved fried chicken that settled in my tummy and made me more aware of my body than was helpful. After several minutes of drumming, though, I suddenly fell backward into my body and found myself scrambling down a thin tunnel, in search of an internal garden that somehow reflected the state of my soul.

There was a fundamental difference between going there and going...other places...that I went. It struck me that it might really be helpful to get a grasp of the different levels of reality that I seemed to be able to access. Being able to name them, for example, could be useful. It might make me sound—or at least feel—like less of an idiot.

Whether I had a name for it or not, the journey to my garden felt distinctly internal, whereas moving to the astral plane seemed to involve leaving my body in some kind of upward fashion. I scuttled through little tunnels, feeling myself drawing closer to the center of me, until the light turned gray around me and I popped out of a mouse-sized hole in one of the walls surrounding my garden. I looked back and the hole was gone, sealed up safely by my meager mental defenses.

The garden itself was—well, it wasn't quite dead, which was something. It was functional, not beautiful, with straight pathways in geometric patterns and grass cropped so short I could see dirt between individual blades. A small pond with its own waterfall bubbled at one end of the garden, more agitated than I remembered it being. I took a couple of deep breaths to see if it would calm the pond, but it didn't seem to help.

"The problem's deeper than your breathing, Joanne."

"I don't have any problems!" There I went again with the juvenile-response syndrome. I waited a few seconds, trying not to blush, then looked for the speaker, who lolled on a concrete bench, his tongue hanging out. I tried very, very hard to modulate my voice into politeness as I said, "Hello, Coyote."

He rolled to a sitting position and shook himself all over, golden eyes bright as he cocked his head at me. "If you don't have any problems, what are you doing shouting for me?"

"I—" I took a deep breath and stood up straighter. "I need some, um, help. Guidance!" I latched on to the word, feeling rather proud of myself. "Please," I added hastily. "If you could." *Nice Mr. Coyote Man,* I thought but didn't say. I didn't have to: he snapped his teeth at me like I was an annoying fly.

"I heard that."

My shoulders sagged. Coyote could hear anything I thought, while I heard nothing of what he thought. Sometimes I thought that meant I'd made him up. Other times I was equally certain it meant I hadn't.

"You did not make me up," Coyote said.

"No," I muttered. "You'd be cuter and less annoying if I had."

He grinned a coyote grin at me and stretched, long and lazy. When he was done stretching, he wasn't a brown and gold beast any longer. Instead an Indian man sat there, his skin as red as bricks and his hair blue-black and long and falling to his hips. He wore jeans and was barefoot, looking incredibly comfortable in his own skin. Only the eyes were the same, bright gold and full of mirth. "Is this better?"

It was certainly cuter. He laughed even though I hadn't spoken out loud, and stood up to go drag a hand through the bubbling pool at the end of my garden. "What do you need, Jo?"

"There've been some murders. And…my mother is alive. Or something. I—can you help me find her?"

He lifted his head in a swift motion, more like a coyote than a man. "Your mother?"

"Is up there in the astral realm or whatever it is, bossing me around."

"Wow."

I was practically certain spirit guides were not supposed to say *wow*. "'Cause you know so much about spirit guides," he said. "I'll see if I can—"

"You won't be needing to, lad."

"Jesus Christ!" I whipped around, unbalancing myself with the motion, to find my mother standing directly in front of the mouse hole that I could've sworn closed up when I arrived. She ignored me momentarily, focused on Coyote.

"Sheila MacNamarra," she said to him. "A pleasure, and aren't you the handsome one. Joanne's a lucky girl."

My dead mother was matchmaking me with a dog. Great.

"I'm not a dog."

"I'm hardly matchmaking, Joanne. You opened up the conduit. I'm just here to say hello."

I set my teeth together and waited a few seconds before I trusted my voice. "Hello, Mother." I waited a few more seconds before it burst out of me: "What the hell are you doing alive?"

A trace of surprise and injury darkened her eyes. "I'm not alive, Joanne. You saw me die."

"Then what are you doing here? Besides kicking my ass back into my body, which hurt, thankyouverymuch."

"Not nearly so much as facing down that enemy would have hurt. Joanne—" Sheila made a small and elegant gesture, bringing her hands in toward her heart, as if collecting sorrow there. "There's very little time, and a great deal to tell you. I'd hoped we could talk before, but you weren't ready—"

"Before what?"

"Before I died," Sheila said, nonplussed. "That was why I asked you to come, of course. I never dreamed you'd be so closed off. If you'd been ready, I could have explained so much."

"Ready for *what?*" I felt very small and young suddenly, a feeling that was reflected in the garden: it grew around me dramatically, until Coyote and my mother both towered over me, and even the sparse blades of grass seemed much larger in comparison to my own height.

My mother cast a glance at Coyote that clearly said she despaired of me, but she brought her attention back to me in an instant. "To accept your heritage, at least on my side. What you've got to face. You're still not ready to hear it, but the moon is changing and I'm out of time. Siobhán, listen to me. I'm a *gwyld,* a—"

"Shaman," I interrupted dully. I'd heard the word before, only directed at me, not my mother. "Some kind of druidic version of a shaman. You came back from the dead to tell me *that?* Like it could possibly matter? Like I could care?" I was not, I knew, being fair. Part of me did care. Part of me cared so much it hurt to breathe, and that was the part that lashed out at her. It was perversely like finding out there was a Santa after all.

Frustration creased her forehead. "I left the mortal world to protect you, Siobhán. I've known since before you were born what you might be, what it was you'd have to face. But you were so unprepared I saw no other choice. You needed protecting."

"What," I said, "if you strike me down I'll become more powerful than you can ever imagine? Is that your gig?"

Complete incomprehension flitted across her expression. I set my teeth together, about to lash out again, but a shriek of wind erupted, sounding in my ears but going unfelt against my skin. My gaze went to the sky even as a shadow, dark and red, fell across my vision again. A full moon hung above me, one that hadn't been shining on my garden moments before. One with blood spilling down its face, and with a piece of darkness falling from it like a scythe. A deep sense of malignancy boiled up inside me, as if a thing of hatred was being born. Cold, raging hands seemed to clench around my heart, and I listened frantically for the rhythmic drumbeat that would let me know I was still alive.

My mother let go an inhuman screech, like a car braking too hard, and flung herself at the sky. Her hair spread out like raven's wings, blocking my view of the bloody moon. The slice of night that had fallen from it was enveloped by the black spiderweb of her hair. I heard another yowl, as gut-wrenching as the earlier ones, and the barbs that had knotted in my heart loosened.

A small, furry bundle of bone crashed into my chest, knocking my heart into pounding again as sweat stood out on my body in cold terror. Coyote stood over me for a moment or two, his golden gaze fixed on mine before he brought his head down to smash it against mine with tremendous force.

For the second time in a single evening, I slammed out of the realm of Other and back into my body, aching all over with pain and confusion.

4

It took the better part of an hour to get Gary out of my apartment, which both made me feel better and worse. When he was gone I sat on the couch with a pillow hugged against my chest, staring blindly at nothing.

It was inconceivable to me that my mother had been some sort of mystic. The woman I'd known for a few scant months had held her cards close to the chest, always judging and never commenting. I'd spent four months with her and, when she died, felt as though I'd known nothing more about her than she liked Altoids. There'd been no real mourning, at least not on my part. Confusion, yes, and, not to be delicate about it, a whole lot of resentment. She'd disrupted a life in which I had not missed her to any noticeable degree in order to have me witness her death. She'd been young, only fifty-three, and in extremely good health. I'd been left with the impression that she was bored of life, and as such saw fit to leave it under her own power.

It appeared that the power in question was more literal than I'd thought. I mean, anybody who could will herself to death wasn't a person whose emotional state was one I wanted to tangle with. She might decide it was time for me to die, and I might not be tough enough to argue. I hadn't even tried arguing in favor of her life, which probably made me a very bad daughter.

Not that there was any really compelling reason to be a good daughter to the woman who'd abandoned me when I was a few months old. We hadn't liked each other as adults. I could only assume she hadn't much cared for me as a baby, either.

A fine thread of emptiness wove through me, an ache that I'd spent the better part of my life resolutely ignoring. I hadn't been given up for adoption by a mother who thought it was best for me. I'd been dumped on a father who hadn't known I existed until that moment, by a mother who evidently didn't like me very much. It was not something I enjoyed thinking about.

Especially as it reminded me, inevitably, of a boy growing up in North Carolina, whom I had known full well I couldn't properly mother. Not at fifteen. Not in the confusion of mourning the sister who'd been born with him, and who'd died just minutes later, too small to live.

I set my teeth together and put my forehead against the pillow, shoving away every thought of family ties that came haunting me. Introspection was not my strong suit. I didn't like to look back, and I wasn't prepared for the past, in the form of my dead mother, to come calling.

I fell asleep sometime after midnight, still wrapped around the scratchy couch pillow.

Monday March 21, 8:20 a.m.

There was a place on the other side of sleep that I'd been to, where I'd walked among the dead and spoken with them. The plan—a plan which I didn't have any intention of mentioning aloud, not even to myself—had been to whoosh through dreamtime, find the dead women and learn who'd killed them, then jaunt off to work like Don Juan triumphant.

Instead I woke up stiff and disoriented the next morning, curled up on the solitary couch cushion, without having had a single moment's otherworldly experience while I slept. An ache of uselessness welled up behind my eyes. Not only did I not understand what was going on, but the baser part of me didn't care. Having it all go away would have been far more within my comfort zone.

I had just used the phrase *comfort zone* with all due seriousness, right inside my own head. I clearly needed to get up, stick my head in a bowl of cold water, and drink a pot of strong coffee. Which I did, except it was a hot shower instead of a cold bowl, and I swear I didn't drink more than three cups of coffee. Honest.

I called a cab—not Gary; he knew too much about me and I wasn't up to facing that this morning—and went to work, my nose mashed against the window. I missed Petite. I wanted to be cozy and safe, driving her instead of taking a cab. I had a better relationship with my car than I had with most people.

With any people, a small and somewhat snide voice inside my head said. I told it to go away, paid the cabby, and stumped through the precinct building to find Billy.

Actually, I was looking for his desk, where I figured I could leave a note explaining my humiliating inability to find anything useful, and then run away before I had to confess my failure out loud. I'd come in early just to be sure I could pull that off.

Billy was earlier. He leaned on his elbow, big palm wrinkling the side of his face until his left eye had all but disappeared into the curves of flesh. He looked like he'd been up all night, which was not only possible, but likely. An attack of guilt grabbed me by the throat. I snuck back out of the precinct building and scurried down the street to the doughnut shop to get him a lemon-poppyseed muffin and an oversize mocha. His face actually lit up when I plopped them down on his desk several minutes later, which made me feel slightly less like a loser.

"You're a goddess." The side of his face was one big red mark from leaning on his hand too long. He unwrapped the muffin, took a slurp of coffee, and squinted up at me. "You didn't get anything about the murders, did you."

"Is it that obvious?" Back to Loserville.

"You look like a kicked puppy. But I'll forgive you anything for the next five minutes, because you brought me the manna of heaven."

"Damn." I looked at the muffin, impressed. "I shoulda gotten me one of those things."

Billy chuckled and sank back in his chair, its unoiled hinge drawing out a creak that slowly lifted every individual hair from my fingertips to my nape. I wrapped my hands around his coffee cup for a few seconds, trying to chase the chill away. He ate half the muffin in one bite, then nodded at his computer screen, speaking around crumbs. "I'd forgive you anyway. I found some stuff out. Not about our dead girls. They all had ID, by the way. We're seeing if they've got anything in common, but so far they look random. Anyway, the murders."

Somehow I was able to understand every word he said. I usually couldn't understand most of what I said when my mouth was full. I twisted around to look at the computer screen. "Interpol?"

"Thought of it this morning. I remembered reading about some kind of ritual murders about thirty years ago—"

"You read them thirty years ago?" Billy wasn't more than ten years older than I was. He gave me a look that suggested I shut up. I pressed my lips together and widened my eyes, all innocence.

"The murders were about thirty years ago. I read about them a few years ago. Pedant."

"Because you what, read about ritual murders for fun?"

"Joanie," Billy said, annoyed. I lifted my hands in apology and tried to keep quiet. Billy glared at me until he was sure I wasn't going to interrupt again, then continued. "These women all had their intestines stretched out, connecting them with one another."

I suddenly wished I hadn't drunk a lot of acidic coffee for breakfast, and looked around for something neutral to eat. There was nothing handy except Billy's muffin, the second half of which he stuffed in his mouth, clearly suspecting that I was about to raid it. A burp rose up through the soured coffee in my stomach and I clamped my hand over my mouth, tasting coffee-flavored bile. Yuck.

"You've got a soft heart, Joanie." Billy gave me a very tiny smile that did a lot to make me feel better.

"I'm not a homicide detective."

"Mmm. Yeah. Anyway, so I remembered this morning reading about a murder like that over in Europe. It's not the kind of thing the authorities like to noise around."

"No kidding." My stomach was still bubbling with ook. "So we've got a copycat?"

"Either that or somebody's changed his hunting grounds. Anyway, the only case there was an eyewitness for was, like I said, about thirty years ago. A woman who was presumably supposed to be the last victim—there's never more than four—fought back and managed to escape. The Garda Síochána—"

"This was in Ireland?" I didn't mean to interrupt. It just popped out. Billy's ears moved back with surprise.

"Yeah. What, you had some run-ins with the cops while you were there?"

"No, I just remember my mother talking about the Garda. She didn't call them the Síochána." I said the word carefully, SHE-a-CAWN-a. "I had to ask her what it meant."

"It means police," Billy said helpfully, then waved off my exasperated raspberry. "Yeah, you know that, right. Anyway, they weren't able to find the guy, and for a while the woman was under suspicion, but she got off when the marks on the victims' bodies had obviously been made by somebody a lot bigger than she was. They're usually strangled into semiconsciousness before the horrible stuff begins."

"Like being half-strangled isn't horrible." It had nothing on having your innards ripped out while you were still alive, and I lifted a hand to stop Billy's protestation. "I know. So what was her name? Maybe we can talk to her, get some kind of information about this psycho that might help us."

Billy leaned forward, chair shrieking protest again, to pull up a minimized screen. "That was my thought. She was from Mayo. I've got some people there looking to see if they can find her. Her name was—oops, wrong window." He pulled up another one, scrolling down. "Her name was—"

"Sheila MacNamarra," I finished, feeling light-headed.

The woman on the computer screen looked more like me than the one I'd known had. There was a ranginess to her that I shared, and our eyes were shaped more alike than I'd realized. I'd never seen a picture of my mother when she was young, and young she was: the photo showed her from the thighs up. She was obviously several months pregnant.

With me.

I closed my eyes, unable to think while looking at the photograph on the computer screen. "You won't—" I cleared my throat, trying to wash away the break I'd heard in my voice. "You won't find her. She's dead."

"Joanie?" Billy sounded bewildered. "You know this woman?"

"Yeah." I wished I was wearing my glasses so I could pull them off. Instead my hand wandered around my face like a bird looking for a resting space: my fingers pressed against my mouth, then spread out to cover the lower half of my face before curling in again. I couldn't stop the little actions, even when I tried. "She's my mother."

I wanted the next half hour or so to disappear into a jumble of confusion, but it adamantly refused to. It was all horribly clear, with an overwhelming babble of questions that I caught every syllable of and a host of concerned, confused, angry expressions that wouldn't let me back up and take stock of the situation. No one had known my mother's name, not any more than I knew Billy's mom's name. Everyone had known I'd gone to Ireland to meet her, and that she'd died, but nobody'd pried beyond that, which I'd been perfectly happy about.

Now, though, Morrison was standing over me—well, trying to. I was on my feet, too, unable to stay sitting while he demanded to know how it was I coincidentally had connections to this woman who'd been a suspect, albeit briefly, in a murder case that was nearly thirty years old. He went on for quite a while, during which Billy tried to be the voice of reason and I watched them both with growing incredulity. Finally I edged between them and said, "Captain," which brought Morrison up short. I rarely resorted to using his actual title.

"Look." This was my reasonable voice. I didn't have a lot of hope for it working on Morrison, but I'd never tried it before, and anything was worth trying once.

"My mother obviously didn't kill those women. She wasn't big enough. The police reports cover all that. I guess I am big enough." I lifted one of my hands, with its long fingers, and shrugged. "And we have no idea when our women died, so—"

"Actually," Billy said. I winced and looked at him. He grimaced back apologetically and shrugged. "The first body has a fair amount of degradation. They figured she died about three weeks before it started getting cold enough to snow so much, probably around Christmas."

Morrison's cheeks went a dangerous dark florid purple. "You're telling me we had a body lying around Woodland Park for three weeks before it snowed and *nobody noticed?*"

"The good news," I said under his outrage, "is that I was in Ireland at a funeral on Christmas. Good alibi."

"How the hell," Morrison shouted, ignoring me, "did a body lie around in a public park for three weeks without anyone noticing?"

"I don't—" Billy began.

Morrison roared, "Find out!" and stalked into his office, slamming the door behind him. Everyone within forty feet flinched. I sucked my lower lip into my mouth and watched the venetian blinds inside the captain's office swing from the force of the door crashing shut.

"Do you think he does that for dramatic effect?" I didn't realize that was my outside voice until nervous laughter broke around me, then rolled over into outright good humor. Someone smacked me on the shoulder and the audience that had gathered for the drama broke up. It never failed to astonish me how there were always people around to watch tense moments unfold. You'd think none of us had jobs to do.

I followed Billy back to his desk, since I still wasn't on shift for another forty minutes. "I really hate to say this."

He eyed me, wary. "But?"

"But I'm pretty sure nobody was supposed to see that body. I don't think it was cosmic coincidence. I think there was…" My tongue seemed to be swelling up and choking my throat in order to prevent me from continuing my sentence. Part of me wished it would succeed. "Power." *Power* was easier to say than that other word, the five-letter one that began with *m* and ended with *agic*. "Involved."

"Yeah?" Billy's eyebrows rose a fraction of an inch. "Can you do that?"

"Billy, I can't even pick my nose without using a finger." Sometimes my mouth should stop and consult my brain before it says anything. Billy got this wide-eyed look of admiration that belonged on a nine-year-old boy. It said, *Wow, that was really gross,* and, more important, *How come* I *didn't think of it?* My mouth consulted my brain this time, and I asked, "I don't suppose you could just forget I said that?"

"No," Billy said, in a tone that matched the admiration still in his eyes. "I don't think I can. I'm going to have to tell that one to Robert."

"Melinda will kill you."

Billy's grin turned beatific. "Yeah," he said happily. "Girls don't get stuff like that. Except you," he added hastily. "But you're sort of not like a girl."

I stared at him. After a while he realized he might have said something wrong, and backed up hastily. "I mean, you are—of course, you're a girl, it's just, you know, you're one of the guys."

"Billy," I said. "Bear in mind that what you're saying is coming from a man who wears nail polish. I'm not sure it's helping."

"See, that's what I'm saying. Have you ever worn nail polish?"

"No," I said slowly. "I started to put some on once, but it made my fingers feel heavy and I hated it."

"Okay then. So what I'm saying is I bet more of the guys here have worn fingernail polish than you have."

"So I'm more like a guy than one of the guys." My tone was flat and dangerous. Well, I thought it was. Billy didn't seem to feel threatened.

"Kind of, yeah. You're like an überguy. You know everything about cars and you drink beer and shoot guns, only then you also clean up pretty good—"

"Billy." I was a hundred-percent cranky, and this time he heard it. He looked up, surprise lifting his eyebrows.

"Solve your own damned case." I turned on my heel and stalked away.

5

I stomped all the way down to the garage beneath the precinct building and peeked around the stairwell wall. Peeking wasn't much in keeping with my stompy mood, but I wanted to see if my archnemesis, Thor the Thunder God, was in the garage before I went in.

He was, of course. I sat down in the shadow at the foot of the stairs—the last flourescent light in the row above the steps had never, to the best of my recollection, been functional—and wrapped my arms around my knees, watching the mechanics at work.

This was where I belonged. I'd gone to the academy because the department had paid my way, but I'd never wanted to be a cop. I was a mechanic and something of a computer geek. The two went hand in hand with modern cars, and I was happy with both labels. But my mother had taken her time dying, they had hired Thor as my replacement, and now I was a cop.

His name wasn't really Thor. It was Ed or Ted or something of that nature. He just looked like Thor, big and blond with muscles on his muscles. He was working on Mark Rodriguez's car, which was forever having the wheels pulled out of alignment. I had a suspicion that Rodriguez went home and beat the axles with a hammer, but I couldn't prove it. Thor wasn't working on the wheels right now, though. He was under the hood, his convict-orange jumpsuit and blond hair bright against the shadows cast by the overhead lights. I put my chin on my knees, watching silently from the shadows. It wasn't as good as being up to my elbows in grease myself, but the smell of oil and gasoline was as soothing to me as mother's milk.

Not that anything about my mother was soothing. I stifled a groan and put my forehead against my knees, listening to the muffled cursing and good-natured banter that went on over the rumbles and squeaks of fixing cars. Tension ebbed out of my shoulders as the comfort sounds and smells vied with my mother's memory for priority in my thought process.

Sheila won out. The image of her pregnant kept invading the backs of my eyelids. She was prettier than I was, and looked serenely confident as she stared back at me from behind my eyes. I could all but see the wind picking up her hair, long black strands that whisked back from her face with a life of their own, but no matter how hard I tried to meet her eyes, I couldn't read any emotion in them. "Come on." I didn't think I was speaking aloud. I was talking to a memory of someone I'd never known. "Tell me what's going on, can't you? What's this guy want? You stopped him once, O Mystical Mother. Give me something to work with here."

She didn't. Evidently not even the memory of her responded well to sarcasm. I sighed and dropped my head farther against my knees. In the garage, metal bit into metal with a high-pitched squeal, a shriek that should have lifted hairs on my arms and made me shiver with discomfort. It had exactly the opposite effect, draining away tension from my neck and making my grip on my own arms slip a little, so that I slumped even more on the stairs. I'd spent far too much time in shops, listening to that sound, to find it uncomfortable. At least, not when I heard it someplace like the garage, where it belonged.

"It's a strange way you have of belonging."

That sound made me flinch, my fingers tightening around my arms again. I could still hear the scream of metal, although as I lifted my head it seemed to blend with a wuthering wind, no less eerie a sound.

Sheila MacNamarra, my very own mother, stood a few feet away, wearing the cable-knit sweater and jeans she'd worn in the photograph taken almost twenty-seven years ago. A silver necklace glinted in the hollow of her throat, all but hidden by the sweater. Her hair was lifted on the wind, moving slowly, as if time was being stretched thin and we were slipping between moments of it.

"Sure, and that's what's happening, now, isn't it?" She took a step forward, the blustery gray sky behind her superimposed over the shop's girders and lights. "Siobhán Grania MacNamarra." My name sounded liquid and lovely in her accent, if I overlooked the fact that none of it was the name I considered mine. "You grew up so tall, my girl." Sheila curved her hand over her tummy and smiled at me. "Your father was tall."

"He still is." My voice was hoarse. I could see blowing grass around her knees, and a white two-story house in the middle of a field. I could also see, with a little more effort, the shop behind her. This was not like any of my limited experiences with worlds that were Other. As much as I wasn't crazy about those, at least I kind of knew what to expect from them. This was a whole new ball game. "Are you real?"

"That I am." Sheila crouched so that she was looking up at me on my stair. "So it's come 'round again, has it? We're back to where we began, you and I. How've we been, girl? Have we had a good life together?"

Cold shocked against my skin from the inside, making my cheeks burn. "What are you talking about? We haven't had any life together at all. You're dead."

Sheila's shoulders pulled back, her face blanching.

"Am I now." She stood, hands pressed against her thighs, and took a few steps away. Her shoulder ended up lodged in the stairwell corner, which bothered the hell out of me and didn't seem to phase her at all. "And how long have I been dead?"

"About three months. What, you don't kn—" Wire contracted around my lungs, forcing air out as surely as a sword could. I rubbed the heel of my hand against my breastbone and tried to pull in a breath deep enough to snap the feeling of suffocation. "You don't know." My words had no strength behind them. "I'm talking to the you from thirty years ago."

"I told you, now, didn't I? That we were between moments of time." Sheila turned back to me, sudden urgency crackling in her movements. "And here I thought this was something done on purpose, but it's not, lass, is it? You've fallen through time and don't even know how you've done it. Have I been such a poor mother to you, then? Taught you nothing of the old ways? Ah, Siobhán, what's gone on?"

"My name is Joanne." Even as I spoke I saw the words cut her, something I hadn't intended. Her eyes lost some of their light and she fell back a step, lowering her gaze.

"I see. Joanne, then. It's a fine name, and isn't it though. Now tell me, girl. You called me, but I think it's my own skill that's brought me here, not yours." She frowned at me, faint and censuring. "I can see the power in you, but it's raw and untempered. I don't understand. You're a woman grown. You should be at the height of your skill by now."

"There's not really time to go into it right now, Mother. You stopped someone, a killer, right?" It was all coming out much more sharply than I meant it to, but I had no idea how to deal with this woman. There was softness in her, kindness. Love. It didn't fit with the mother I'd known, and I was afraid distraction would keep me from ever understanding what was going on. She was already dead. It seemed a little late for her to be getting the answers she needed. "He's back, or somebody like him is back. What's going on?"

I watched it happen. The gentleness drained from her, leaving behind something much colder and more stark. Lines that I hadn't seen in her face a second earlier now etched themselves around her mouth and between her eyebrows. The serenity washed away, leaving behind nothing more than resolution.

A wave of sickness and sorrow hit me in the stomach and overtook my whole body, making tears sting at the back of my eyes. My throat tightened up and my hands cramped from cold. The girl in the photograph was gone, and the woman I'd known as my mother had replaced her. I wanted to say I was sorry, to take the words back, because I'd liked the confused, light-voiced young woman from the photo, and I'd made her leave.

I was never going to escape that. With a handful

of sentences, I'd taken the joy out of my own mother's heart and turned her into someone whose focus was so strong that she could will herself to death while I sat by her side and watched. The shriek of metal penetrated my awareness again, combining with the wind to scream in banshee cries that I thought would wake me up every night for the rest of my life.

"I've yet to fight the Blade. Those poor women, their lives lost and to no avail." Sheila curved both her hands over her belly now, then made fists of her hands. "Damn him, damn them both to Hell."

"Me?" There was something about an Irishman cursing someone to hell that carried far more conviction than an American making the same damnation. My voice came out a childish squeak, betraying a fear I thought should be absurd, but which seemed very real at that moment. Sheila jerked her head up, then yanked her hands away from her pregnant tummy.

"No." The softness was gone from the Irish lilt, leaving cold edges. "Not you, Siobhán. Joanne. I thought I had the strength to banish him and lock away his master forever, but there are things I will not risk."

"Me," I squeaked again. Sheila flattened her hand against the curve of her belly again, the gesture more than answer enough. My head began to pound, a throb that fit into the beats between the rise and fall of the wind and tearing metal. "You didn't stop this guy who rips out people's entrails for fun and profit because you were protecting me?"

"Sure and I thought I'd be stopping him, girl." Hard, dissonant notes sounded in my mother's voice. "I'd thought this plan through for so long. Break his power circle and push him so far out of time he'll be lost for good. But I can't follow him to the ends of the earth to make certain, for the life within me can't withstand the journey, my fragile Siobhán."

Time blurred with a squeal of sound, a too-fast babbling of voices being sped up. The light changed, winter sun dropping and darkening into night. Clouds whisking above Sheila faded to an ominous red, as if the shadow of an eclipse was slipping over them. Even the prosaic flourescent lights burning behind the memory of clouds began bleeding. I twisted in my stair seat, looking behind me at a low red moon. Dread prickled up through the soles of my feet, itching like bee stings, and spread higher into my body. The bleat of time fast-forwarding slowed, and avaricious malevolence crawled over me, pinning me in place like an unfortunate butterfly. My lungs filled with blood, pain slicing my cheek as I clapped my hand against a healed-over scar there. My fingers came away coated in red wetness.

A piece of darkness fell away from the crimson moon, plunging tip over tail to the earth. In the instant before it smashed to the ground, blackness flared and it became a man, or at least a thing that looked like a man. Emaciated and pale, it moved too smoothly to be human, gliding across the Irish field and through the garage walls faster than a man could run. My belly contracted, the knot of power hidden there flaring, ready to be used if I could think of a way to use it.

I couldn't think at *all*. The thing, the man—I saw in a flash of moonlight how sharp and narrow his features were, like the rest of him, and remembered that Sheila had called him the Blade. It seemed like a good name, and the choking sensation of blood in my lungs only brought home the accuracy of it. The Blade swept toward me, moving ever faster while I sat frozen, feeling as if I was wrapped in safety, unable to free myself even with the best of intentions. The Blade reached out long bony fingers, curling them as if he'd throttle me, and I sat and watched him do it.

Sheila MacNamarra did not. I never saw her move, but then, I was transfixed by the Blade and looking the other way. She put herself between me and him, a human woman vibrant with life. She flared golden, like a moment of star-born glory, and the Blade shrieked a sound of torn metal and moaning winds. He leaped forward, fingers clawed for her throat. She caught him with a foot in the stomach and they rolled ass over teakettle, thumping through the field and the bodies of police sedans.

I felt each jolt as they hit the ground, smashing

through my body as if I was encased in water. Despite myself, I let go a little giggle: I felt no personal danger, only fascination and curiosity as I bounced around with the two combatants. I could feel Sheila gather her will and insist upon *change*. The air itself responded as she flung up her arm to block the Blade's attack. His hands crashed against a shield of air as solid as steel. Sheila scrambled to her feet, still wielding her invisible shield, and smashed it in a backhand swing, catching the Blade by the face and knocking him backward.

Again I felt her gather her will. Bars that I couldn't see but could sense began to spring up around the Blade. This wasn't just the essence of healing, the thing I'd been told I could do as a shaman. It was something more, something far beyond not just my capabilities, but even my skill to imagine. I watched, round eyed with admiration and astonishment, as the world seemed to leap at her command. *My mom can beat up your bad guy!* a little part of my mind crowed. I clamped a hand over my mouth to prevent another giggle from escaping.

The bloodred of the sky deepened like a warning bell. The Blade shot taller, more narrow, as if gaining strength from the wrongly colored world. Sheila faltered, a creature of light weakened by its absence. The Blade shrieked pleasure and crashed through the bars she'd built, shattering her will as if it was nothing. For the first time I saw her cower, a moment of weakness in the woman with an indomitable spirit.

I had nothing to give, but I had nothing to lose, either. I reached out to the place I sat in the real world, my garage, a place of safety and comfort to me, and begged for power to help save the woman who protected me. The very cars themselves seemed to respond, filling me with the knowledge that I was—or had been—one of their caretakers. The walls of the place, in a building meant to house those who safeguarded the city, gave to me what I asked, their own strength and certainty in the role they filled. For a moment it overwhelmed me, raw power from things that had seemed lifeless to me before.

Then the Blade was bearing down on Sheila, fingers locked around her throat, making her the fourth victim of his murdering spree. I took what I'd been granted and coiled it up with my own core of silver-blue power, then wound up and threw it overhand, like a baseball, into Sheila MacNamarra's hands.

Power erupted like an electric line cut loose, snapping and flailing. The Blade shot backward, landing dozens of yards away on hands and feet, still skidding back. Rocks in the field tore up under his long fingers, furrows grooved in the concrete garage floor. For an instant, the banshee cries stopped, leaving a silence so profound it hurt me in my bones.

Then even I saw the flash of silver thread that lay between myself and the roundness of my mother's belly. It pulsed with the power I'd just thrown, crackling and popping like a trapped snake. The Blade's gaze snapped to me, focusing on me for the first time since Sheila had placed herself between us. He howled a victorious shriek and pounced toward me, forgetting Sheila in the moment of triumph. As he reached me, Sheila rose up behind him with her hands wrapped around a column of light, a weapon shaped from her own will and nothing more. She drove it into his spine, sending him arching backward with a scream that brought rupturing agony to my ears, and then blessed silence.

The blood red light cleared. I slithered down the last few steps into the garage, stickiness trickling from my ears. Sheila's face appeared above me, round eyebrows drawn down with concern, long black hair tucked behind her ears. She had her hand pressed over her stomach, fear narrowing her green eyes. Rushing clouds whirled behind her head, and I managed a tiny smile.

Relief swept her face, her lips shaping words I couldn't hear. I said, "Thank you," feeling the words vibrate in my throat even if they didn't echo in my ears.

Then her face blurred into Thor the Thunder God's, and I decided that was as good a time as any to pass out.

6

I woke up to a weirdly silent world in which Morrison's face was hovering worriedly over mine. Morrison worried was distressing. Much more distressing than Morrison yelling. There were certain constants in my world.

Hearing, for example. Up until this very moment, hearing had been one of those constants. Now there was nothing. No ringing in my ears, no ocean of blood thrumming, no background traffic noises or cops arguing over topics ranging from doughnuts to politics.

One missing constant I could deal with. Two was too much. I frowned at Morrison and said, "Why aren't you yelling?"

At least, I think I did. I never realized how much I depended on hearing myself to know I was talking. I mean, I could feel my voice box working, but the astounding silence into which the words fell really, really made me want to begin shouting. I didn't, but only just barely. I thought shouting would look a lot like giving in to panic, and since it appeared that half the precinct was standing behind Morrison, I didn't want to come across like a wussy girl just because of a little thing like shattered eardrums.

I felt very much like a wussy girl just then. It was possible I owed Billy a very small apology for being bent out of shape over the one-of-the-guys comments. A very small apology. Minuscule. I closed my eyes, cleared my throat—another thing that I could only feel, not hear—and said, "I'm okay."

I got my eyes open again in time to see everybody sag with relief. Even Morrison, although he covered it nicely by scowling magnificently and, judging from the color of his face and the fact that I could see his uvula, yelling.

It made me feel a lot better about not being able to hear, actually. I sat up very slowly, not at all sure that broken eardrums didn't equate to a broken sense of balance. It didn't seem to, which was nice. Vomiting on my boss after all this fuss would have been embarrassing. Especially since he was being nice, and had a hand between my shoulderblades, keeping me steady as I sat.

"I'm okay," I repeated silently. "I just, ah…" Something tickled along my jaw. I reached up to scratch it and came away with sticky, drying blood under my fingernails. "I can't hear," I said to nobody in particular, especially myself, since I couldn't hear me, "and the thing we're after looks and sounds a lot like Munch's *Scream*."

I suspected I was glad I was looking at the gook under my nails instead of the gathered crowd. "I'm going to need a little time," I said, still to my icky fingers. "And maybe a sandwich."

The room cleared like I'd fired a shot. Ten seconds later the only people left were Morrison, Thor, and Billy, the middle of whom looked like he'd rather be somewhere else. "I'm fine," I told him. "Thanks for, um. Whatever you did."

He gave me a tight smile, nodded, and followed the rest of the crowd like he'd been given a reprieve from the firing squad. I wondered why my mind was wandering down the aisle of shooting similes. I'd never been completely deafened by firing a gun.

Billy looked at Morrison in a way that made me look, too. The captain said something I didn't catch— obviously—and Billy cast me a worried glance, then nodded and left the room. I finally figured out I was in the broom closet, which was nice. It was the station's flop room, kept meticulously clean for cops who'd been on the job too long and needed a rest break. I hadn't known it was big enough to hold more than two people, much less the eight or so that'd been in there.

Morrison touched my shoulder. I nearly jumped out of my skin, then drew in a sharp breath through my nose and turned to face him, eyes wide. Not hearing sucked a lot. He said something and I focused on his mouth, concentrating.

"If you think," he said, slowly and clearly enough for me to read, "that you're getting out of work today just because you collapsed with blood running from your ears, think again."

I had never heard—or not heard—such reassuring words in my life. I split a grin that turned into laughter, and leaned forward to give the police captain a hug. A tiny dimple that I'd never noticed before quirked at the corner of Morrison's mouth, and he returned the hug somewhat gingerly. I sat back, still grinning, and felt my face fall long and googly with dismay. "Oh, shit."

Morrison's eyebrows shot up and he followed my focus to his shoulder, where his formerly impeccably white shirt was now stained with sticky red residue. "Oh, for Christ's sake, Walker," he said, and he didn't even have to say it slowly for me to understand. I wrinkled up my face in apology. He sighed explosively and waved it off. "What the hell happened to you?"

"I ran into the bad guy." I was trying so hard not to shout that I suspected I was barely more than whispering.

"In the *garage?*"

It was amazing how easily I understood him. Amazing, and somewhat alarming. I frowned at his mouth and nodded, then shook my head. Not being able to hear made me feel like I wasn't able to talk, either.

"In Ireland. In the garage. It's complicated. Morrison, I'd really like to get my ears fixed before anything else happens."

"You think something else is going to happen?"

"Something else always happens."

His eyebrows rose and fell in an acknowledging shrug. "Do you need a doctor?"

I shook my head. "Just some time and some food." I felt like somebody'd turned me upside down and shaken every last bit of energy out of me. Thinking about it made it worse. Morrison's hand found its place at my spine again, supporting me, and it took everything I had to not lean over, curl my fingers in his shirt, and snivel on him for a minute. "I'm a little tired." That time my voice felt so low I wasn't at all sure I'd spoken out loud. Morrison tipped my chin up so I could see what he was saying. It struck me as an unbelievably intimate gesture, and I felt myself blushing. Morrison ignored it, which was somewhere between relieving and insulting.

"Lie back down, Walker. You're white as a sheet."

I *felt* white as a sheet. I felt like all the energy that I usually ignored had been bleached and left out to dry. Part of me wanted to argue, because Morrison was the one telling me what to do. The other part thought falling asleep for the rest of the day sounded like a good idea. I started to nod, but Morrison's finger under my chin kept my head from dropping.

"I sent Holliday to get your drum. That'll help, right?"

I nearly kissed him. Instead I closed my eyes and bit my lower lip, nodding. "Yeah. Thank you." My nose prickled with embarrassing tears. "Thanks."

I didn't hear him answer, but I felt the rumble of his voice through his touch.

"I'll just lie down until Billy gets here, or food does." I didn't need to hear my own voice, either, to know that it was full of stings and thorns; that was how my throat felt. I hoped I just sounded tired, not angry or about to burst into tears. Morrison wrapped a strong hand around my biceps and helped me lie back down. I pulled a pillow over my head and knew nothing for a little while.

Billy didn't just come back with my drum. He came back with Gary, who found me in the laundry room, washing the broom-closet sheets. By the time he found me I'd eaten and rinsed out my ears, which made me feel considerably more human. I was leaning against the washing machine, feeling it do its thing, when Gary poked his head in and said something I couldn't hear. I grinned a little and pointed at my ear, which made him huff and puff like the big bad wolf.

Getting anything useful out of the drum when I couldn't hear proved to be awkward as hell. I eventually sat down directly across from Gary and kept my fingertips on the drum's edge while he knocked out a beat.

I'd never felt the drum actually call up energy inside me before. It was like a well filling, a few bubbles in the depth of me turning into splashes and then into a steady trickle. I said, "Faster," and Gary increased the beat until the power of the drum made me laugh with the feeling of life well lived. It was an entirely internal celebration that took my breath and made my blood run thinner and faster in my veins. I wanted a hundred drums all around me, so their vibrations shook the very air, making it safe for me to dance even without being able to hear the beat.

I burst through the top of my head and into clear sky so cold even the blue was leached from it. I could hear my own labored breathing as I tried to catch oxygen from the thin air, but I knew with great certainty that I was hearing an illusion. My spirit might be unharmed—at least with regards to this particular instance—but the body I'd left behind needed repair work.

The first analogy that slid through my mind was that of blown-out stereo speakers. I folded my legs and sat in the clear thin air, just as I might have within my own garden, and began the process of removing the destroyed stereo components and replacing them. I overlaid the idea on my own body, and called for the renewed power that lay coiled inside me. It sprang up, eager for the call, and swept through me.

I had a completely horrid sensation in both my ears at once, as if bugs were crawling out of them. I stuck a finger in one and wriggled it, coming away with a tiny smear of bloody flesh. I let out a ragged yell and flapped my hand frantically, getting rid of the icky bit, then repeated the whole ritual, including the frantic flapping, on the other side.

That part didn't hurt.

The next part did. I could feel the power in me rebuilding my eardrums, fitting the right amount of newly created flesh into the cavity in my ear. It felt like an inkjet printer was zipping back and forth inside my ear, making one tiny line of new eardrum after another. Heat ran down my eustachian tubes and into the back of my throat, tasting like blood and feeling increasingly like someone had poured molten gold into the delicate tubes.

I kept coughing and trying to gag the feeling away. Nothing worked, the boiling feeling continuing to zip around in my ears, until they popped abruptly and wind shrieked against my new eardrums. I fell back inside my head, the ringing of the drum suddenly impossibly loud, and yelled again, this time scaring the bejeezus out of Gary, who stopped drumming and threatened me with the drumstick. Then he leaned over the drum and hugged me without warning, mumbling, "You get in all kinds of trouble when I'm not around, lady. You oughta watch yourself."

"Yeah, well, you should see the other guy." I wrinkled my face. "Actually, I guess that's the problem. We can see him now."

"Am I s'posed to understand that?"

I gave him a lopsided smile. "Not really. C'mon. I need to go talk to Billy."

"My mother called it the blade. Blade." I tried it out without a capital letter and with one, wrinkling my nose. "Its master's blade, specifically."

"And its master is?"

I shrugged. Billy looked at the ceiling like he was asking strength from God. I spread my hands. "I thought getting any kind of name from a woman who's been dead for three months was pretty good."

"Well, can you go get more?"

I slid down in my chair, glaring futilely at Billy's computer screen. "What have I done for you lately, huh?"

"It's the nature of the beast, Joanie. Can't get no satisfaction." He gave me a sideways look. "Are you really okay?"

"Right as rain." I scratched my jaw where the blood had been. "I don't know how real this thing is, Bill. I'm not sure if it's something you can catch. Whatever Mother did to it set it back a lot of years, but she thought she'd have the power to destroy it, and that was a big fat bust. And whatever it is has got a master."

"Forget about the master. The master isn't the thing stringing girls out by their guts, right?"

"Right." God, I hoped I was right.

"Then he's not our problem right now. By the way, Melinda wants to know if you're still coming over for dinner."

I blinked. "What?"

"It's the equinox tonight. She invited you last week, remember?"

"And you think to bring this up in the context of masters? Or was it being strung out by your guts?"

Billy fashioned a crooked grin. "You know Mel. She's a slave driver."

I laughed. "So a little bit of both. Yeah, I don't see why not. I mean, you tell me. I know it's the first forty-eight hours of a murder investigation that are most critical, but we're kind of way the hell past that. Is taking the night off going to make a critical difference?"

"If it does, it's my ass in the hot seat, not yours. You're just a beat cop, remember?"

"A beat cop who isn't doing her job today. Crap." I got to my feet. "Did Morrison put somebody on the Ave to cover for me, or am I going to get beaten within an inch of my life the next time he sees me?"

"You're fine, Joanie." Billy's voice was gentle. "People who spontaneously rupture eardrums, even if they follow it up with a little lay-your-hands-on-me action, are generally considered out for the day."

I sat back down. "Yeah? That happens enough to have a protocol for it?" Probably only with me around. Great. "Can I bring Gary to dinner? Petite's still in the shop."

Billy looked around. "Where'd he go?"

"Back to work. Some of us," I said in my best gruff Gary voice, "gotta work for a living, darlin'."

"Oh. Sure, bring him. Mel cooks enough to feed an army anyway."

"That's because you have four kids, Billy. That *is* an army." I scooted forward, nodding at his computer. "Okay, so I'm Detective Holliday's personal assistant for the day, I guess. What do you want me looking for?"

Billy snorted. "I can look up weird shit on the Net, Joanie. You're the one with the direct line to higher powers."

"Jesus H. Christ on a pogo stick, Billy. Don't say things like that. Higher powers my ass." I actually shuddered.

"Whatever you want to call it, you've got a bead on something I can't access. Even the captain knows it."

A fact which did not fill me with joy and glee. I sighed, dropping my chin to my chest. "Last time I went into the wonderful world of the weird, my eardrums exploded, Billy."

"Look at it this way. At least nobody shoved a sword through your lung." He gave me a sunny smile that held up to the glare I shot his way.

"Thank you. Thank you, Billy, that really helped a lot. Bastard."

"Hey." Billy looked injured. "My parents were married."

"Mine weren't." Huh. I'd never thought of myself as a bastard before. Interesting, what you can get through almost twenty-seven years of living without thinking. "Look, Billy?" I heard myself get all quiet, like I was about to impart something important. Billy heard it, too, and leaned forward.

"My mother had the chance to eliminate this guy back when she faced him. She didn't because she was pregnant with me and she didn't want to risk me. So this whole thing is kind of my fault." I wrapped my arms around my ribs, staring at a broken corner of tile beneath Billy's desk. "I mean, the fact that there are more dead women now. I know I'm being sort of a jerk, because I hate all this crap, but…I really want to get this thing solved. I need to. Whatever it takes."

Billy clapped his hand on my shoulder, solid and re-assuring. "We'll figure it out, Joanie. We'll get this guy. You'll get your piece."

Or maybe he said *peace*. I wasn't sure.

7

The drumming hadn't been enough to fill me up. Not all the way, at least. Maybe a hundred drums would've poured so much energy and power into me that I'd have been good to go for the rest of the day, the rest of the week, as long as it took. But by midafternoon I was stumbling like Petite did when she ran short on gas, and nothing I did brought me even one whit closer to figuring out what the Blade was or how to stop him from killing someone else.

So I did what any sensible woman would do. I went—no, not shopping. My idea of an ideal shopping experience was walking into the store, finding exactly what I wanted on the first rack I stopped at, buying it, and being out of there in five minutes. I was a retailer's nightmare.

But I was also a well-trained Seattleite. When the chips were down, I went for coffee.

The Missing O was half a block down the street from the precinct building, run by an entrepreneurial young fellow who thought the idea of opening a doughnut and coffee shop next to a police station was pretty funny. After a while the cops started thinking it was funny, too, and began to take a certain pride in being the O's number-one clientele.

A barista greeted me not by name, but by drink: "Tall hot chocolate with a shot of mint?" I waved an agreement and went to pay without ever having to say anything. A minute later I was ensconced in the corner, hands wrapped around the drink.

A coffee shop with a mug of hot chocolate was no place to solve the world's problems from, but it beat a sharp stick in the eye. I let my eyes half close, watching the world through a blur of lashes and waiting for inspiration to strike.

Inspiration, last I checked, did not come in the form of Captain Michael Morrison. Well. He was certainly inspiring in some ways. He frequently inspired me to mouth-frothing argument, for example. At the moment, though, he stood a few feet away, frowning down at me as if unsure how to approach. I untangled my eyelashes and looked up at him. "I don't bite." I thought about that statement, then nodded, determining it was true. I couldn't remember having bitten anyone in my sentient years.

Morrison let out a fwoosh of air and shrugged his

shoulders. He was wearing a seaman's coat with big black buttons, so out of fashion it looked like haute couture. "That's a great coat."

He looked as startled as I felt. To the best of my recollection, nothing like a compliment had ever passed my lips when I was speaking to the captain. He shrugged again, hands in his pockets, which made the whole coat move like a woolen wall with a purpose in life, and sat down. "Thanks. Belonged to my father."

"Seriously?" I supposed it was unlikely Morrison had sprung fully formed from the forehead of his mother, but I'd never given much thought to his family. "He was a sailor?"

"Merchant marines. He died when I was twelve."

Neither of us knew what to say after that. I slid down in my seat and wrapped my fingers around my hot chocolate tightly enough to bend the cardboard. "So," I said after a while, just as he said, "Your hearing's back." I twitched a grin at the plastic top of my cup and nodded. I didn't see if Morrison smiled, too.

"You and Holliday learn anything yet?"

"We would've mentioned it if we had." It came out sarcastic. I hadn't meant it to. I saw Morrison's bulk move back a few centimeters, like he was responding to my nasty tone and putting extra space between us. *Good, Joanne. Antagonize the boss. Again.* "I'm trying, Captain. I really am."

He muttered, "You certainly are," under his breath, making me look up in amused offense. His expression hadn't changed. Maybe I was the only one who thought he was making a joke. Great. Just great.

"I really want to solve this." I kept my voice low, afraid he'd think I was kidding. After a moment something relaxed in his gaze, a little gleam of approval coming into it. I annoyed Morrison for a variety of reasons, starting with knowing a lot more about cars than he did, and ending, emphatically, with wanting a career as a mechanic when it was his opinion I could be a good cop. It was possible I'd taken one tiny baby step toward a better relationship with him by genuinely wanting to solve this case.

"Has it occurred to you that you might be in danger, Walker?"

The chocolate was hot enough to keep my fingers stinging with warmth, or I'd have dropped it in my lap, hands suddenly numb from surprise. "Sir?" I never called Morrison *sir*. I don't know which of us liked it less.

"Your mother turned this killer in thirty years ago. If he puts you together with her—"

I sat there staring at him, slack jawed with stupefaction. "It's unlikely," I finally heard myself say. "Different country, different names, pretty much no connection…."

"Except whatever the hell you've got going on up there." Morrison pointed a thick finger at my head. I touched my own temple guiltily. The man had a point.

Crap. He had a point, and I had no idea what to do if he was right. I blinked at the table, hoping it might come up with a brilliant answer or two.

"Is this going to turn out like the last case?"

Then again, maybe I hadn't taken any steps toward him approving of me at all. I curled a lip at the top of my hot chocolate, doing my best James Dean impression. "You mean with a dead body and no actual proof of guilt aside from the word of a semihysterical teenage girl?"

Morrison gave a credible growl that rumbled up from the depths of his chest. I took that as a yes, and shrugged uncomfortably. "I'm putting my money on 'probably.'"

Silence stretched over the table long enough to break. I looked up when it snapped, to find Morrison glaring out the window, his mouth set in a thin line. At least he wasn't glaring at me. "Get me some answers, Walker. Tell me how to stop somebody else from dying."

I lowered my gaze to the cup again. "For what it's worth, Morrison, I don't like this any more than you do."

He stood up, the chair feet squeaking back against the wet floor. "That's the only thing that makes it bearable."

I didn't feel any less alone, watching him leave, shoulders broad and strong in the seaman's coat.

I locked myself in the broom closet back at the station and struggled to get inside my own mind. When I finally did, my garden looked like somebody had dumped ash all over it, making it as tired and gray as I felt. It was not reassuring. Nor was the fact that it took Coyote a very long time indeed to show up, or that he looked distracted when he did. How a dog could look distracted, I didn't know, but there you had it.

"I'm not," he said for the umpteenth time, "a dog."

One of the few thoughts I seemed to be able to keep to myself around him was the private glee at being able to get on his nerves with something as simple as calling him a dog. It made me feel better right away. I even managed a bright grin. "Sorry. I need your help."

"God helps those who help themselves, Joanne."

I startled. "What, you're a Christian now?"

"Is that so strange?"

"Is it strange that my shape-shifting coyote spirit guide is a Christian? You tell me."

He finally looked at me, little spots of brighter-colored fur above his eyes lifting like eyebrows. "No," he said. "It's not. You've got too many preconceptions, Walkingstick."

"I wish you people would stop calling me that." I didn't like having my original last name bandied around. Especially not when I was dealing with psychic realms I didn't really understand. The idea that names had power was one I could grasp, if nothing else. Which actually brought me to my point: "I need to know how to protect myself, Coyote."

He snapped his teeth at me and got up to pace toward me, looking alarmingly like a predator instead of a scavenger. "You should've been learning that for most of the last three months."

"So sue me. Are you going to throw me to the wolves just because I'm slow on the uptake?" More than slow, I admitted. One might go so far as to say recalcitrant. Deliberately recalcitrant.

I could live with that.

At least, I could live with it as long as he gave me the help I needed now. Possibly, very possibly, this was not a good long-term game plan. I promised myself I'd think about that later. Preferably much later. I did my best puppy-dog eyes on Coyote.

Note to self: puppy-dog eyes work better on people who do not actually possess puppy-dog eyes themselves. Coyote looked disgusted. I retreated on the puppy-dog defense and tried a verbal one. "All I need to know is how to protect the very core part of me, Coyote. My name. That kind of thing. I don't want the bad guys to be able to get to it easily."

"A thought which only strikes you now that a bad guy is looming."

"Yeah."

Coyote dropped his head in a very human motion, and sighed so deeply I was surprised he didn't start coughing. "You know how to do it, Joanne. Think in metaphors."

"What?" I found myself grinning just a little. "Like airbags and steel frames keeping my little ol' name safe?"

He gave me a look that would reduce a lesser woman to blushes of embarrassment. I valiantly ignored the burning in my cheeks and mumbled, "Oh."

"I don't know why I put up with you." He snapped his teeth at me again, and was gone.

"Because I'm cute and irresistibly charming," I said to the empty garden. No one, not even a mockingbird, responded.

"Please tell me dinner isn't going to suck as much as the rest of today has." I leaned over the top of Billy's computer, sighing. He looked up, offended.

"Are you dissing Mel's cooking?"

I snorted a laugh. "No. I just feel useless." I put my hands on his desk, letting my head hang. "Find anything about the Blade?"

Billy let out an explosive sigh and creaked back in his chair, hands folded behind his head. "Comic book references. Stuff about some swordsman named Bob Anderson. Wesley Snipes pictures."

"Really?" I perked up, edging around his desk to try to get a look at the screen. "Any half-naked ones?"

"Joanie!"

I drooped. "I didn't think so. There wasn't nearly enough half-naked Wesley in those movies, anyway."

Billy gave me a flat look. "Any luck with the psychic stuff?"

My cheeks went hot with discomfort. "No. I…can't get there." My jaunt to see Coyote had tapped me out. I couldn't get any further out of my body than your average caterpillar could. In fact, a caterpillar, with its whole transformation process, was probably going to have more success than I was right now.

"Oh." Billy's silence stretched out a few long moments. "All three of the dead women are from the greater Seattle area," he said eventually. "The Captain went to visit their families. To tell them. I was hoping we'd have something for him when he got back."

"Way to lay the guilt on, Billy." I slumped again, my head heavy enough to strain my neck. "All right. Look. I'm going to go down to the park and, um…" I wet my lips. "You remember that thing I did in the garage in January?"

Billy let out a huff of laughter. "How could I forget?"

"A lot of people seem to have. Or they're trying hard to." I shook my head. "I thought maybe I'd try something like that again down at the park. Having you along would be helpful. You, uh. Know how to put your energy out there." Pulling my tongue out with forceps would have been more fun than saying that sentence. Billy, bless his pointy little head, didn't laugh. He just stood up and grabbed his coat.

* * *

Fresh snow glittered over paths that had been stomped down by a lot of police officers in the past twenty-four hours. The sky was clearing, leaden gray clouds parting to let sparks of sunlight through. I squinted at the ground, kicking up sprays of snow as I tromped through the park, a few steps ahead of Billy.

I could feel Billy walking behind me on a more than physical level. In January I'd asked people to offer up their energy to help me net a god. Billy was getting ready to do that again, coiling his own essence into a ball that he'd be able to share with me when I needed it. Not, I thought, unlike what I'd done for my mother, in the memory/dream connection that morning. I blurted, "Sheila didn't defeat that thing by herself," filling up the silence of the snow-covered field with my voice. "I was there."

"Of course you were there." Billy sounded confused. "She was pregnant with you."

"No, I mean, I was there...twice." Such a gift I had for explanation. "He was kicking her ass. I threw her some power. It went right through...me...into her."

"You boosted your fetal self so your mom could draw enough power to defeat the Blade?"

Billy made it sound so succinct and sensible that I had to look over my shoulder at him to see if he was kidding. He wasn't. I nodded. "Yeah. And then he noticed me, the adult me, and came after me, which distracted him enough that Sheila could…get him." I didn't really know what she'd done, besides stab a sword of light through his spinal cord. Maybe that was enough to set your average evil minion back thirty years.

"So," Billy said, "when you've got this time-travel thing down pat, you want to slip back to about, oh, '85 and tell me to invest in Microsoft?"

I laughed. "Only if you promise to share the proceeds with me." I hunched my shoulders, trying to rid myself of the itchy sensation between the shoulder blades. My interference with Sheila's confrontation twenty-seven years ago felt important. I just wasn't sure why.

I bounced off a wall that wasn't there and crashed back into Billy's chest. He oofed, catching me, then frowned down at me. "Joanie?"

"I have no fucking clue." I put my hand out and encountered resistance. I prodded, then stepped forward and leaned into it, feeling like a mime. Billy fought a grin and completely lost the battle.

"Gonna grow up to be Marcel Marceau?"

"I sure as hell hope not. Can you, um…?"

Billy, showing a remarkable ability to understand Jo-speak, edged around me and walked through the wall I'd hit. He turned, eyebrows lifted.

"Shit," I said in my best thoughtful tone. And, "What the fuck." Apparently crashing into invisible walls brought out the naughty words in me. Curious, I pulled my glove off and put my hand against it directly.

A dangerous burst of dull red flashed around the entire baseball diamond, so quickly it was gone almost before I registered it. A tingle of malicious familiarity made the nerve in my elbow ache.

Morrison was right. The Blade had found a way to recognize me.

8

"Joanie?" Billy stepped back through the barrier as if it wasn't there. I leaned harder on it, prodding at it with my hands and trying to do the same with my mind. It failed miserably. I did not think of my mind as a poking instrument. There was no scalpellike wit here, no sharp-as-a-knife insights. Nor could I come up with a car analogy that would let me slide through the wall. Cars and walls, in my experience, smashed together, not phased through one another. Not that I'd ever smashed up a car myself. Petite was the only vehicle I'd ever owned and I'd have killed myself before running her into anything.

"Joanie?" Billy asked again. I took my hand off the wall, my nerve quieting as soon as I broke the contact.

"I can't get through." Obviously. "He put up some kind of firewall."

"A firewall."

"Yeah, you know. To keep unfriendlies out of your computer network?"

"I know what a firewall is, Joanie. I'm just questioning your usage. How come it let me through, if it's a firewall?"

I lifted my eyebrows at him. "It doesn't recognize you as an unfriendly. It's programmed for me." It was a *lot* easier to think in terms of computer protocols than magic. I thought I might be on to something here.

"Right. So can you still do the thing you were going to do?"

I pursed my lips and looked through the invisible barrier. "One way to find out." The core of power in me was waking up, the wall providing some kind of challenge it felt ready to stand up to. I was pretty sure it was a false high, but I was willing to take it.

"Last time I did this," I said, more to myself than Billy, "it didn't actually do a damned bit of good."

"You're older, wiser, and stronger now." There was an unexpected resonance to Billy's voice, a depth of faith that I knew full well I didn't deserve. Still, it made me straighten my shoulders and drag in a deep breath of cold air. I closed my eyes momentarily, feeling the steam from my breath beading into water on my eyelashes.

When I opened them again, I wasn't quite in my own body anymore. The core of silver-blue energy was alive inside me, pushing me out as though there wasn't enough room for the two of us in this town. For a moment I felt like I was being given a gift I didn't really deserve: I hadn't done any of the training Coyote thought I should, and I wasn't sure I ought to be able to slip out of my body so easily.

The flip side to that, equally frightening, was that if I could do it without any training, then maybe he was right, and it really was something I should be doing with my life. I didn't like that possibility any better at all.

Right in front of me, the Blade's firewall glimmered dark red, like blood seeping out from the heart of the world. It cut off my ability to see anything inside it with more than ordinary eyes. I turned my head very slowly, unsure if my body was doing the same thing, but afraid to move too quickly for fear of jarring myself out of the double vision. Beyond the firewall, the world was full of neon colors, pulses of life that looked like a kid with fingerpaints had gone wild. Billy was just to my right, a swirling ball of orange and fuchsia energy held in his hands. I whispered, "Thanks," and though I was pretty sure I hadn't said it out loud, he crooked a grin and nodded his head once in acknowledgment. I reached out for his colors, calling them to me as politely as I could. They leaped out of his hands, whirling together like agitated kittens, and spun into the silver and blue core of me.

I felt, instantly, a dozen times stronger. My mind cleared, focus spilling through my limbs as if the blood had just remembered that it was supposed to be running. I didn't expect the sudden boost in clarity. It suggested my power really hadn't recovered from the run-in with the Blade that morning. Or almost thirty years ago. Whichever. The point was, if Billy's energy was bringing the world into that much sharper relief, I was even more tapped than I'd thought.

Buoyed by his dancing fuchsia and brilliant orange, I spread my hands, sending tentacles of power darting over the Blade's shield. Silver slithered over red, trailing my and Billy's colors like banners, testing and tracing the barrier. I went up, not around, looking for weak points that would allow me to hack into the system.

Giggling while out of body was an interesting experience. It felt like champagne bubbles in my nose and fingertips, little sparkles of glee that didn't require containment.

As if in response to my laughter, the red wall faltered.

My giggles cut off as I jumped to take advantage of the weakness, a thin spot in the barrier that began to strengthen again even as I slid threads of power into it. I envisioned taloned nails that could grasp and tear more efficiently than my own, and worried at the spot like a determined rodent. I found myself grinning again, wondering what Coyote would think of me throwing over the car analogy in favor of using psychic rats to claw my way through a magical firewall. Even as I grinned, a silver tendril punched its way through the wall. Other colors, Billy's and mine both, leaped to the spot, squirming through and braiding together to strengthen each other without ever blending or losing any of their own distinctive coherence.

My hands lifted of their own accord, making claws that wrenched apart from one another, as though prying open a bear trap. The wall above me groaned and then tore, great jagged chunks ripping free with the same metal-on-metal shrieks I'd encountered that morning.

I was abruptly very cold, sweat standing out on my face and beading into my eyes. A dispassionate part of my mind suggested *shock?* and for a dizzying moment I considered stopping before I found myself facefirst in a snowbank, dying of exposure. The power I was using gasped and shriveled, the jaws I'd forced open in the red wall beginning to crash shut again. My knees gave out and I dropped to the snow. The chill helped me focus, and I used the energy that had been keeping me on my feet to try to keep the wall torn asunder. It had life of its own, forced and vicious, with no purpose beyond keeping me out. Destroying me, if it could.

And it was going to. I crumpled farther into the snow, pressure bearing down on my weakening breach in the wall like so much newspaper. I knotted my fingers in snow, feeling icy chunks bite into the lines of my ungloved hand and then melt into bone-aching cold. I was going to be pulverized by someone who wasn't even there. What an embarrassing way to die.

At least Morrison wasn't there to see it. For a moment I went in a mental circle, annoyed that that was my last thought, then realizing it couldn't be, because *this* was my last thought—

Power slammed into me, drawn from a depth that I could barely fathom. Deep purple, burnt sienna—Billy's colors, but at their most profound. I could feel the love he drew on, lacing his colors with such gladness I was happy to stop breathing, so long as I could do it for *them*—

I didn't come to my feet. My body was irrelevant, left behind as I sprang forward on the force of the power Billy gave to me, unstinting. I slammed my fingers, all swirled with dominant purple, into the barely existent crack—all that was left of my opening in the wall—and tore it apart.

Redness shattered all around me, breaking in huge chunks of raw-edged power that collapsed into fragments as they hit the ground. I boiled through the opening and stood against the waves of blood rage that had gone into the killings. The bodies were gone, but the black power that linked one woman to another was still there, seeped in the earth beneath the snow like their blood. I could see lines that hadn't been there the day before—or that I hadn't been strong enough to see. Billy's outpouring of energy made my skin tingle, even if I'd left my actual body behind.

He can't keep this up forever, Joanne. Stop fucking around. Did other people have little voices in their heads that said things like that? I could stretch myself out a little and touch a hundred thousand minds in Seattle just to find out, but I was afraid the answer would be no. I refrained, instead focusing on the thin lines rising up from each of the three points where the women had died.

They came together in thready blackness, like oil-smeared string that glimmered and twisted with unhealthy light, making three points of a pyramid. They joined at the apex and braided together, reaching higher until the braid grew watery and distant. I could see it cut through the clouds and into the blueness of the sky beyond, but it faded before it reached the dark curve of space above the world. I was almost certain it faded, not that my vision was failing. The power diamond wasn't complete. The Blade needed one more body to finish building his stairway to heaven. That was the good news.

The bad news was it obviously didn't matter that the bodies themselves were gone. The power their deaths had bought was there, seared into the ground. Taking the three women away from the park hadn't broken the spell, and I wasn't sure what would.

The worst news was I could only think of one way to find out. The rich colors of Billy's power hadn't faded at all, memories coalescing around me: moments of love, laughing until the tears came; moments of holding sick children, afraid of what the night might bring. The bright spark of his wife's smile; the open acknowledgment that his girls had him wrapped around their little fingers, that his boys made him puff up with a fatherly pride he felt a little silly about, in this enlightened day and age.

What he was giving me was the part of him that would never, could never, give up. It was his center, his family, the core of all his strength, and just as surely, the center of all his weaknesses. He embraced every bit of it, flinging it toward me with everything he had, giving me the power to reach all the way to the stars. He knew what he was doing: he could protect himself from the lethal drain but chose not to. Instead he offered up power far beyond the limits of safety. I could take it and follow the Blade's black thread into the heart of its darkness, and learn what lay behind him.

This morning and almost thirty years ago, my mother had had the same choice.

I fell back into my body with a jolt so hard it made my teeth ache, refusing the maelstrom of power offered to me by my friend. Refusing to take what he would give until the moment his system went into critical failure. I wouldn't take it, not even to fight the thing that wielded the murderous Blade.

Weak with exhaustion, I was still able to turn in time

to catch Billy as he fell, the very life of him drained almost to the sticking point.

The earth itself had power to spare, a thin green-and-blue flow far beneath its frozen surface. I reached for it with a worn-out plea, dragging the offered trickles of energy up through the snow and into myself. I couldn't reach even as far as the scattered trees, much less beyond the park's boundaries to beg for some of Seattle's teeming life energy. I had to wait, bent over Billy's chilled form, drawing in tiny spurts of strength until the swirling core of silver-blue inside me gave a little groan, and let power flow into my hands.

I fell back on the analogies I knew best. Billy's battery was drained and needed a jump. The thought of jumping Billy made me burble a snicker. His wife would beat me up.

The logical side of my mind said that if part of a person was the battery, it would probably be his mind. My hands drifted over Billy's heart without paying any attention to the logical part of my mind. I actually made little pinchers of my fingers, like jumper-cable heads, and clumsily stabbed one hand against my own heart, the other staying over Billy's.

It was a long and slow transfer of strength, my eyes half-shut and my head bowed over his. I was gaining very little for myself; what I could draw from the frozen ground beneath the snow I simply siphoned into Billy.

His color improved gradually and he finally chuckled, more shaking his body than sounding in my ears. "Think we can walk out of here if we lean on each other?"

"Mngrnf." I thought that was supposed to be "maybe." Billy seemed to understand, and we took a couple of long minutes to climb to our feet, giggling with exhausted clumsiness.

"You find anything out?" he asked once we were both on our feet.

"Yeah." I tried out this whole walking thing, one shaky step. I could feel weary relief spill through him and into me.

"What?" His first step wasn't any steadier than mine. I smiled wearily and pulled myself up a little straighter, letting him lean on me.

"I found out I've got the best friends in the world. C'mon. Let's go, Holliday. Your wife's expecting us for dinner."

9

"I swear on my wife's grave." Gary herded me up the stairs to Billy's front door, maneuvering Billy into line behind me. Mel stood in the open doorway, looking bemused. Gary spoke to her, not to me or Billy, which was just as well, because we'd gone well past punch-drunk sometime in the past hour of work and were howling with laughter every time anybody moved. "I swear on Annie's grave," Gary repeated to Mel, "this ain't my fault. They were like this when I picked 'em up at the station."

"I'd ask why Billy wasn't driving," Melinda said, getting out of her husband's way as he snickered and staggered through the door, "but I think I see why. I'm Melinda Holliday." She threaded a hand between me and Billy to shake Gary's, then fixed me with a gimlet eye. "Have you two been out drinking, Joanie?"

An eruption of giggles escaped through my nose and

squirted tears from my eyes. I clapped both hands over my mouth and tried to wiggle a finger up to clear my eyes. "No. Swear to God. Hi, Mel." I bent to give her a hug, hoping I wouldn't lose my balance in doing so. She was nearly an entire foot shorter than I was and better dressed than anybody I'd ever met, including Billy. "This's my friend Gary. Gary Muldoon. He," I said extravagantly, "is a *hero*."

"Where 'hero' equates to 'designated driver'?" Melinda asked archly. "Get in here, all of you." She sounded like she was herding cats, or her four children. We all straightened up and scurried inside to the best of our ability, more obediently than either cats or her kids would have done.

"Joooooooaaaaanne!"

That was the last thing I heard before I went down in a pile of elbows and knees and squirming bodies. "Oh, sure," I heard Billy say, somewhere above my head. "Joanie gets all the hugs, but your old man gets nothing?"

"We see you all the time, Dad," a voice from the pile of squirmy people on top of me pointed out. The oldest kid—Robert-who-didn't-like-to-be-called-Bobby, that-was-a-little-boy's-name—extracted himself from the pile to give Billy a proper hug. He was eleven, not quite old enough to have too much dignity to show such blatant affection.

That left two kids squishing me, and one toddler

slapping his barefoot way down the hall with the clear intention of finishing off the dog pile. Melinda scooped that one up, eliciting a howl of dismay while the girls, Jacquie and Clara, clambered off me, pulled me to my feet, and attached themselves to my sides like leeches. "Joanne, we haven't seen you since *forever*...how come you don't come over more often...did I show you my friendship pins...no I want to show her my Xbox it's cooler than the dumb pins—"

I didn't even know which of them wanted to show me what, but I promised, as loudly as I could, that I wanted to see both the pins and the Xbox and anything else they had to show me, which satisfied Clara, who released me and went tearing off down the hall shouting about the computer games. I grinned after her and gave Jacquie an extra hug. She beamed and clung to my side even more enthusiastically. I had no idea why they liked me so much, but I adored them and it made me feel I'd done something right in a prior life.

Except, the annoying little voice in my head said, brightly, *you haven't had any. That's what Coyote told you, remember?*

I told the annoying voice to shut up and tried to get my boots off without letting go of Jacquie. It was partly self-preservation; I still wasn't doing so well at the whole standing-on-my-own thing, and neither, it seemed, was Billy, who leaned against the now-closed door and smiled wearily. This was what he needed more than any power I could have jumped his battery with: the rambunctious noise and love of his family.

Erik, the toddler, yowled, "Dooowwn!" and then added, in a snuffle, "Pease?" Melinda laughed and put him down. He crawled over to my feet through the snow we'd tracked in and helpfully began yanking on my shoelaces.

I'd been ushered out of the hall and into the kitchen, and had a glass of wine in my hand before I was entirely sure I'd gotten my boots off. Erik came trundling after us with one of the boots wrapped in his arms, which I took as more or less a good sign. Mel was exchanging pleasantries about it being nice to meet you with Gary, who scooped Jacquie—she was only five—off the floor and turned her upside down. Jacquie shrieked with unholy glee, narrowly missing kicking Gary in the nose. For an old guy with no kids of his own, he ducked well.

The first sip of wine hit me behind the eyes like a bowling ball. I let slip a startled giggle and lifted the glass to peer at it, as if I might see a miniature bottle of whiskey hidden in the rich dark liquid.

"Are you all right, Joanne?" Mel somehow heard my giggle through the general noise and turned to look at me, her eyebrows lifted and a teasing smile in place. "What have you and Bill been up to?"

"All kinds of weird sh—tuff." I caught myself just in time, but Robert, sitting on the counter where he wasn't supposed to be, smirked and rolled his eyes as if to say, *grown-ups*. Mel, without having to look his way, said, "Off the counter, Rob. Go set the table," which was apparently his punishment for thinking himself superior to adults. He thumped down with another eye-roll and I winked at him in sympathy as he skulked into the dining room.

"We've been misbehaving horribly," I assured Mel. "I'll tell you about it after dinner."

"You'd better. I get huffy when strange women bring my husband home acting drunk on holidays."

"I'm not that strange," I protested. She laughed and went to open the kitchen window, sending a blast of cooler air into the hot room. I stepped closer to it, taking a deep breath as I leaned over the sink and peered at their backyard. It looked like a Thomas Kincaid painting, down to giant snowmen and half-buried swing sets. Moonlight turned it all purply-blue. I lifted a toast to the man in the moon, the hard edges of his full disc reddened and mellowed by the wine in my glass.

"You're pretty strange, Jo," Gary said.

I looked back over my shoulder. "You're not helping."

He shrugged, grinning, and turned to Melinda. "Anything I can do to help, ma'am?"

"You could start by not calling me 'ma'am,'" Melinda suggested. I shook my head.

"Don't say that. He'll start calling you 'dame' and 'lady' and 'broad' if you're not careful."

"It's parta my charm," Gary said. I laughed.

"You keep saying that."

"And you keep hangin' around. I figure I must be right."

Melinda arched a curious eyebrow at me. I put my nose in my wineglass, suddenly aware that my cheeks were staining pink from something other than the warmth of the kitchen. I heard her under-the-breath, "Mmm-hmm," before she clapped her hands together, making herself the picture of efficiency. "All right. Jo-anne, you get the roast beef, Gary, you can get the potatoes. Jacquie, get in here, thank you dear, would you get the corn and where's your sister? Erik, not under the table, sweetheart. Erik, not under the—Erik! Get out from under the table!" She went to pull her errant child from beneath the dining room table while Gary and I followed Jacquie around, all of us picking up our charged items.

"I don't know how she does it," I whispered to Gary. "Four of them. I can't even find my own shoes some mornings."

"That's 'cause you leave 'em in the bathroom."

"Gary, how do you *know* that?"

He gave me an unrepentant grin and put the potatoes down on the table as he headed back into the kitchen. I put the roast beef down and smacked a hand against my forehead. Robert appeared at my elbow, looking curious. "Is he your boyfriend?"

"No!"

Robert got a grin that looked suspiciously like his mother's, said, "Uh-huh," and sauntered off. I had the distinct feeling I'd been had.

"You can sit next to *me*," Jacquie announced from behind me. I spun around, blinking down at her. At least she probably wouldn't tease me about Gary.

"Okay. Where are we sitting?"

"Here and here." She dragged two chairs out and looked at me expectantly. I sat and she scrambled into her own chair, looking smug. A moment later Mel appeared in the doorway, carrying Erik on one hip and an enormous bowl of gravy in the other hand.

"Jacquie, you're supposed to be helping set the table."

"I'm keeping Joanne company," Jacquie said virtuously. I gaped at her and Mel laughed out loud.

"I see how it is. All right. You keep Joanne company." She put the gravy down and disappeared back into the kitchen as I yelled, "I'm being used!" after her. Jacquie giggled, pleased with herself, and tilted her chair precariously so she could lean on me. By the time I got her straightened up, the table was set and everyone had gathered around. I lifted my wineglass and my eyebrows, looking to Billy for permission to make a toast.

"To Mel," I said cheerfully. "A miracle of modern efficiency. Thank you for inviting us to dinner." I lifted my glass a little higher, watching the wine catch the bright white of one of the chandelier lightbulbs and turn it red as the full moon. "Oh, *shit!*"

I dropped the wineglass and ran for the door.

10

I didn't actually get my boots all the way on until Gary had us halfway to the park. I kept fumbling my stupid damned cell phone as I tried to call Morrison. Finally, on the fourth try, I got the right number punched in and he answered in with a worn-out hello.

"Morrison? You've got to get everybody out of the park, right now. Do we have anybody there? Call them out. He's going to be there. The Blade. It's the full moon. Mother said the moon was changing. Can you call them out?"

Gary gave me a sideways glance of concern. Billy leaned over the front seat of the cab, hanging on my every word. I had no idea what Mel must think. I hadn't managed to say anything coherent between grabbing my boots and running for the cab.

Apparently I still wasn't saying anything coherent.

Morrison was silent on the other end of the line for a few moments, then exhaled heavily. "Walker?"

"Of course it's Walker! Does anybody else do this kind of shit to you? Can you empty the park? They're never going to see him coming, Morrison, they're just going to get killed. You've got to move now!"

Another moment's silence, and then, "I will call you back in two minutes. Do not do anything until you hear back from me." Morrison hung up. I finally pulled my second boot on, wishing my foot weren't soaking wet and cold from melting snow.

"Hurry-hurry-hurry-hurry, Gary, hurry."

"If I hurry any more we'll be dead." It was true. The roads were coated in black ice, and he was driving as fast as I would have, which didn't bode well for anybody.

"Joanie?"

"It's Blade, dammit, it's the full moon." I twitched around to look at Billy, then twitched forward again. "I'm going to have to explain it to Morrison, I don't want to explain it twice." I leaned forward, as if my doing so would urge the cab to a faster pace. "Dammit, dammit, dammit, stupid stupid stupid Jo."

"Hey," Gary said, surprisingly quiet under my litany of abuse. "You got no reason to be callin' yourself stupid, lady."

Unexpected sniffles hit me right in the nose. "No right," I mumbled. "Not no reason."

"Close enough for this old dog."

The cell phone rang and I nearly jumped out of my skin as I answered it. "God, I *hate* these things."

"I assume you're talking about the phone," Morrison said. "The park's clearing out. What the hell is going on, Walker? You'd better not be screwing with me."

"I would not screw with you," I promised fervently. "It's the full moon, Morrison, my mother died on the full moon. It was the solstice, now it's the equinox and the moon is full again. Check the records, I bet that's what it was twenty-seven years ago, too."

"How the hell am I supposed to check the records on the full moon from thirty years ago?"

"There's this really cool Web site," I started, then screwed up my face and grabbed the oh-shit handle as Gary took a corner by use of the Force, without looking where he was going and with no apparent regard to life or limb. "Look, it doesn't matter, I know I'm right. He's killing people on the full moons of winter. This is the last one. Tonight's the equinox. I'm going to stop him."

"How?"

"I have absolutely no idea." I hung up, not wanting to hear Morrison's response to that. To my utter surprise, the phone didn't ring again. Less than two minutes later we pulled into the park's lot. I tumbled out of the cab almost before it stopped moving and ran for the baseball diamond as fast as I could. Gary and Billy came after me, shouting.

I expected to slam into the Blade's red barrier with such force that it'd throw me back. Instead I flung myself at it so hard that I skidded ten feet in the snow when I hit nothing at all. I said something witty and intelligent, like, "Da fuh?" around the mouthful of snow I got for my troubles, and scrambled to my feet, waiting for all hell to break loose.

Somehow, despite everything, I didn't expect it to break loose by way of crimson falling down the face of the moon to cast a bloody shadow on the earth. Everything real seemed to go away: the bite of cold air, the shine of moonlight on fresh snow, my friends' voices yelling somewhere behind me. I stood there with my jaw hanging open, staring up at the bleeding moon, while a sliver fell from it and tumbled all the way to earth.

Just before it hit the ground, it flared a cloak of blackness that cut the air with a banshee scream. Then the cloak settled, the Blade walking forward, tall and thin and hatchet faced. I could feel power rolling off it, heavy as the sea, and with as much concern for the threat I provided as the ocean itself might be.

Right about then it struck me that I was so low on power I'd been punch-drunk and giggling less than an hour earlier, and that out of all the days to pick a fight with something that looked like Morticia Addams's incredibly evil older brother, today might well be the worst possible choice.

The Blade came toward me, faster than a run, without any visible means of locomotion. He simply glided over the blood-colored snow, picking up speed that was all the more eerie for its silence. I did a mental check over my list of available weapons.

There weren't any.

I was going to die.

To my surprise, I discovered I could live with that. I let out the best war cry I could manage—it had nothing on Jacquie's gleeful yelling, but it wasn't bad—and flung myself at the Blade with everything I had.

Which was nothing.

The Blade wasn't prepared for that.

I hit him in the stomach, a shoulder-first tackle Gary would've been proud of. It was like smashing into a flexible block of ice: cold split straight down into my bones and made the marrow into something that carried icy death. He screamed—for the first time I realized the metal-on-metal shriek I'd heard time and again was actually coming from the Blade, a banshee wail straight out of hell.

A banshee wail.

If I'd had time, I'd have stopped to beat my head on something. I'd called the haunting shrieks *banshee cries* without thinking it through all along. The Blade *was* a banshee. Harbinger of death.

My death, specifically, if I didn't gain the upper hand.

We rolled and thumped across the frozen field, struggling for sheer physical dominance. For a moment I had him, but he wrapped bony fingers around my wrist and cold seared into my skin again, numbing my arm all the way to the elbow. I was going to have a dandy case of frostbite if I got out of this alive.

He flung me backward over his head, using my arm like a fulcrum. I actually cartwheeled in the air, watching the blood moon zip by before I smashed into the snow and skidded. I staggered to my feet, turning just in time to catch the Blade's shoulder with my gut, an excellent reversal of my tackle a moment earlier. All the air wheezed out of me and I hit the snow again, doing less skidding and more sinking with his weight on top of me. He was *heavy* for such a skinny thing, as if he'd been emptied of bone and muscle and had cold iron poured into his skin instead. His fingers wrapped around my throat, driving me further into the snow. It felt so warm compared to his hands that for a few seconds I stopped caring, cozy in my snow bed and ready to sleep.

A tiny, offended burst of power flared in my belly, reminding me what real warmth was.

I opened my eyes again, looking up into the Blade's grimacing rictus. I couldn't tell if it had ever been human. Skin stretched across its bones so tightly it might've been a mummy, eyes with bloody fire lighting them staring wide and empty at me. Its teeth—*her* teeth, I finally realized: it was, or had been at one time, female. Of course. Banshees were. *Her* teeth were bared, dry lips pulled back from them. I wasn't sure she needed to breathe, but her chest was expanding.

Wait. I knew this part. This was where she screamed until my eardrums ruptured. I thought twice in one day was a little much, so I took what warmth the power inside me offered, forced it into my arm, and jabbed upward with two stiffened fingers. Right into her throat.

My fingers went all the way through to her spine with a horrible sound of flesh tearing as easily as paper. The scream turned into an aborted *glerk* and the banshee loosened her hold on me. I kicked her off and rolled away, clapping my hand to my throat, coughing through bruised muscle for air. For a few seconds we stayed there, both swaying, watching each other warily. The hole in her throat sealed up, not like human flesh would, but like paper was being stretched back to fit into a hole it'd been wrinkled away from.

She pounced again and I ducked, absurdly smug at the startled look that brightened her flame-colored eyes as she went flying over my head. Then she tackled me from behind, smashing my face into the snow. I thought, very clearly, *damn, that thing really corners,* and had a brief, irrational moment of wanting to try Petite out against her.

Instead I dragged in a lungful of snow and ice as I shoved so deep into the snow that I hit the earth below it. The banshee's knee was in my back, bearing down with too much weight for me to move. I scrabbled for the worn-out center of power within myself, and came up dry. Apparently I'd blown my one chance when I didn't finish ripping her head off a minute earlier. I pounded a fist in the snow, weak flailing as I tried to buck her off. It was about as effective as threatening to catch a storm in cotton candy.

She bent forward, bony knee pressing into my spine between my shoulder blades. I thought about screaming, but I couldn't get enough air to. She hissed, right there behind my ear, and I had the horrible idea she was spitting maggots into my hair. Why maggots were a problem when I was about to be dead, I didn't know, but the idea completely grossed me out. "In the womb I heard you die, for no one lives when a banshee cries."

I wasn't just going to die. I was going to be rhymed to death. That simply wasn't fair. I flailed again, wishing my arms didn't feel so heavy. Wishing my legs would kick, instead of lying there getting colder. Wishing I could wake up enough energy inside me to reach out for more. I didn't even have enough to ask the city to hit me with its best shot, a tactic I'd tried once before and had sworn I wouldn't do again. That I even thought about trying told me I was in dire straits.

"The pregnant gwyld was clever and wise, took you away from prying eyes. Should have known it couldn't last, power like yours can't be passed." Her voice was singsong and scaly, grating against the ringing in my ears. I tried jerking my head back. Not even a banshee could like a head butt to the bridge of the nose, right? But the weight of her hand was too much to move. I considered giving up and dying. It was pretty clearly in the books. On the other hand, she was saying something interesting, if I could get enough oxygen to my brain to work my way through her bad poetry. "Master sees and Master hears, gains his strength through bloodred tears. Thirty years he's gone unfed, shaman's gifts protect the dead."

The words burrowed into my brain, extracting details about my life in exchange for my fumbling grasp of what the banshee was telling me. I whimpered into the snow and tried hard to hang on to the idea of my name wrapped safely up in airbags and seat belts. I felt the scrape of her voice slide off that thought, and nearly laughed with relief. I could keep her away from the most important things. At least if I was going to die, I wasn't going to die with my soul eaten.

Power erupted in my belly like molten gold being poured into me. I straightened my arms, suddenly filled with strength, and shoved up, lifting the Blade's weight as if it were inconsequential. I whipped around, flinging her off me, and she landed yards away, skidding through the snow on hands and knees, back arched like an angry cat. For an instant, the banshee cries stopped, leaving a silence so profound it hurt me in my bones.

I had no time to wonder where the new strength was coming from. I drew on the memory of my mother, throwing up a jail cell made of her own will, and copied it. Bars of blazing silver flashed up out of the snow, slamming closed around the banshee. She threw her head back and keened, a high piercing note that shivered all the way to the bloody moon. My bars wavered under the onslaught, and her voice strengthened, the moon itself seeming to hang lower in the sky the longer she wailed.

Black threads of power, the sacrificed lives of three women, wound together and responded to the banshee's cries. They leaped through the bars I'd built, piercing her bony body. She grew in size and in power, feeding from the blood lines, which throbbed and pulsed like arteries as they spread across the snow. I dug deeper into the fresh power I'd found, discovering an ocean's depth of energy waiting to be tapped. It ran deeper than I did, the same kind of power that Billy had tapped into earlier that day. The love of family, the protective streak that went beyond what a single person could encompass. I could use it, but I doubted I'd live through it.

It didn't matter.

The ocean of blue crushed down upon the banshee,

pressing down to sever the blood lines. They flattened, carrying less sustenance but refusing to shatter. I felt half-moon cuts opening up on my palms, my hands fisted so tightly that blood couldn't escape the tiny slices my fingernails made. The banshee kept screaming, her voice muffled by the weight of my power, but not yet broken. I set my teeth together and reached deeper into the core of power I'd tapped, willing to die as long as I took the other bitch with me.

Sheila MacNamarra put her hand in mine, pale and wraithlike in the bloody moonlight. There was no substance to her, only a terrible force of will, and with her touch a heart of coldness broke inside me. I gave her one shocked look and she returned it with a smile as warm as the summer sun.

"We started this nearly thirty years ago, now didn't we?" The lilt in her voice turned thirty into *tarty*. "Let's put an end to it, shall we?"

That morning, and almost thirty years ago, I'd thrown her a fastball of my own power. Now she made good on the gift, returning it threefold. The depth I'd reached, the unexpected strength, wasn't mine at all, and it wouldn't, in the end, tap me out. It was my mother who would die for it. My mother who had already died for it.

Golden strength and red temper flowed into me, blending with my own silvers and blues in a way I hadn't seen before. She shored up the silver bars of the cage

I'd built, added her weight to that of the deep blue sea. Out of the corner of my eye I saw her nod, and found myself walking forward, my fingers trailing in the golden depth of her strength.

I slipped between the bars of the cage I'd built, putting my hand all the way into Sheila's power, and withdrawing a sword made of fire. I recognized the shape of it: a rapier with a sweeping guard that flickered and warmed my hand without burning me. Flames shimmered to a deadly edge along the slender blade. The Banshee's screams erupted all over again, but the power bearing down on her muffled them and left my beleaguered ears in no real danger.

The black lines of blood magic that fed her parted under the sword's blade where they'd refused to disintegrate under raw force. *A scalpel,* I thought. *My mother was a scalpel. And I came so close to never knowing that. To not understanding.*

The banshee stopped screaming when the lines were cut, her gaze fixed on the red moon, as if waiting for rescue to come. I glanced up at it, then shook my head. "He's still locked behind bars." Not bars. Behind a fallen cave mouth, the broken stones held in place by my mother's will. My mother, who, with my help, had disrupted the sacrifice that would feed him, almost thirty years ago. And with her help I'd done it again tonight. "Still hungry, too." I leaned in, my hands shaking. "Too weak to help you, bitch."

Surprise creased the Blade's narrow face as I took her head, the fiery rapier ripping through her neck with the sound of paper tearing, loud in the absence of her cries. I caught her falling head with a grace that bewildered me, fingers knotted in her thin hair, and walked away from the dusty bones with a spot of emptiness building inside me. All the power that had been brought to bear, both mine and the dark stuff birthed by the banshee's murders, faded, clear moonlight reestablishing itself over the frozen fields. My mother, wearing the cable-knit sweater and jeans she'd worn in her youth, folded her arms beneath her breasts and smiled at me.

"Mom…" I hadn't ever called her that before. It made my throat tight, and her smile fragile. "You brought me to America to protect me from that thing, didn't you?" The banshee's rhymes finally made sense. "So it couldn't find me."

Her smile flickered, still fragile, and she lifted her chin. I saw, quite clearly, the silver Celtic cross of a necklace that rested against her collarbone, momentarily exposed by the shift of her sweater. I pressed my fingers against my throat, where the same necklace now rested.

"I thought it was for the best, lass. You told me, you see. Before you were born, you told me I hadn't succeeded in destroying the Blade. It was all I could think of to do, to protect you."

I closed my eyes briefly, remembering the way joy

had bled from her expression and left resolution in its place. I nodded in a jerky motion, and made myself open my eyes again. "Thank you."

"I thought I could explain when you were grown. When you came to see me. But you weren't ready." Grief colored the shadow of her smile. "So closed off, Siobhán. Whatever happened to you, that turned you away from the wonders of the world?" She lifted her hand, staying my answer before I had a chance to give it. "There's no time, not anymore. There hasn't been since the beginning. Bitter ashes, isn't it, but that's the price of Gaelic blood, my Siobhán. For all their wars are merry."

"And all their songs are sad," I whispered. Surprise brought out her smile and let it fade into pleasure at my recognition of the quote.

"It was all I could think of to do, loose myself from the world. I could see it in you, Siobhán. Joanne. My Joanne. That the moment was coming when you'd have to choose. I thought if I could hold on in spirit, I might protect you for a little while. Distract the darker things while you grew to understand your gifts."

"You did." My throat was still tight. I tried swallowing against it, but came up dry. "You were here. I would have died tonight. Thank you. I…will I see you again?" She was fading around the edges now, like the Cheshire Cat. I knew the answer even before she shook her head, and looked away to hide the shock of loneliness I felt stab through me.

"The space of the winter moons was all I could bargain for. I was afraid even it might not be enough."

"Bargain?" I looked back at her, what was left to see. She looked younger somehow, the smile that curved her mouth belonging to a woman I'd hardly known.

"Goodbye, Siobhán. Know that I love you." There was nothing left but her smile, and then even that was gone.

Morrison had joined Billy and Gary at the bleachers when I walked back to them. None of them seemed to see me coming. Gary clutched his chest and sat down with a thud, glaring at me as I clumped up to the bleachers. "What the hell happened out there, Jo?"

"What'd you see?"

"Not a goddamned thing! You ran off and now you're back!"

I looked up at the sky. The moon seemed higher than it had been, more solid and real somehow. "It didn't seem that long to me."

Morrison was staring grimly at the head I still carried. "Is that the killer?"

I lifted the head a few inches. "Yeah."

"Where's the rest of it?"

"Out there." I turned around, waving the banshee's head at the field.

There was no body lying in the snow, nor any sign of the wrestling fight I'd had with her. The only footprints at all in the new snow were mine, leading up to the bleachers. Even they only seemed to begin a few yards away, just on this side of the closest blood line that had been drawn with one of the victim's entrails. I stood there a few seconds, waiting for a clever explanation to pop into mind.

Nothing did. After a moment I looked at the head again, then over my shoulder at Morrison as I hefted it. "Do you want me to bring this in?"

It took a long time for him to say no. I nodded and gave it a swing or two, then threw it back the way I came. It arched and hit the snow with a soft poof, powder flying in the air. When it cleared, there was no mark that suggested anything had landed on the smooth white surface.

"It's over." Morrison said, almost a question. I nodded. Billy let out a whistle that split the air and shoved his hands in his pockets with an air of finality.

"So who wants to come back to the house for dinner? I bet Mel kept it warm. Why don't you come with us, Captain? There's plenty."

Gary stomped down the bleachers, Billy a step or two behind him. Morrison looked at me. I kept my head turned a little to the side, meeting his eyes. He finally nodded and jerked his chin. "Let's go."

Tension ebbed from my shoulders and I dropped my chin to my chest. "Captain." Not Morrison. I didn't know why.

Morrison turned, eyebrows lifted. I swallowed, trying to figure out the right thing to say. Neither "thank you" nor "sorry" seemed exactly appropriate. I stood there gazing at him until he developed a faint, surprisingly understanding smile. "Come on, Walker," he said, more gently. "We're done here." He tilted his head again and walked down the bleachers after the other two.

I let out a deep breath and followed them all, smiling at the moon.

* * * * *

Don't miss the next phase of THE WALKER PAPERS
THUNDERBIRD FALLS
will be available in May 2006!

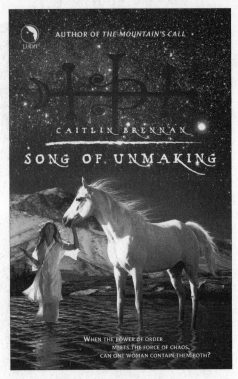

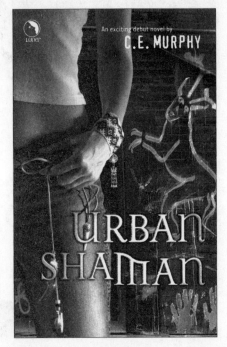

LCEM223TRR

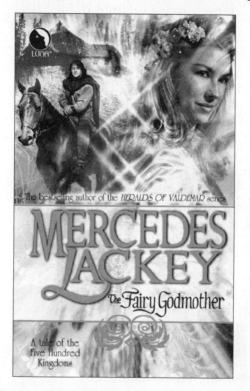

THE TEARS OF LUNA

A shimmering crown grows and dims and is always reborn. Luna has the power and gift to brighten dark nights and lend mystery to the shadows. She will sometimes show up on the brightest of days, but her most powerful moments are when she fills the heaven with her light. Just as the moon comes each night to caress sleeping mortals, Luna takes a special interest in lovers. Her belief in the power of romance is so strong that it is said she cries gem-like tears which linger when her light moves on. Those lucky enough to find the Tears of Luna will be blessed with passion enduring, love fulfilled and the strength to find and fight for what is theirs.

A WORLD YOU CAN ONLY IMAGINE ™

LUNA™

www.LUNA-Books.com

THE TEARS OF LUNA MYTH COMES ALIVE IN

A WORLD AN ARTIST CAN IMAGINE ™

This year LUNA Books and Duirwaigh Gallery are proud to present the work of five magical artists.

This month, the art featured on our inside back cover has been created by:

Amoreno

If you would like to order a print of Amoreno's work, or learn more about him please visit Duirwaigh Gallery at www.DuirwaighGallery.com.

DUIRWAIGH
Gallery

For details on how to enter for a chance to win this great prize:

• A print of Amoreno's art

• Prints from the four other artists that will be featured in LUNA novels

• A library of LUNA novels

Visit www.LUNA-Books.com

LBDG0905TR